Psychic Surveys Book Nine

The Devil's Liar

ALSO BY SHANI STRUTHERS

EVE: A CHRISTMAS GHOST STORY
(PSYCHIC SURVEYS PREQUEL)

PSYCHIC SURVEYS BOOK ONE:
THE HAUNTING OF HIGHDOWN HALL

PSYCHIC SURVEYS BOOK TWO:
RISE TO ME

PSYCHIC SURVEYS BOOK THREE:
44 GILMORE STREET

PSYCHIC SURVEYS BOOK FOUR:
OLD CROSS COTTAGE

PSYCHIC SURVEYS BOOK FIVE:
DESCENSION

PSYCHIC SURVEYS BOOK SIX:
LEGION

PSYCHIC SURVEYS BOOK SEVEN:
PROMISES TO KEEP

PSYCHIC SURVEYS BOOK EIGHT:
THE WEIGHT OF THE SOUL

BLAKEMORT
(A PSYCHIC SURVEYS COMPANION NOVEL BOOK ONE)

THIRTEEN
(A PSYCHIC SURVEYS COMPANION NOVEL BOOK TWO)

ROSAMUND
(A PSYCHIC SURVEYS COMPANION NOVEL BOOK THREE)

THIS HAUNTED WORLD BOOK ONE:
THE VENETIAN

THIS HAUNTED WORLD BOOK TWO:
THE ELEVENTH FLOOR

THIS HAUNTED WORLD BOOK THREE:
HIGHGATE

THIS HAUNTED WORLD BOOK FOUR:
ROHAISE

REACH FOR THE DEAD BOOK ONE:
MANDY

REACH FOR THE DEAD BOOK TWO:
CADES HOME FARM

REACH FOR THE DEAD BOOK THREE:
WALKER

THE JESSAMINE SERIES BOOK ONE: JESSAMINE

THE JESSAMINE SERIES BOOK TWO: COMRAICH

CARFAX HOUSE:
A CHRISTMAS GHOST STORY

THE DAMNED SEASON:
A CHRISTMAS GHOST STORY

SUMMER OF GRACE

Psychic Surveys: Book Nine

The Devil's Liar

The truth isn't always black and white.

SHANI STRUTHERS

Psychic Surveys Book Nine, The Devil's Liar
Copyright © Shani Struthers 2022

The right of Shani Struthers to be identified as the Author of the work has been asserted by her in accordance with the Copyright, Designs and Patents Act 1988. All rights reserved in all media. No part of this publication may be reproduced, stored in a retrieval system, or transmitted in any form or by any means, electronic, mechanical, recording, photocopying, the Internet or otherwise, without the prior written consent of the copyright holder, nor be otherwise circulated in any form of binding or cover other than that in which it is published and without a similar condition being imposed on the subsequent purchaser.

ISBN: 979-8-3597-8720-8

www.shanistruthers.com

Authors Reach
www.authorsreach.co.uk

All characters and events featured in this publication are purely fictitious and any resemblance to any person, place, organisation/company, living or dead, is entirely coincidental.

Acknowledgements

Writing a Psychic Surveys book is always like catching up with old friends. Ruby, Theo, Ness and Corinna seem far too real to be simply fictional characters. Thank you to every one of you that has told me you feel the same, and that you avidly await where the team find themselves next. Certainly, events can get very dark for them, and this book is no exception. Thank you also to my beta readers, those that comb through initial drafts of the book and give me feedback on what they liked and what needs fixing. For Psychic Surveys Nine these are Rob Struthers, Kate Jane Jones, and Lesley Hughes. Thanks also to Rumer Haven for knocking it further into shape via editing. We've worked together for a number of years now and always in perfect harmony. Also, big thanks to Gina Dickerson for producing another fabulous cover, plus formatting and other graphic skills. Again, we've worked together for years and I'd be lost without her.

Nine books in and we're reaching the end of the series, although…never say never. I'm constantly surprised where the team take me, and they seem to be in charge of that aspect, not me! Already they're banging on the door with ideas for Book Ten…

The brighter the light, the darker the shadow. *Carl Jung*

Prologue

A terrible case. One of the worst Theo had experienced. Scrub that. She *hadn't* experienced it. She'd refused to. Why? Because she wasn't herself at the time, she wasn't…equipped. Family life hadn't been so good, not her husband Reggie's fault, though, entirely hers. Her gift could weigh heavily, dealing with the dead when life itself was often enough. There were just so many in need, everywhere she looked, their desperation a tidal wave constantly threatening to deluge her. She'd learnt to handle it, of course, to keep herself from drowning, but it had taken many, many years. It had taken help. But back then, when she'd been young and only recently married, with a baby to look after, the first of three boys, it became one responsibility too many. As for Reggie, he'd also learnt to handle it but, again, only in the ensuing years. Recalling this, she breathed a deep, nostalgic sigh. He'd become quite blasé about it, in fact.

"There she goes again," he'd say, "talking to the dead," but only to himself, never to others. He wouldn't embarrass her like that. Times had been different then. It *would* have been an embarrassment. "Theo, darling, as much as this is your calling, don't forget about us, eh? Your family. We need attention too. Just a bit, mind. We're happy with that." And then he'd laugh, that big throaty chuckle of his that she adored, settling back down in his favourite fireside chair with his paper, the pages rustling as he turned them. She loved him and had done from the very first day they'd met, both taking shelter from a sudden rainstorm in the doorway of a Woolworths in their mutual hometown. Playing on the shop's well-known catchphrase, they'd often say afterwards the true wonder of Woolies was that it had brought them together. A heady romance followed that initial meeting, then a ring on her finger, and a house. It was bewildering how fast it had progressed.

Her gift, her talent, her psychic ability, she'd had it since she could remember. It was as much a part of her as her humour and her sometimes wry take on things. She could sense the recently and not so recently deceased, see them too, often mere shadows, but other times they were more substantial than that, just as a living person was, imploring her wherever she went. Although not brought up in an overly religious family, she knew all about heaven, that place where departed souls were supposed to go when the shutters came down. So how come so many didn't go there and stuck around the living instead?

Whether in town shopping with her mother or at the cinema with friends, or even in the park, kicking back after the school day was done, she'd known lost souls would be there, wandering by. Such forlorn figures, shoulders slumped and heads hanging low. Not always dressed in the clothing of the day either. That was the sixties, when women wore miniskirts and men chose paisley. The spirits, though – even then she'd called them spirits as opposed to ghosts – could look really old-fashioned, wearing the sort of attire only seen in picture books. They'd be drifting by, and then they'd turn to wherever she was, by the swings, the slide or the roundabout, as if a piece of string had jerked their heads sharply in her direction. They'd stare, their eyes widening and mouths opening because they knew they could be seen, they'd sensed it, and then they'd change direction, come towards her, arms lifting and hands outstretched. *You can see me?*

Their confusion, shock and pain would rush at her too, a black wave containing all the human emotions but more intense somehow, as if death did that, made them more potent.

At first, she'd turn on her heels, both as a kid and a teenager, make any excuse to whomever she was with and run back to the sanctuary of her home, her own room, throwing herself onto the bed there, covering her head with pillows and hiding. Trying to drown out their words, how many times they'd asked her, *Why am I like this?*

How was she supposed to answer when she didn't know? No way she could carry this burden alone. She told her parents what was happening, came clean, and thank God for them, they believed her, her mother even saying that she'd known something was different about her right from the off, that they'd get her seen by the 'right people'. Spiritualists, as it turned out. How her parents knew of such people, they never said, but they were true to their word. At age fourteen, she was introduced to Margaret Cuttress – such an ordinary-looking lady, somewhere in her seventies, who lived in a 1930s semidetached in Eastbourne. Although Margaret Cuttress ran a spiritual group, she didn't claim to be psychic. What she was, though, was kind and so very wise. She had a *belief* in the spiritual, and, as Theo came to realise, sometimes that was more than enough.

It was Margaret who taught her about boundaries and about the light.

"You're special," she once said as she took Theo's hand, the skin around her pale eyes crinkling as she smiled. "And it *is* a gift. You're here to help people that others can't."

"They're spirits," Theo amended. "Not people."

"They were people once. *Now* they're spirits, clinging on to the human journey." She released Theo's hand and leant back in her armchair. "And what a tough journey it can be, hard to make sense of. But some of us at least try. It's good, though, isn't it? To know that there's something else. That there has to be a point to all this. Imagine…if there wasn't." She shook her head, silver hair like a halo. "No, I *can't* imagine. That's the thing. Oh, it's a privilege to have met you, darling, to try to help."

And then they practiced again, drawing light straight from Source – the brightest, whitest, *gentlest* light – and wrapping it around themselves as though it were a blanket. Gentle it might be, but it was tougher than steel.

"Don't be afraid to speak back to the spirits," Margaret said. "Not in words. Goodness, no! That would draw some queer looks! Communicate in thought. You *can* say no. Everybody has that right. 'No, I can't help. I'm sorry. I can only do so much.' Come on, practise with me. That's right, project those words: *No, I can't help. I'm sorry…*"

Sitting there in the chintz of Margaret's living room, the smell of roses always in the air – her mother's favourite perfume, she'd told Theo once, thrilled that she could detect it – Theo would practice and practice and practice. Whilst other girls were learning the latest dance moves and obsessively following the movements of bands such as The

Beatles and The Hollies, she was doing this, learning to live with herself.

Margaret's halo suited her. She'd been a godsend. An angel sent at the right time. One that eventually gained her wings, as the saying goes, no trace of her lingering spirit ever detected. She'd flown. Returned to her spiritual state. Gone home, which was a type of heaven after all.

Life, however, continued for Theo. The journey. And she could do it thanks to Margaret, erect boundaries, protect herself, helping where she could but not to her own detriment. Gifted she might be, but she was not superhuman. She did her best, though. Always. And when she talked to a spirit, when she persuaded one of them to leave their earthly woes behind and go home too, there was elation. She'd been born to do this. It was her vocation.

And then she'd met Reggie and somehow taken her eye off the ball. Too consumed with material matters, with all a young woman must do to support her family. The boundaries had come down. Even today, so many years afterwards, sitting alone in the living room of her Lewes home, Reggie gone and their three boys with houses and families of their own, she didn't know how, but the boundaries had just…evaporated. Maybe she'd grown complacent. But there was also the fact she'd been lucky. Overbearing the spirits might be, but at that point she'd never encountered anything dark. Contrary to popular belief, the spiritual world wasn't something terrifying, merely another dimension which existed right alongside the material world, the veil between the two not as thick as some wished it to be.

The darkness was no match for the light. The light simply…absorbed it. That's what Margaret had told her and also what she now knew to be true. Dear, sweet Margaret, whose eyes had held such conviction.

Maybe depression had caused the boundaries to fade. Postnatal depression that overwhelmed everything, that terror of being wholly responsible for another human, and Reggie working so hard he was barely there. Just as she knew no one else with a psychic ability, she knew no one else with a young baby to care for either. She was isolated and scared, in some ways more than she'd ever been. And Wayne – oh, she loved him now! – but back then, he never stopped crying. And nor did she. She was *plunged* into depression. A void. A melancholy place in which she became over-comfortable with all things bleak. Addicted to stories in newspapers, to murders committed and one murderer in particular, the *unlikeliness* of her. It had been such a dreadful case that had hit the headlines, keeping the newspapers busy for months. The TV too, and Theo glued to it, forgetting another lesson Margaret had taught her, that like attracts like.

"Focus on the darkness," she'd said, "and it's the darkness you'll encounter. And we don't want that, now do we, Theo dear? We want to help the needy, not the opportunistic, the mimics or the deceivers." She'd halted only a second before adding, "The evil."

Was she evil, this killer? Because that's how she was portrayed. A demon clothed in girlish innocence. Her victims two other children, both toddlers.

Her image – aged only ten – was everywhere, but nowhere more so than in Theo's mind.

Mary Bell had dark hair framing a pale heart-shaped face with wide, knowing eyes, also dark, that bore into you, froze you right through to your soul. That's how it felt for

Theo, at any rate, that her heart, once bursting with love and excitement, was now suspended in icy numbness. A dreadful feeling, and so when Reggie was home, she would take it out on him, scream at him for the slightest thing, rage and rage, trying to feel something. Deep down she *was* hurting; she was mystified and bewildered, and so she shouldered the world's hurt and made it her own. What a mistake! The little girl in the newspapers was locked away in a remand home, Theo wondering about her victims and whether she should she try to seek them out – see if they lingered? Poor wretched lambs.

But in the end something sought *her* out instead, no victim of crime, rather another perpetrator, this one a little older than Mary Bell, but unlike her, she seemed to have got away with murder and had since died. She was so…damaged, as any child capable of committing such acts would be, so tortured that Theo couldn't help. Already on the edge, she'd fall further if she did, clarity coming to the fore at the last minute.

The spirit came out of nowhere, and on a day when the sun was shining too – when Theo was alone, thank God, some rare time off from the baby, her mother taking care of him, realising she needed a break.

She'd been on a bench in town, just sitting, staring into nothing when the girl manifested, when she flew at Theo, her mouth cavernous, wide open and screaming, *Help me! It wasn't my fault, what happened. Was it? Is there something inside me? Something poisonous? Something rotten? Here, in my chest. A voice keeps whispering in my ear, telling me it's my fault. All of it. No! No! No! It can't be! Am I the devil? Is this hell? Is it?*

Theo immediately fled back to her marital home, but

the girl would often materialise, day and night, Theo just so thankful no one else could see her, the blood that dripped from her hands, the clothing she wore splattered in it.

The only thing Theo could do at that stage was help herself, Reggie growing more impatient with her, not understanding why she wasn't embracing her role as wife and mother as every other woman seemed to. Wayne screaming more and more. There was always such noise in her head! A cacophony that refused to ease.

No! Finally, she'd told the girl. *I will not help you. I won't! You've hurt people, you've...killed them, haven't you?* Children, it had to be, just like that other one. For how could a mere slip of a girl overcome an adult? *If so, you are evil. A devil. Born that way.*

Theo winced as she recalled this, but it was a long time ago. She simply hadn't known then what she knew now, what life taught you alongside your mentors. Margaret had been right when she'd said life was a journey, that throughout it you learnt, you evolved, or were meant to. The older you got, the more you realised there was a reason for everything.

The spirit had finally vanished. Theo had even managed to forget about her eventually. Her mind lifting out of depression as she'd indeed got used to her new role as the baby grew, became less fretful, she and Reggie continuing to forge their way ahead through thick and thin. The turning point had come when Reggie got her help, just as her parents once had. A home help this time, and again an older woman, someone vastly more experienced who'd had several children and knew the ropes.

Daphne Blunt had guided her through what seemed like another minefield. She was also as cheap as chips, Reggie'd said, asking only a very basic wage, which had allowed them to afford her. Another woman put here to help, but this time the living. God bless Margaret, and God bless Daphne – and all the people that a more mentally stable Theo had come to know since those bygone days: Ness Patterson, as psychic as she was herself; Ruby Davis, another remarkable talent in the psychic world; and dear, sweet Corinna, a developing psychic she thought of as her fourth child, the girl that she'd always longed for. The four of them had formed Psychic Surveys, helping so many in the spiritual world. Together.

Blessed. Truly blessed. More ups than downs in life, when she reflected on it. Glorious ups. That life in its twilight stage now, but such happiness in her heart.

Such guilt too.

The spirit who'd begged her, where was she now? Gone to the light, Theo hoped, somehow, someway, despite her tortured nature. Or was she festering? Theo didn't use that word lightly, for the girl *would* fester. Therein lay the danger.

The reason she was on her mind again was because of something that had happened only recently, an incident in her local newsagent, of all places. A *deliberate* incident?

Theo had been in there, grabbing a magazine, a Bounty bar and a packet of crisps – the weekend's guilty pleasures – and had brushed past a shelf where some secondhand books for sale were stacked, her shoulder catching the edge of one and it falling to the floor. Huffing, puffing, cursing even, albeit silently, she'd bent down to retrieve it. *Forgotten Murders* was its somewhat dubious title, the cover picture monochrome, dark and grainy, designed to be foreboding. Her spine had tingled as she'd held it, and then she'd opened the book at precisely where a case of two murdered children was documented. Eliza Brooks had been aged twelve, as had Danny Bailey, the other poor unfortunate. Their deaths had occurred in the same manner, in the same area of Sussex, only days apart. Her eyes glued to the page, she'd taken a deep breath. *Don't search for the darkness*, she warned herself. She mustn't. Trouble was, the darkness often searched for her.

Finally, she'd closed the slim hardback book, taken it to the counter and paid for it, then hurried home to read more. The two children had been crudely and cruelly murdered, bludgeoned with a rock and also strangled – but then, she reasoned, can murder be anything other than cruel? Who'd carried out such heinous acts remained unknown.

The dates they'd been killed – 1970 – it fit. It was within the same timeframe that the child spirit had appeared to her, covered in blood.

Was it another cry for help, this book falling at her feet? After so long? *It wasn't my fault, what happened.* That's what the girl had said. *Is there something inside me? Something poisonous? Something rotten?*

Finally, Theo had closed the book and sat there in her armchair, long after daylight faded, her mind full of possibilities, constantly contemplating.

There are things that truly haunt us, memories being one of them.

Also, the realisation that you should have done something but hadn't, becoming more regretful as you reached the end of your own time on earth.

Finally, in the comfort of her living room, all white and airy, just the way she liked it, full of sacred space with no husband or sons to mess it up – more's the pity – she lifted her head.

"Child, are you nearby still? Can you hear me? If so, I'm ready to talk to you now, to work with you. I'm…equipped. If you can, give me another sign that you're with me."

The silence tore at her.

Chapter One

Ruby was trying hard to keep a straight face. She loved her job, truly. Regarding some cases, though, she couldn't help but wonder what the heck she'd got herself into, starting up and running a business such as hers, specialising in domestic spiritual clearance. Theo was clearly feeling the same, her lips clamped so tightly together they were white, as were Corinna's. Of the four of them, only Ness remained poker-faced, making it impossible to guess how she felt. Hats off to her, though. She'd got that particular expression down to a fine art. The other three…not so much.

Theo was the first to crack, to the surprise of no one, emitting a bellow of laughter that was nothing less than infectious, Ruby and Corinna quickly caving in. Not so straight-faced now, Ness sighed heavily. Even Jed put in a brief appearance, barking and wagging his tail, clearly curious as to what all the fuss was about before deciding nothing much and disappearing again. Thank God the clients who had appointed Psychic Surveys weren't on the premises. Roger Edwards and his much younger partner, Skylar Muldoon, had left them to it, practically skedaddled out the door, heads down and clutching at their respective shoulder bags. The memory of which made Ruby laugh all the harder.

She couldn't blame them, though. This was a troublesome spirit that haunted their home. Responsible for banging and crashing at unsociable hours, apparently, an attention-seeker. He was also rude, or as Theo might term it, *bawdy*, the insults hurled their way ever since they'd entered eye-watering. *You hideous bunch of wart-infested witches*, the disembodied voice had spat at them. *You fat old blunderbuss!* That was for Theo. *As for you, you're as sour as a lemon! A right old vinegar tits!* Ness had been on the receiving end of those particular lovelies. *Need someone to plumb your depths?* Corinna had shaken her head when he'd asked her. As for Ruby, the spirit had come right up and whispered in her ear, *I'd give you a bun in the oven anytime.*

The house was an ordinary one. A tiny Victorian mid-terrace in Brighton, down a little lane off the main shopping artery in town, an equally small theatre at the end of it, a place for art-house productions. The owner who'd called them in, Roger, was also arty. He just had that vibe about him, dressed in linen trousers, a loose pinstriped shirt and a cravat, his white hair longish, a foppish fringe pushed to one side. Skylar fitted the cliché of a Brighton creative too with her long flared skirt, also linen, a blouse tucked into its waistband, and brown hair flowing. Ruby didn't actually know what they did for a living; neither had said. The only thing he'd talked about since getting in touch was the haunted cottage they'd recently bought. That whoever lingered there was 'a bloody pain in the arse'.

"I don't care what it costs," Roger Edwards had declared when they'd been summoned to his doorstep, "pull out all the stops. Get rid of it. Send it back where it belongs, to hell."

Ness had baulked at that. Even Theo had raised an eyebrow.

"I don't know if you've read the information on our website," Ruby had replied whilst being ushered into the kitchen, "but it's not hell we aim to send them to."

Skylar, who'd been standing beside him, raised her hand and waved it dismissively. "Yes, yes, yes, we read all about that. Something about the light or whatever. Frankly, I don't care where it goes, just as long as it's gone. It's really violent. Terrifying, in fact. I just want it over. Come on, Rog, or we'll be late meeting Noah and Fleur."

Roger had duly nodded. "We'll be back in an hour or so," he'd said to Ruby. "If we're satisfied some sort of progress has been made, we can sort out payment then."

"An hour?" Theo had muttered. "Go us, eh? So we're on a budget after all."

All cases that the team took on varied. Some actually took no time to clear, as if the spirit had been waiting for them all along, yearning for words of gentle encouragement: *There's a light, can you see it? That's right, in the distance. Go towards it. Don't be afraid. The light is where we come from and where we return. It's Source, our true home.*

And then off they'd go, gliding happily towards it, sometimes turning back for a farewell wave, sometimes not, just…disappearing to the other side.

Other spirits, though, could be far more resistant. They were afraid, usually. Terrified that the light was a trick and that in it they wouldn't be a part of something, become whole, but cease to exist. They had to be persuaded, *firmly* persuaded: *You simply cannot stay here. This isn't your home any longer. You're out of time and out of dimension. And quite frankly, you're also a nuisance, scaring the living like you do. Now, go on. Go. We will walk with you to the light. We can guide you all the way there.*

Other types of spirits were those that feared retribution for their earthly sins. Again, it took time to explain that while all harm inflicted on others in life would have to be examined intricately, there was no such thing as a place filled with fire and brimstone where you'd burn forever. Acknowledging what you'd done, owning it, was necessary for redemption. Basically, you had to man up, be willing to experience the sorrow you'd heaped on others, which, admitted, could be agonising, but eventually you'd evolve.

A complicated job, when Ruby thought about it. So many shades of grey involved. They swung from one end of the spectrum to the other, but today, it was all about the giggles.

"He definitely used to tread the boards, this one," she said.

"A badass diva," Corinna agreed.

"Lord knows we've dealt with badass divas in the past," Theo interjected between snorts. "Remember Cynthia Hart from Highdown Hall?"

Ness sniffed. "Hardly going to forget her, are we?"

"Try as we might," Theo continued jovially.

Ness then made a show of checking her watch. "We've precisely twenty minutes left. We've made a connection with the spirit." Here she paused, grimaced slightly. "A *dubious* connection, but we're getting nowhere fast."

"Okay, all right." Theo gave a slight cough before adjusting the floaty scarf she wore. They'd all agreed the spirit was somewhere in his mid-fifties and, given the slightly old-fashioned language he was using, had died around thirty to forty years previously. "Now, look here, matey-boy," she continued, "we've enjoyed your company, really we have. If you weren't something on the stage in life, then you missed your calling, because one thing you are is entertaining. The trouble is, you can't make up for it now, not in your current guise, so do us a favour and have a good look around, will you? There's a light. Can you see it? You may have to squint, but it's there, I can assure you, and the more you look for it, the more visible it'll become. Head towards it, dear chap. I'll tell you something, you'll keep 'em rolling in the aisles where you're going. They're fond of a good joke there."

Fuck off, you flabby old whore! Who d'you think you are anyway, telling me what to do? I'll tell you something, stuff another pork pie in your gullet. That'll shut you up.

As Ruby and Corinna collapsed into fits of laughter again, Theo shook her head and sighed rather theatrically herself. "I've been called some things in my lifetime," she said, "but a 'flabby old whore' is up there with the finest."

"Oh, this is tedious," Ness complained. "He's just not listening."

"He's all mouth is what he is," Theo countered. "We give it another shot, but if no cigar, what say you we go to the pub? I could murder a G and T."

"Down for that," Corinna replied, Ruby also nodding her head.

The remaining twenty minutes Roger Edwards had allotted them passed quickly. When he'd initially phoned them, Ruby had done some research on the house but could find no mention of a death there, nor of a single man who'd lived there that fit the bill of this character. No matter, not everything was recorded in black and white. What if he'd been a renegade from the theatre, gone walkabout? Perhaps she'd need to do some research into that next. He could have been an usher or a backseat lurker, growing increasingly bitter since he'd never been the one taking centre stage. But c'est la vie. That was how it went sometimes. Maybe a custodian of the theatre might remember something, shine a light on him that way, at least.

She was busy thinking this whilst simultaneously getting ready to wind down, head home to Cash and baby Hendrix after that G and T Theo had mentioned, when the front door burst open, Roger, his partner and two other people standing there. The ones they'd mentioned before, perhaps, Noah and Fleur? The man held a small video camera in his hand and the woman some kind of microphone.

As all four Psychic Surveys team members turned towards the door, a flashlight causing Ruby to blink rapidly, Roger was the first to open his mouth.

"Aannd…action!" he cried out before adding, "I presume there is some kind of action by now. You've had long enough."

Ruby was about to answer, her colleagues no doubt forming replies of their own, when taunts and insults courtesy of the spirit became something far darker. An attack. Not on her but Ness, whose hands lifted to her throat as if trying to release some pressure there.

"What the hell?" yelled Theo, bustling towards her, Ruby and Corinna also quick to close the gap.

"I knew it!" declared Roger, such triumph in his voice. "Didn't I tell you, Noah? It's an old thespian we have on our hands here. Knew he'd play to the cameras. YouTube is going to love this! It'll go viral, make our name. Go on, Bob, carry on, do your darndest!"

Ruby swung round to face him. "Bob? Who the hell is Bob?"

"Bob Darnell," Roger happily replied, while, by his side, Skylar clapped her hands with glee. "Reputed to haunt the theatre at the bottom of the lane here, an actor, or he wanted to be, from the fifties and sixties. I used to sit in the theatre when it was quiet, trying to make contact with him, managed to coax him back here eventually, told him I'd make a star of him yet. And…well…it worked! He's been here ever since. Then when I found out about Psychic Surveys and what you do, I knew I could fulfil my promise, make a star of him, and in turn—" Roger gave a somewhat insolent shrug "—us."

"Um…hello," Corinna interrupted, "could I just say Ness is really struggling here. If it is Bob responsible, he needs to let her go."

Noah and his camera darted forward. "Oh no, no, no, don't let go yet, Bob! This is incredible footage. Groundbreaking. *Most Haunted*, eat your heart out."

"Shit!" Ruby gasped. "Ness's face. It's like…"

"She's going to explode?" offered Fleur, who'd joined Noah, that microphone of hers held high. "Now, wouldn't that be something?"

"Bloody hell!" It was Theo, all trace of amusement gone. "A setup! That's what this is. One that we blindly walked into." As she addressed the spirit, the fury in her voice increased. "Bob, stop what you're doing now! Don't you see? They're lying. They're using you. This will make *them* famous, not you. Only they will reap the rewards.

You're dead, Bob, you know that as well as I do, you've croaked it, and I'm sorry if life wasn't what you wanted it to be, that you never hit the heady heights of stardom, but this isn't the way to go about it now. I repeat, you have nothing to gain from this. There's no benefit for you whatsoever. Now, listen to me. Stop what you're doing and let Ness go."

Whilst Theo pleaded, Ruby and Corinna had their hands at Ness's neck too, trying to help but grasping only at thin air. Unable to speak, her eyes were also closing.

"Shit," yelled Corinna. "What are we going to do?"

Ruby tried hard to think, aware too that Theo's words were bouncing off Bob, having no effect. As for Roger and his cohorts, they were milking the situation for all it was worth, having no care that someone was getting hurt in their quest for more followers on YouTube or TikTok or wherever the hell they posted their videos – a snuff video at this rate.

How fast the situation had changed had stunned her, but now she was rallying. She had to; Ness's well-being depended on it. Although it was thankfully rare, she'd been in a situation similar to the one her colleague was in now, knew how serious it could be.

Before she could contemplate further, she lunged at Noah, wrenched the camera from his hand and threw it to the floor, proceeding to stamp on it, anger giving her the might she needed to cause quite some damage.

Noah was the one stunned now, so much so it rendered him immobile, but Fleur was on the attack, every bit as much as Bob and Ruby, casting the microphone aside as she pounced on Ruby. Entwined, the pair crashed against the wall, Corinna now trying to disentangle Fleur from

Ruby while Roger and his partner drew out their phones and started filming on them instead.

Again, Theo stepped in. Theo, who was just over five feet and as wide as she was tall, in her early seventies too, and right now more formidable than Boudica of the Iceni tribe. She roared at them all, the living and the dead, demanded they get a grip.

Even Bob listened this time as Ness at last gasped out loud, whatever pressure there'd been released, Corinna rushing over to offer support.

"Incorrigible," Theo continued. "The lot of you. The behaviour of imbeciles! You!" she said, turning to Roger Edwards. "You were aware of this spirit. You *coaxed* him from the theatre to your house, made all sorts of empty promises, effectively preying on him."

"Well…I…um—" But Theo refused to let him speak.

"Because you're a failed thespian too, by the looks of it. Am I correct?"

His cheeks suffused with colour, at which Theo nodded.

"I thought as much. It's a case of the blind leading the blind. Pathetic! And believe you me, if I see my face or those of my colleagues on any form of social media, I will sue, do you hear? I do not consent to starring in anything. Frankly, I've better things to do with my time, such as offering help to those who truly need it."

Warthog! The only light I want is the limelight!

Theo turned on her heel, a nimble move, and gazed, basilisk-like, at a spot just beside Ness, who was busy recovering.

"Is that correct, Bob?" she replied, a sneer on her lips. "Then what I suggest is this: attack away. But not my colleagues or I will summon the hounds of hell and set them on your tail, do you hear? They will chase you all the way into Hades, where the only thing you'll be is infamous. Instead"—she lifted a hand and indicated those in the room who were not members of the Psychic Surveys team—"take your pick amongst these little beauties -- Roger, Skylar, Noah and Fleur – and do your darndest. What is it they say in the theatre? That's it. Break a leg. Any leg. You've eight to choose from." As gasps filled the room, from Ruby as well as Roger and his friends, Theo addressed Ness. "Are you okay?"

"Yes," she answered. "I'm fine. Really."

To prove her point, Ness staggered forwards to stand by Theo's side, Corinna and Ruby joining them. Somewhere in the great unknown, Ruby could hear barking, Jed having returned to enjoy the sideshow but from a safe distance.

"Good," Theo decided, "then we'll take our leave."

"Ow!" It was Skylar complaining. "What was that? Did one of you just shove me? Ow!" she said again, stumbling slightly. "What the hell's happening?"

"Quick," Fleur said to Noah, "grab your phone. Bob's at it again!"

Roger swung round to face the Psychic Surveys team standing en masse. "You said break a leg. What if…what if he takes it literally?"

Ruby was concerned about that too. "Theo," she said, "turns out Bob's not that much fun after all. He's dangerous. We can't just leave them here with him. At his mercy."

Theo eyed her directly, such steeliness in her expression. "People have to evolve," she said. "And look at them. Go on, see what they're doing."

Roger was trying to help his partner but getting shoved too by the invisible force that was Bob. Yet even as he was, his eyes were alight when addressing Noah and Fleur: "Did you get that? Oh my God, did you get that? Ow! Bob, wait. We need to choreograph this, make it count. Shit! Shit! Shit! We're going to go stellar! Make sure you record everything."

Ruby returned her gaze to Theo. "So what you're saying is…"

"Once they've all ended up in the hospital with a broken arm or leg or whatever, perhaps we'll come back then. When Bob realises breaking limbs is all he's good for, he may be more conducive to moving on. Come on, our job here is done. For now."

"Did someone mention a G and T earlier?" Ness said, the first out the door.

"I believe that was me," replied Theo, following her.

"Then make mine a bloody double," she said as Ruby and Corinna exited too, closing the door behind them as another cry rang out.

Chapter Two

Of course they went back. They had to. They'd left for a good half hour, though, by which time Roger Edwards and his cohorts had abandoned any hope of social media stardom, begging the team to intervene once more, to end the spirit's onslaught. There were no broken limbs, although some bruises had been inflicted – primarily by them all feeding off the situation and running around in circles, bashing into each other – and all phones had long since been discarded, broken even, by the looks of it, lying forlornly on the floor.

Oh, they had to get firm with Bob. Well…Theo did. If ever there was a limelight, she stole it that afternoon, standing there in the centre of the room, alone and truly magnificent, the reigning queen. Ruby was in awe of her, and so were Roger Edwards and his friends. And Bob too, it seemed, for he finally dispensed with venting the anger and frustration that had followed him into the spirit world and listened as Theo once again sold the idea of the afterlife to him – basically a place where he could fulfil his true potential, be all he was meant to be. Very few living, breathing people, although reincarnated, retained memories of what it was like on the other side, but, by God, Theo painted a vivid enough picture. In short, and after another hour or two of Psychic Surveys' time, Bob was sold and just…disappeared, went backstage, another bark accompanying him, Ruby'd swear it: Jed's version of applause.

As soon as he'd gone, the atmosphere in the house calmed, Roger and his cronies able to sense that too and, much to Ruby's dismay, immediately reaching for their phones, stabbing at the screens and shaking them, seeing if they could retrieve any footage as Noah's camera was beyond help.

Their faces fell when they realised the futility of their actions, that Bob was not, by proxy, going to make them media sensations. Their expressions were even more hangdog when Ruby informed them they'd be billed for three hours of Psychic Surveys' time.

"And there'll be no quibbles with payment," Theo told them, "or I'll be having a word with Bob, maybe get him to do an encore."

Roger swallowed, Skylar rubbed at the bruises on her arms, and Noah climbed to his feet. "Don't worry, Roger, we'll all chip in," he said before turning to Theo. "It's not a problem. Really, it isn't."

"Good," she replied, giving Ness a run for her money in the poker-face stakes. "And here's another tip for you, this one free of charge: try using your own talent to get yourself noticed in future. Dig deep. I'm sure you'll find something of use."

Once again, the team took their leave, all intent on heading home this time. It had turned out to be a long day, and Ruby was itching to see Hendrix, her baby, who was just over six months old now and chubby as hell. She couldn't wait to give him a squeeze, and Cash too, in the home they shared on Sun Street in Lewes.

A sanctuary, that's what the house was – a retreat from the world, the people and the spirits in it. A workspace too, her office having relocated from the high street to the attic there. That evening, having got home and completing the obligatory squeezes, Ruby then took a long, hot shower, after which she rocked Hendrix to sleep – something that took all of five minutes, the boy thankfully as keen on slumber as his father.

With the child settled in his cot, Ruby padded down the narrow staircase to the kitchen, where Cash was preparing dinner.

"Hard day at the office?" he quipped as she entered the room.

She took a moment to answer, instead surveying him as she pulled out a chair and sat at the table. He was tall, over six feet, and had a handsome face – chiselled, she always thought of it – his skin slightly darker than hers courtesy of his Jamaican-born mother, Cassy. Thirty-one to her twenty-eight, they'd been together a few years now, such a lot having happened during that time, both good and bad. Cash had everything to do with the good, and now Hendrix too – the icing on the cake – but some of the bad, some of what she'd experienced, what she'd *discovered*, during that time was so bad she couldn't countenance it, shaking her head even now as certain memories tried to resurface.

Cash clearly noticed.

"Rubes?" he said, stopping what he was doing, frying onions and garlic in a pan to make a tomato sauce for the pasta he was boiling. "You okay? Shit." He left the spatula in the pan and hurried over. "It was a bad day, then? You look really tired."

"Do I?" she said, rubbing at her eyes, imagining all too well that their green was slightly faded. "Yeah, I am tired, I suppose, and yeah, it was an…unusual case we worked on. Got it sorted, though."

He ruffled her hair. "Got that pesky ghost packed off, did you?"

"Eventually," she said. "Almost became a media sensation whilst we were at it." Remembering the 44 Gilmore Street case, where that had almost happened too, local press determined to paint them in a grim light, she frowned. "Like I said, though, all was fine in the end. I'll explain over dinner. Will it be long? I'm starving."

"Nope, not long at all. Reckon I'll be dishing up in about ten minutes. See that bottle of Shiraz there? Crack it open, pour yourself a large one and the same for me too. It's arrabbiata we're having, with Barilla rigatoni. It'll make the long day seem worth it."

She smiled at his quirky insistence on using particular pastas, and he returned to the hob and got on with the cooking. *He* made it worth it, him and Hendrix. And Jed, of course, her spirit dog companion – her familiar, those given to the old ways might say – a shining light in the darkness, a beacon. Where was he? He'd made a brief appearance earlier at Roger Edwards's house, but since then there'd been no sign of him. That was Jed, though. He came and he went. Maybe he was a guide for others too, not solely her. Who knew? She might sense, see and hear grounded spirits, but what lay beyond the veil she, like so many others, had no clue – although quickly she amended that to no *conscious* clue.

The evening passed, and it was, as expected, a very pleasant one. Dinner was followed by a movie on Netflix, the red wine relaxing her bones as she snuggled up to Cash. He loved the old black-and-whites, and so they'd often dig around the channels to find one. Sometimes, for nostalgia, they'd watch one of the golden greats starring Cynthia Hart, the spirit the Psychic Surveys team had moved on from Highdown Hall, a case which Cash had helped them with when she'd first met him. He claimed not to have a psychic bone in his body, and sometimes Ruby believed him but sometimes not because Cash, he could be a great help. Theo's take on it was that *everybody* had psychic ability, that it wasn't called a 'sixth sense' for nothing. How good you were depended on how much notice you invested in it, and, like all talents, the more practised you were, the better you became. But…she was glad he was interested only up to a point, was otherwise firmly anchored in the material world. He was the yang to her yin. He provided the balance. If she was with someone as psychic as her – and *rarely* had she met another as psychic as her, her team excepted – it could tip the scales in one direction only. Never a good thing.

They had indeed ended up watching an old Cynthia Hart film – *The Elitists* – where she'd starred with her real-life lover, John Sterling. God, the chemistry between them on-screen was explosive. It made Ruby feel quite raunchy, actually, something Cash was grateful for. Unlike the spirit they'd encountered earlier, Cynthia and John had soared right to the top, been revered all around the world, and then – for Cynthia, at least – it was over, her life cut dramatically short just as she'd been about to star in *Atlantic*, the biggest budget film of all time, at that point in history, anyway. Poor Bob, who'd never made it at all, and poor Cynthia, a girl from a humble background who'd struck lucky, who'd held the world in her hands and then lost it – Ruby couldn't decide which was worse.

Later that night in bed, Cash gently snoring, Hendrix in the second bedroom now but his snuffles audible courtesy of the baby monitor she kept in her room, Ruby tried to sleep…and failed. She hated sleepless nights. Just lying there, tossing, turning…thinking.

The past…sometimes it wouldn't leave you alone. This was one of those nights, so many thoughts tumbling through her head, so many different subjects that craved attention. She didn't want to do this, not now. Hendrix would wake around six, wanting a feed and a cuddle, and then she had a busy day planned, not work this time. She was meeting a friend – a *new* friend, Michelle, who had a baby boy the same age as Hendrix, Leo. She'd met Michelle at a mother-and-baby swim class at the Lewes Leisure Centre, the pair of them terrified of ducking their precious babies' heads under water, the boys loving it, though, emerging from the deep spitting out water and giggling, the instructor clapping her hands to witness it. 'See,' she'd told them, 'babies come from the womb. They're familiar with being in water! This will get them used to it all over again, teach them not to be afraid of it. Oh yes,' she'd continued, beaming at them, 'we'll make champion swimmers of them yet!' And Michelle and Ruby had looked at each other, exchanged rueful smiles and, after the lesson, grabbed a coffee in the café there, chatting about everything to do with babies whilst the two boys were jiggled happily in their laps.

That's what she should focus on – the joy and excitement of meeting Michelle and Leo. They lived in Lewes too, in the Malling area, around a fifteen-minute walk from Sun Street. Leo wasn't Michelle's first child; she had an elder daughter, Willow. She was the only other young mum Ruby knew and someone she could imagine continuing this thrilling, sometimes overwhelming adventure with for a while yet. They got on so well, which was something to be happy about, relieved even. And yet…as always, tendrils of darkness pushed through the light to probe the minefield of her mind, a shrill voice always screaming at her, *Look at me, remember me. By God, girl, don't you dare forget about me!*

Ruby squeezed her eyes shut, only to see yet more darkness. Oh, how she wanted to forget! She tried so hard. Family. Forming one of her own was miraculous – a *new* family – but she came from family too, and that was what demanded to be remembered. A troubled family. Her mother, Jessica. Her father…

No! I won't do this! You can't make me! I won't let you ruin what I have.

A man she'd met only once. Whom she'd longed to meet, ever since she could remember. And then when it had happened, wished she hadn't.

Someone who was troubled most of all. Insane.

That word – that admission – made her gasp, the sound causing Cash to stir, to roll towards her. He remained asleep, though. Thankfully. She didn't want him to wake, reach out and ask her what was wrong, worm out of her the thoughts that always troubled her in the dark depths of the night. *What if it's hereditary?*

She wasn't insane. If anything, her friends and Cash kept her sane. Jed too. But madness, she'd always feared it, and yet hadn't known why until she'd met her father. She hadn't understood the reasons for battling against such wild thinking – there was so much light in her life! That's what had to be remembered. She must draw on everything she'd been taught, silently repeating in her mind, even now, words that were so familiar: *Draw the light straight from Source, Ruby, pure white, gentle light made entirely of love, which is the greatest force of all. Wrap yourself in it, and it'll swallow the darkness. Always.* She knew that; she believed that. And belief was everything, was power itself.

So why did the battle continue? Why the constant nagging fear? That feeling that something terrible was waiting just out of sight, ready to lash out, to destroy her.

Having a family was indeed a miracle, but it made you feel vulnerable too. *She* might not be mad, but what if…what if…

A yelp…a cry…

Ruby turned towards the monitor. Was Hendrix okay?

She didn't stop to think but leapt from bed, hurried to the door and out of it, crossing the landing to the second bedroom, tiny like the rest of the house, doll-sized, but perfect for a baby, for the child he would grow to be.

Moonlight flooded the room as she entered, the curtains having been left slightly open. There he was, in his cot and fast asleep. He must have cried out whilst dreaming.

What kind of dream, though? A nightmare? Do babies even have nightmares?

Immediately, she reprimanded herself.

Of course not! Babies are full of sweetness, full of light, and nothing else. Pure.

Even when they came from something hellish?

Tears blurred her vision as she reached down and gently stroked his plump cheek.

Why all these thoughts? Despite her happiness – and she *was* happy, happier than she'd ever been – why did they continue to plague her? Not just that, multiply?

Was this normal? Could it be down to hormones, even? Did motherhood make you fear because the thought of losing a child, something so precious… No, she wouldn't go there. She couldn't. Just kept thinking of the light as she stood by the cot, wrapping them both in it this time. *You'll be all right, baby. We will, you, me and Daddy. And Jed's here too, somewhere, even when he's not. The best guard dog ever.*

But what was he meant to guard them against, not today, perhaps not even tomorrow, but sometime in the future?

The answer came quickly, inevitably, causing tears to drip from her cheeks, to land on the woven cotton blanket below.

Unfinished business. That was what.

In every life, in every human experience, there was always something that needed completion, and if not, then perhaps, just perhaps, the soul wouldn't be able to rest easy, and the battle would replay, over and over through the ages, through different lifetimes, in different realms, even, until finally, finally, there was a victor.

Chapter Three

"Ruby, hi! How are you today? How's the little man? Oh my God, he looks so cute in that outfit! Leo's covered in the remains of his turkey bolognaise, I'm afraid. I tried to clean him up, but I didn't want to be late meeting you, so, yep, he's gotta wear his food with pride!"

Michelle Bayliss was the same age as Ruby, the same height, the same situation, the same…almost everything. A godsend. Meeting in Southover Grange Gardens, a place where squirrels chased each other and birds sang in the treetops, they could grab a coffee and a sandwich from its handy outdoor café on such a beautiful spring day.

"My shout," Michelle said, causing Ruby to protest. Michelle was adamant, though. "You get it next time, okay?"

Ruby relaxed. More than that, she beamed, glad to hear there'd be a next time. After requesting a tuna mayo sandwich and a green tea with lemon – the latter a new favourite recently – she guarded both buggies as Michelle duly went to place their order.

Leo was asleep, such a sense of contentment emanating from him. Hendrix, however, was wide awake, though quiet and just staring back at her with those big dark eyes of his.

She reached into the buggy and stroked his cheek, just

as she'd done the previous night. "We're going to be all right, eh?" she murmured. "We're going to be just fine."

And she meant it – in the cold light of day, at least. It was funny, really, how the dark played on your fears, brought every gloom-ridden, obscure thought to the surface. And yet, on a day such as this, with the sun high in the sky, it was all so totally different. The cold fear that had clutched at her heart as she'd stood by Hendrix's cot had faded to nothing. All she felt now was happy and hopeful, successful even, having got her personal life on track and her business life too, achieving everything she'd ever wanted, and all before the age of thirty. *Too good to be true, perhaps?*

She retracted her hand. "For God's sake, Ruby," she muttered. "Don't start."

"Sorry?" Michelle asked, returning with a tray.

Ruby looked up, surprised at first, unaware she'd spoken out loud. "Oh…nothing. Nothing. Just having a word with myself, that's all."

Michelle maintained her smile as she sat down. "About what?"

Should she do it? Ruby wondered. Tell her? That was the thing with Michelle. They might be relatively new friends, but she felt she could trust her, sensed she'd understand.

Ruby tore off a crust of sandwich so that Hendrix could gnaw at it before answering.

"Anxiety," she said. "I get a bit anxious sometimes, you know, about…stuff. No reason. Life's sweet. Actually, maybe that *is* the reason. I feel so lucky, and then…then…"

"You worry it'll all get taken away?" Michelle guessed

before adding, "I feel that way too, especially since having children. It's normal, though, only natural. With little ones to protect, you become more sensitive to the world and its dangers. That's the maternal instinct coming out in you. You'll do anything to keep your kids safe."

At Michelle's words, Ruby sighed with relief, felt even more of a fool for the direction her thoughts took her on occasion. She lived in the light, and because of that, she attracted the light. Yes, she had to deal with the darkness too, that was all part of the job, *such darkness*, but she'd triumphed over and over, she and her team.

Michelle took a bite of sandwich before continuing, chewing thoughtfully. "Yep," she said, "it all started when Willow was born," referring to her older child, aged eight, who was currently at school. "That euphoric happiness coupled with the most crippling anxiety. Ruby, you've said you had a hard time adjusting when Hendrix was first born. Do you think you could have postnatal depression? It's very common."

"Maybe. A little. At first, perhaps. But I'm okay now. Mostly."

"Good to hear, but monitor it, okay? Keep…a balance. And remember, it's normal to feel anxious." She glanced at her sleeping cub. "We're responsible for another human being entirely. It's awesome but bloody overwhelming. And you know what?"

"What?"

"I think it always will be."

Ruby nodded, eating some of her sandwich too. "Willow's such a pretty name. Does she have the same red hair as you?"

Michelle reached a hand upwards, fluffed at her hair,

worn short and neat. "She does. You'll have to meet her one day."

"I'd love to."

"Really?"

"Yeah, why not? Gain an insight into what lies ahead!"

Michelle laughed and averted her eyes as she took a sip of coffee. "Oh, Willow's a good girl, no trouble at all. Honestly."

Ruby leant forward. "You know, I admire you. You were so young when you had her."

Again, Michelle didn't meet Ruby's eyes, not at first. Instead, she stared into the cup she held, swirling the coffee around inside it. "It was a tough time for sure. I had no idea how I was going to cope, alone and with a baby. Her dad…yeah, he didn't want to know, refused to stick around. I wasn't especially close to my parents, not then, although they've turned out to be great grandparents. Funny that, isn't it? They've kind of grown into the role, matured. But…you know, you do cope. You have to. You've got to get on with it, for their sake. The kids, I mean, not my parents." She laughed. "But seriously, things fell into place eventually. I met Tim, and he was willing to take us both on." She nodded towards Leo. "Then this one put in an appearance."

Ruby nodded and smiled too. So Leo's father wasn't Willow's? She hadn't known that, and no reason she should at this very early stage of friendship, but it caused her now to wonder if Willow saw her father or, like her – once upon a time – didn't know who he was. Musing on that, it took a moment to realise Michelle was speaking again.

"Sorry, I didn't quite get that."

"Oh," Michelle said, waving a hand in the air, "I was just saying, if we're talking about admiration, what about you, starting a business so young, and a successful one at that."

"Ah, right, yeah." She had of course told Michelle she was a working mum and mentioned what she did, but, boy, had she played it down, leaving out all the stuff about the darkness and other entities, those that were non-spirit and so damned persistent. There was only so much her new friend needed to know. If Ruby were to come clean, tell the truth, the whole truth and nothing but the truth, she risked sending her running in the opposite direction. "It's a way to earn a living, I suppose."

"And if you have such an incredible gift, a brilliant way to make use of it."

"Yeah, that too," Ruby said just as Hendrix started whimpering, but she didn't mind; she was glad of the distraction. Reaching into the buggy, she released the restraints so she could lift him out onto her knee.

"He really is so handsome," Michelle said, reaching across to rub at his arm.

"Like his dad," Ruby replied, although mainly to herself, continuing to jiggle him.

"It's amazing that ghosts are real," Michelle continued, pushing her half-eaten sandwich to one side now, and Ruby's heart sinking to see it, knowing what it meant: that, finally, she wanted more details. "For so long I didn't think so. Didn't think at all about the paranormal and the possibility of it. It just wasn't on my radar. Don't do religion. Never liked horror films, you know, stuff like that, preferred romance and drama. And now…well, now…it's different. It really is amazing to think it's real.

That the paranormal is…you know…legit."

As she talked, Ruby's mind wandered yet again. Michelle was a full-time mum and her partner an electrician, able to support entirely his young family, their decision that she should be there for the kids a mutual one. Ruby and Cash tried to be there for Hendrix too – both self-employed, they were able to work around taking care of him most of the time – both their mothers also willing to help out, Cash's mum especially, who simply adored babies and couldn't get enough of him. Jessica, Ruby's mum, also loved Hendrix, but her life with Saul was a gentle one; it had to be, for the sake of their precarious mental health, the darkness and the way both had played with it responsible for that. They had a routine, which Ruby didn't like to disturb too much, fearing they weren't out of the woods yet, that just like something lay in wait for her, it did for them too, what they'd conjured, an attachment, not banished at all but ready to drag them back to the bleak place they'd once inhabited. *Ruby! Come on! Focus on Michelle.*

She'd been saying something about ghosts being real, now waiting expectantly for a reply.

"Well," Ruby said, trying to find a succinct and rational way to explain, "there's the material world that we know, but there's also a spiritual world, and they exist side by side and often in perfect harmony. But sometimes, just sometimes, in certain places and due to a whole variety of reasons, the curtain between the two thins or gets damaged."

"Stuff breaks through?"

"Yeah, kind of. It sounds exciting, I know, but mostly it isn't. Mainly we investigate houses where there's supposedly a presence but there's nothing. It's squeaky clean. Comes down to air locks in pipes or mice and pigeons in the attic, that kind of thing."

She'd said all this before to Michelle, used the very same words – her standard speech. And Michelle had gladly accepted it, hadn't had the time to probe too much as they were always so busy, the babies demanding their attention or the swimming tutor at the pool insisting they listen up. Now, though, despite Ruby not being fully focused, Michelle was.

"Are ghosts ever…evil?" she quizzed.

"Evil?" Ruby couldn't help but swallow.

"Yeah. I mean, you seem so laid-back about it all, and I'm sure a lot of cases are false alarms, but do you ever get frightened? That anxiety you mentioned, does it…feed it?"

Ruby frowned whilst tearing off more bread for Hendrix to chew. Where was Michelle going with all this? Or was it normal to ask such things? After all, the spiritual world was indeed portrayed as evil in films and in books. That aspect was played upon yet hardly ever the good, and certainly not the magnificent. Maybe it was human to err towards where the thrill lay.

"What I'm trying to say is," Michelle continued, not waiting for Ruby to reply this time, "are you scared, you know, by stuff that happens? By stuff that even you can't understand." Again, she rushed on, emitting a short burst of laughter too. "Oh God, look at me, interrogating you. Sorry, you must get this all the time. And you're not scared, are you? Like you say, it's mostly pretty mundane. And that's reassuring, it really is. I love that you're not scared, that you describe all this as normal, because…yeah, it could be."

Ruby was confused, more so than ever. Michelle was swinging from one point of view to another. Hendrix having settled, she reached across and briefly touched Michelle's arm. "Are you okay, Michelle? Is there something else you want to say? Something specific?"

Was it her imagination, or had Michelle flinched when she'd touched her?

"Michelle?" she pressed.

"What? Oh no, no. I'm fine. I'm just…interested, that's all. Oh, come on, don't tell me people aren't interested once they find out what you do for a living."

Truth was, outside her family and her team, Ruby didn't have many friends. Not close friends, anyway, her skills of communication perhaps better with the dead than the living. And she was fine with that. Didn't really have time for much more than her life was already crammed with. Having a baby, though, had changed that. She needed others in her situation, a case of like calling to like once again, because she needed to learn how to be a mother, how to cope. Michelle was the first of those friends, the first of many, Ruby hoped. But would that seriously transpire? Would she be accepted once people knew what she did for a living? Would she forever be thought of as…odd?

Anxiety. There it was again, flaring in her chest, a great bloom of it. The fear that the normality she craved would always be just out of reach.

She was about to respond to Michelle, who was gazing at her earnestly, the green of her eyes trying to look beyond the exterior, it seemed, to somewhere deep inside, to see the true answer she'd give, revealing another fear, maybe even a universal truth, that people were fascinated by what she did for a living rather than just plain old Ruby Davis. Might even take advantage of her because of it. Would Michelle too?

Hendrix had had enough jiggling, enough chewing on a crust, was bored too of park life in the afternoon. He let out a howl, one of his bloodcurdling finest, causing both girls to wince, Michelle to cover her ears, even.

"Blimey," she said whilst laughing, "that's enough to wake the dead."

"Sorry," said Ruby, jumping to her feet and jiggling him harder. "He's tired, but unlike Leo, he always seems to fight it."

Leo was also stirring, wrenched from the arms of Morpheus by the scream. As if fearing he was missing out, he too opened his mouth to join in the caterwauling.

Ruby apologised again. "Hendrix must have woken him."

"No problem," Michelle said, quickly extracting Leo from the buggy and doing the same as Ruby, rocking him back and forth. "The idyll never lasts for long when they're babies."

Ruby forced a smile back. "Yeah, yeah. Something I'm learning."

"Maybe we can meet without them one day, during the evening, have a few cocktails."

"Sounds great."

God, she could do with a cocktail right now, a martini of some sort, something that would really hit the spot. Numb her. Another thought that startled her. What was this? She was so fed up with motherhood-induced anxiety she was considering alcoholism?

As Michelle placed Leo back in his buggy, Ruby did the

same with Hendrix, the baby kicking and arching his back in protest every step of the way. Finally, with both boys strapped in, the girls turned to look at each other, their cheeks red with exertion.

"Shall we meet again soon?" Michelle suggested, Ruby's heart leaping to hear such words. Here was one woman who wasn't put off by what she did. Even so, Michelle would ask more about it, delve deeper. Ruby could sense that as strongly as she could sense spirit on occasion. It was there in Michelle's eyes when perhaps it hadn't been before. That intrigue.

"Yeah, sure. Now that swimming lessons are over for a while, perhaps we could take them to the pool anyway? Just for a splash around."

"That would be great. Or…"

"Or what?" prompted Ruby when Michelle stalled.

"Or something else. I'll have a think."

Ruby chanced a laugh. "Hey, you haven't got a haunted house, have you? Want me to come over and take a look?"

"A haunted house?" Michelle repeated, but, to Ruby's surprise, her laughter wasn't returned. Instead, Michelle was serious suddenly. Thoughtful. "Oh no, no, nothing like that. Tell you what, leave it with me and I'll have a think about what to do."

"Okay," Ruby answered, confused again. What was wrong with the pool? Both boys loved splashing about in it, and that was one time Hendrix wouldn't fight sleep; he'd go spark out afterwards. "So, you'll call me, or I'll call you?"

"I'll call you," Michelle said, her hands on the buggy and pushing it. When they'd met, she'd come from one direction and Ruby the other. Now she turned that way again, murmuring as she did, "I'll definitely be in touch."

After taking a few steps herself, Ruby then halted and looked over her shoulder. Eight or nine times they'd met, including the swimming lessons, that was all. Michelle had been the driving force behind their budding friendship, Ruby grateful, though. In the class, there'd been three other sets of mothers and babies, but they'd all seemed to know each other, were cliquey. So it was natural she and Michelle would gravitate towards each other, being the outsiders. Entirely natural. Wasn't it? It was Michelle who had broken the ice, offered the hand of friendship, Ruby practically biting it off. And it was going well, great guns. Swimming lessons had taken a brief hiatus, but they were still meeting up, she and Michelle, Leo and Hendrix, a new phase for Ruby unfolding.

Michelle disappearing from sight, Ruby continued walking, Hendrix thankfully having calmed down, now staring up at the clouds and cooing.

Life's encounters were amazing, really. Who you clicked with and who you didn't. All those people who surrounded you, who you *never* knew, strangers. But those you did, you formed a network with, a web of sorts. Encounters that were…fateful, perhaps?

Yes. Michelle had been very keen to pursue their friendship.

Patient too.

Only now was she asking more about Ruby's profession; only now it interested her.

Hey, you haven't got a haunted house, have you? Want me to take a look?

That's what Ruby had said, or words to that effect.

And Michelle had replied, *Oh no, no, nothing like that.*

As she emerged from the park onto the street, feeling paranoid, anxious, or whatever the hell she was, Ruby couldn't help but think Michelle had left something unsaid. That she was still patient, still waiting for the right moment to broach another subject.

Her house was fine. She'd said so.

So what wasn't?

Chapter Four

"Theo? Is that you? What are you doing here?"

Ness frowned as she approached the figure sitting on the bench. It was late in the day, nearing dusk, and this particular cemetery was a good drive from Lewes, on the edge of a small village known as Peasham, a peaceful place, but then cemeteries tended to be – even for the psychic – those laid to rest normally doing just that and resting.

Despite this being the case, sometimes if Ness was at a loose end or if her partner, Lee, was working late – which, as a police officer, he tended to do – and she still had some energy to burn, she'd pick a cemetery and sit there. Just for an hour or two, just to check. To make sure all was well and nobody did indeed linger, those recently departed, perhaps, or those who had met an untimely end still clinging on. She'd muse too, meditate on life and death, what lay in between and beyond. Sometimes, she didn't think at all; she simply sat there, listening to birdsong, losing herself in its sweet rhythm.

A lifetime dealing with the dead. Some people would think that a dreadful waste. Ironic, even. In the western world, at least, death wasn't supposed to be acknowledged, not while you had breath in your body. You should make the most of each day and be grateful for it, pretend even that death would never happen to you because you were invincible, the one who would live forever. Certainly, Ness remembered days when she'd felt like she'd live forever, that dealing with death was indeed a travesty when there was so much life on offer. But that had been a long time ago. In her late fifties now, the years were blurring into one, not necessarily a bad thing, she conceded. What's more, she increasingly loved her job, wanting to help others, the living *and* the grounded, and fulfil what she was put here to do.

And so, if not on an active case, this is what she did, went to places the dead were likely to be. She knew Theo did the same. But to wind up here, the pair of them, at the same cemetery? That hadn't happened before.

Theo lifted her head in response to Ness's address. "Oh good grief, dear girl. Hello!"

Ness closed the gap between them and sat down. "Having a contemplative moment?"

"Something like that. You?"

"Had a bit of time to kill, nothing on the TV. I'd finished my book, so…"

"You thought you'd come here?"

Ness nodded.

"Been before?"

"Not to this cemetery. You?"

"It's a first for me too." There was a wistful smile on Theo's face as she returned her gaze to the landscape. Crammed with headstones, some were pristine, others peeped out from behind tall grasses, granite and concrete reminders of those who had come, who had experienced, then left again. There were other benches dotted around, and at the heart of it all a tiny stone church, its doors locked, as all church doors were nowadays, it seemed.

Theo was definitely contemplative, Ness thought. She looked…sad. Distracted. Regret rose in Ness for disturbing her. Everyone needed time alone.

A few moments passed before Theo spoke again. "Where'd you park?"

"On the south side of the cemetery."

"Oh right. I parked on the north side."

"Hence why I didn't see your car."

Theo nodded, and more silence fell. Ness broke it this time.

"Theo, are you okay?"

"What?" Briefly, Theo glanced at her. "Yes. Why?"

"I don't know, you just seem…engrossed."

Theo attempted a snort. "Not my usual jovial self?"

"Well…"

"The perennial joker in the pack?"

"Maybe."

"Shouldn't that please you? I know how I can grate on your nerves."

It was true. The pair of them did tend to clash occasionally, but Theo also knew Ness wouldn't change a thing about her. Not just friends, they'd connected on a much deeper level than that. Theo had explained it once, said that she, Ruby and Corinna were all part of her soul group, that they were meant to come together in this life and had probably been together in past lives too and likely would be again in the future. 'We've got work to do and things to work through too,' she'd said, 'and although we're four separate people, we're also a unit. That's how we work best, when we work together.'

It was good to belong. For many years, Ness had felt alone, and this despite coming from such a big family. A family who'd viewed her psychic ability with nothing less than contempt, her mother especially. But that was all over now, in the past, and not something to dwell on, at least not here, not now. She'd created another family comprising friends and colleagues, and now Lee was added to the mix, the man she was in love with.

"Funny how we met. Do you remember?"

It startled Ness when Theo said this. Had she been picking up on the thoughts running through her mind? Theo could do that. Ness could do it too, although it was also entirely possible to guard your thoughts, keep them private.

"Of course I do," Ness said with a smile. "Although it wasn't exactly earth-shattering."

"As it should be when two meteorites clash."

"Oh? Is that what you'd call us, something as mighty as meteorites?"

Theo gave a wry laugh. "I've told you before, own it, Ness, how special you are."

"Yes." Ness was a little more subdued now. "You have told me, many times. And I'm grateful. But as to how we met, trolley wars in a supermarket, of all places."

"You having a go at me because of it."

"I did not! I was polite!"

"I'm sure I heard you mutter something like 'look where you're going, you daft old bat.'"

Ness remained indignant but then had to admit, she'd been in a bad mood that day and so might well have uttered something she usually wouldn't.

"Well, whatever," she replied. "That shove you gave me in my back certainly got my attention. And you swear it wasn't deliberate? That you didn't know what I was?"

"Who, Ness, not what," Theo amended with a sigh. "Who."

"You know what I mean," Ness said, equally terse.

"No, I had no conscious clue. This gift we share, we know well enough it's not an exact science. I didn't know until we got talking, but, my oh my, when I clicked on…it was the Fates conspiring, as the Fates often do."

"Or it could just have been coincidence."

"You know my take on coincidence! No, no, no, I've told you a dozen times, we were meant to meet, you and I, a thorn in each other's sides that really we wouldn't be without."

Each sat silently again, mulling this over. Ness agreed with the sentiment Theo had just uttered, wholeheartedly. She'd hate to be without Theo, but Theo was getting older; her health was a rollercoaster ride. There'd come a day…

"Easy to think such sombre thoughts, especially in a graveyard."

Ness turned to Theo. "Will you stop reading my mind? Besides, you're going nowhere, not anytime soon, at any rate. You're in the pink of health"—she glanced at her friend's hair, the soft pastel shade of pink she dyed it—"quite literally."

Theo smiled. "We all have a sell-by date. Why fight it?"

"Theo!"

"Oh, don't fret, dear girl, don't fret. Okay, all right, I'm going nowhere yet, but…"

"But what?"

Theo raised her hands, rubbed at her eyes. "Oh, I don't know. I'm somewhat prone to reminiscing at the moment, that's all."

Further intrigued, Ness cocked her head. "Theo, what are you really doing here?"

"Thinking," was the immediate reply.

"About what, though? Anything specific?"

"*Someone* specific, yes."

"Who?"

"No one you'd know."

"Theo!" Ness said again, growing exasperated. "Look, if you believe in fate so much, then fate brought us both here this evening, to a place I've certainly never been before, and you say you haven't either. Who are you looking for? Tell me. Someone here?"

Theo hung her head, sighed. "I fear for where she is. That's the honest truth."

"Who, Theo? Who?"

Now Theo raised her head and looked directly at Ness. "That's just it, I can't tell you! I never asked her name. I just…banished her. A bit like you did with Lyndsey."

Ness was shocked, not least because of the mention of her twin. She had to sit back and focus on something other than Theo and their conversation. That stuff with her twin, it was resolved now, but it had taken its toll, nearly crushed her. Who now was crushing Theo? Ness had talked about Lyndsey to Theo over the years they'd known each other, but Theo had never talked of any such similar figure in return. Then again, Ness had always had a sneaking suspicion she was holding on to something, that she was not entirely the hail-fellow-well-met character they all knew.

"That you all know and love, dear girl."

"Oh, for goodness' sake," Ness said, shaking her head. "You just can't help yourself, can you? It's rude to read someone's mind if they've asked you not to! But yes, you're right, that we know *and* love. Very much. Theo?" There it was, a whine in her voice that she'd tried to keep out, but she was just so desperate to know. "Tell me all about it."

Theo patted at Ness's hand. "All right, all right. What there is of it. Which isn't a lot. I just…I feel guilty, you know. Weighed down by it. It's something I should have done, that I was put here to do, only…I was drowning in my own stuff, struggling. Really struggling. And so, perhaps I *couldn't* help, not back then. But I can now, that's the thing. I think I have to, especially after what happened recently in my local newsagent."

Ness still didn't have a clue what her friend was talking about, but rather than interrupt again, she waited patiently for the story to unravel, which it did, bit by bit, the sun sinking slowly on the horizon, the night air, the *cold* night air, taking hold, and still Theo talked as if a dam had burst. When she was done, they both leaned back on the bench, the headstones silhouettes now and softer for it. Theo was spent, clearly. Ness could feel exhaustion rolling off her. As for Ness, she was stunned, horrified and saddened.

"A child killer," she whispered eventually.

"A child that killed children," amended Theo.

"Yes, but—"

"No buts, Ness. We know from other cases, high-profile cases – the likes of Mary Bell, for example – there are reasons a child would do such things. Terrible reasons."

"Yes. Of course. I realise that. Even so…"

"What? You think we shouldn't help her?"

"It's just—"

Still Theo spoke over her. "We've helped some questionable types find the light in the past, Ness. To find peace, ultimately. It simply isn't our job to judge them. There are others that will do what is needed once they cross the great divide. That's our philosophy, and it always has been. Are you now saying you don't…*believe* that philosophy?"

Ness swallowed. "Of course I do! But this girl, she may well have crossed over by now."

"Lyndsey didn't, not entirely, not for a long while."

"No, but she wasn't where I thought she was either, 'festering', as you've put it regarding this girl. That was just my imagination at play. My fears."

"And this is my imagination, my fear."

"We can only do so much," Ness countered.

"I know, but I feel I was meant to help her, and I didn't. She was so frightened, so confused. She thought there was something rotten inside her. What if there was?"

Ness frowned. "Possession?"

"We know it happens."

"Yes. Sadly."

"What if she was a conduit for something, a tool? An innocent, really. And now…now I'll never know, unless…"

"Unless what?"

"Unless I find her. Actively seek her out. She's dead, and what do we do with the dead? We bury them."

"Hence why you're here."

"Why I've sat in so many cemeteries day after day, evening after evening lately, trying to find out where she's buried, to feel some kind of connection again, to tell her I'm here, that I'm ready, that I'll help her. The murders took place in Eastbourne. She was a child and therefore not likely to travel, so it figures she has to be somewhere in this vicinity."

Ness looked around. The gloom really was increasing, shadows darting here and there, flighty things. The dead? Possibly. Or just the shadows of night and therefore benign. "Detect anything?" she said after a while.

"Not a dickie bird."

"And you've no idea what her name was?"

"None."

"But you know the victims' names?"

Theo nodded. "Yes. Yes, I do. Eliza Brooks and Danny Bailey, both aged twelve."

"And this was in the early seventies?"

"Yes." There was a slight pause, and then Theo spoke again, her voice completely different, more charged with energy. "Oh God, Ness! I've been so focused on my lost girl, I've pushed those two into the background. We know *their* names, at least. And so we *do* have something to go on. Who knows, they may be grounded too."

"They may be, but even if they're not, it gives us a lead, a beginning."

Again, Theo nodded. "A beginning," she repeated. "Yes, yes, it's exactly that. From which we can hopefully reach a satisfactory conclusion. That's what this is all about, isn't it?" She nodded towards the headstones. "Beginnings and endings."

"Yes," Ness said, wistful. "And don't forget, new beginnings too."

"Ha," Theo exclaimed. "A journey, an endless one. One that can be…interrupted."

Ness reached across to Theo. "We'll do our best to find this girl again, to find them, Eliza and Danny. There'll be a record of where they're buried, at least."

"Of course there will be, silly old fool that I am for not realising before. I'm losing my marbles, clearly, just not…thinking straight sometimes."

Alarm bells rang in Ness's head. "You forget things?"

To her surprise – and delight – Theo burst out laughing. "Because of old age, Ness! Because I'm getting on. Not because dementia's kicking in. I hope not, anyway. I should have thought about the victims, using them as a line of enquiry."

"Well, I thought of it for you. The benefits of being part of a team in action."

"You think this is a case for Psychic Surveys?"

"Absolutely. All hands on deck. We need to call a meeting, and you tell Ruby and Corinna everything you've told me." She shivered, this time unnerved by it. "Look, it's getting cold. We need to go home, get some rest. I'll walk you back to your car."

Theo rose. "You will not! I'll walk myself, thank you."

"So bloody stubborn," Ness muttered through gritted teeth.

"You wouldn't have me any other way."

Ness rose from the bench too. "No, I suppose not."

"We'll call a meeting tomorrow, then?"

"At Sun Street? Yep, it's a fairly free day for me, so if that's the same for the rest of the team, we'll get a time sorted."

"Perfect. Well…I'll see you, old friend."

"Tomorrow," Ness elaborated. "I'll see you tomorrow."

Theo smiled at her, and then, before Ness knew it, she was being hugged – hard.

"Oh," she exclaimed, trying to bite back surprise. Theo didn't do this, not to Ness, anyway. Rarely did they have physical contact. And yet she was grateful for it; it chased away some of the chill that had crept into her bones as they'd sat there and talked. Theo was right when she'd said they'd dealt with some terrible people, along with some people who'd met terrible ends, their psychic careers nothing if not chequered. But this latest case, if it became one, she had a feeling about it. A bad one. Possession. When evil worms its way in and gains a stronghold. A child being used. As Theo had said, a conduit. There was danger involved in dealing with someone like that. Maybe even mortal danger. They'd have to tread carefully. Call on the light for protection and be careful not to assume anything.

Tonight, though, all was peaceful. The hug over, Theo at last picked her way down the path. No choice but for Ness to turn in the opposite direction and do the same. Just one last scan around the grounds, ensuring no one was silently watching her, someone frightened, sad or just plain lost. Another soul who'd lost direction.

The way was clear.

Chapter Five

"Eliza Brooks and Danny Bailey. Okay, right, we can head to The Keep and find out more about them there. See if that gives us any leads to any suspects at the time."

Ruby having spoken, Corinna then took the book that Theo had bought in the newsagent's and opened it at a place where there was now a Post-It note.

She began to read, tossing curly red hair over her shoulders, her green eyes growing wider. "Christ," she said, "these two met a murky end, didn't they?"

"A *similar* end," Theo said, "hence why the same person could be responsible."

"That person being someone that begged you for help all those years ago, having died herself?"

Theo nodded in response. "Everything fits, by which I mean the timeframe. But more than that, I just…*know* it fits."

Corinna closed the book, then hugged it to her chest. "You think she's still out there, the girl who killed these kids, waiting in the wings, trying to reach you?"

Ruby frowned. "But if that's the case, why doesn't she show herself to you again? Why act all cryptic instead, knocking that book off the shelf? She wasn't exactly shy before. Bloody hell, Theo, it sounds terrifying the way she appeared, covered in blood and screeching. The stuff of nightmares."

As much as Ruby sympathised with Theo's plight and would of course do anything she could to help, she was also surprised by how long this experience had been bugging Theo, lying suppressed, then rising to the surface again, *forcing* its way through.

Theo just shrugged in reply to Ruby's question. "I don't know. Maybe she thinks I'll reject her again. Maybe it's because she believes in her own hype, that she's truly something evil. There could be a million and one reasons. I just think, given the book incident, the time has come to throw some energy her way, see what we can find out, if we can indeed get a lead to her identity and what happened to her, how she died too."

"I took the liberty of having a word with Lee," Ness said, quickly stifling a yawn, which she then apologised for. "Sorry, I couldn't sleep last night for thinking about it all. But yes, I had a word with Lee this morning before our meeting to see if he could find anything out about Eliza and Danny. I also Googled Sally Williams, the author of the book."

Theo nodded. "I've Googled her too."

"So as you know, she's dead. The book was written in the late eighties, and she died in the late nineties, according to what I found, so there's nothing to be had from her."

Corinna made a show of flipping through the book's yellowing pages. "Jeez. Has it really been hanging around the newsagent's all this time?"

"As if she was just waiting for an opportunity," surmised Theo, "the courage to try again. We have to remember, dear girl, time isn't linear on the other side. It's not even a 'thing'."

"So," said Ruby, trying to get it straight in her head what they knew so far, "two children were murdered, only days apart, in the same area, in some woods in Eastbourne, and in the same manner, bludgeoned, then strangled. I wonder if they knew each other?"

"Sally Williams only goes into so much detail," Theo informed her, eyeing the book which Corinna was still holding on to. "To be honest, it's really only a summary, one of many summaries of unsolved murders in Sussex from the nineteen forties to the late eighties – giving a fascinating morsel, but that's all. I tend to think the book was something of a passion project for Williams, a way to keep the poor victims relevant, should anyone bother to read it, that is. I checked on Amazon, and while it's listed, it's long out of print, so this may well be a rare copy, which makes the incident even more significant. No, no, no," Theo continued, sighing, "Sally doesn't offer any theory about what happened with Eliza and Danny. I'm afraid she's left that entirely to us. Ness, has Lee come back to you already?"

"He has. He's only had time to have a brief look at the case, I'm afraid, whatever there is that's been digitised. Basically, as with all child murder cases, it was family members that were initially key suspects, but investigations went nowhere."

The sound of barking distracted Ruby. "Oh, Jed's here," she said as he appeared on the floor beside her, wagging his tail.

Theo's, Ness's and Corinna's smiles were indulgent, although they couldn't see him; only Ruby could.

"How's his mood?" Theo enquired.

"He seems happy enough," Ruby told them. "He's just

settling down by my feet. His ears are alert, though. He's listening in, as usual."

"Dear Jed," Theo said, still smiling.

Corinna was eager to get back on track. "You say nothing concrete, Ness, but were any arrests made? If the unnamed girl was guilty, she wasn't, like, a daughter or cousin of one of the families affected?"

Ness shook her head. "From what I know so far, no arrests were made and certainly no other child suspects. If the girl who appeared to you, Theo, was guilty, she would have to have been bloody strong to fell two others the same age as her, one of them a boy. If ever a child was suspected, it would likely have been a boy, not a girl."

"She was possessed," Theo said. "Like I said."

"Something rotten inside her," Ruby mused.

"Her words, remember? Not mine," replied Theo.

"Are Eliza or Danny's parents still alive? Or siblings?"

"Again, that's something we have to find out," answered Theo.

"But if they are," Ness warned, "we approach with care. As Lee said, raking up people's pasts isn't something they'll be grateful for. Not when it's a past like this."

Ruby nodded. She understood that. But surely it would eat away at you, not knowing the identity of the person who stole something so precious from you. If there was a chance you could find closure, would you take it? Or sometimes, as she felt in her own case, was there no resolution to be had because the prospect of facing it all again — reliving it — was too painful? As the police had done, you had to eventually file it away just to survive.

"Ruby?" Theo said, clearly noticing her colleague had gone quiet. "Are you okay?"

"Yeah, yeah." Ruby did her best to muster a bright smile. "I was just thinking…well, I was thinking that these children's deaths are a stone-cold case now, and there might be more information on them that can be dredged up with modern methods, but, really, they're as Sally suggests – forgotten about. If we do find a lead, we have to keep at the forefront of our minds that not everyone wants their past raked up, for sure, but also not by people like us, by psychics. Some people are still horrified by that notion."

"Not usually the desperate, though," Theo pointed out.

Glancing at her, Ruby could only agree. "Yep, okay, not usually the desperate. We always stand more of a chance with them." Clapping her hands together, the resultant boom satisfyingly loud, she added, "The Keep's open for another couple of hours. What say you we get the investigation underway right now? Jed, you coming along for the ride?"

* * *

The trouble with the murders having happened in Neolithic times, as Corinna put it, was there was only so much information recorded. What The Keep was useful for, though, was birth and death records and, of course, obituaries. As the team scoured through newspapers from the early seventies, there it was, an obituary for Eliza Brooks, who was to be buried at St Martin's Church, just outside of Eastbourne in Sussex, and, only a short while later, one for Danny Bailey, who was also to be buried at St Martin's.

"Well, would you credit it?" Theo said on discovering this. "That's one of the few churchyards in Sussex I haven't performed a vigil. St Martin's," she mused. "I've driven past it on occasion. It's the home of an Anglo-Saxon church, I believe, set close to a small stretch of river. If, and I realise it's a mighty big *if*, the children are still grounded, or one of them is, at least, then maybe we can get a name from them, see if they knew their murderer." Before anyone could comment, Theo sat back. "Oh, I know, it all sounds crazy and perhaps just a bit too easy. I don't think for one moment any of this is easy. It's ruddy hard, it's…awful. And it may be too late to solve, that's the thing. Far too late."

Ruby looked at Theo, who had bowed her head. How grave Theo sounded, how…hopeless. And that wasn't like her. She seemed resigned to failure before they'd even got started. Usually, she was so gung ho about things, so positive, but now she was just sitting there in front of them, shoulders sagging and inert. A different Theo to the one she was used to, a side to her rarely seen.

Ruby edged her chair closer, Ness surreptitiously nodding her approval. Jed, who had declined Ruby's earlier invitation to accompany them to the archive's office, reappeared to sit by Theo's foot, nudging her, although she didn't seem to feel it, doing his utmost to cajole her. Ruby reached out to rub at Theo's arm.

"What is it you're always telling me? We do what we can to help. We try our best. And our best is pretty damned good." She chanced a laugh. "I'd go so far as to say it's the best of the best. *We* are, the team. Look, we'll give this a shot. Go to St Martin's, and…we'll see. If we get a name, we can focus on it, call her forward again, this girl, help her. You know, it's strange. I feel sorry for anyone that's a victim. Christ, who wouldn't? But sometimes I feel sorry for the perpetrator too because to align yourself with that much darkness, it has to be terrifying. Deep down they know there'll be a reckoning. The realisation that all the darkness does is prey on you. And, well, I guess that's why so many hide from the light and why we sometimes have such a hard time. But no one can hide forever. Which means you're right, Theo. There's a time for everything. A time for *her*."

Theo had raised her head during Ruby's pep talk; she was smiling, but her eyes still held such sadness.

"Theo, are you okay?" Ruby checked, Jed whining now, doing that thing he did when distressed, turning in a circle and chasing his tail.

"I'm fine," she assured Ruby. "I just…want to help. While I can."

Ruby swallowed, glanced at Corinna, saw the look of worry on her face too.

"You are all right, aren't you?" she checked again, her voice slightly choked.

Theo rallied, straightening her shoulders, her chin slightly higher than it was before.

"Oh, for goodness' sake, of course I am! Now, are we heading to St Martin's or what?"

Chapter Six

All squashed into Ruby's Ford, they reached the churchyard at dusk. It was tiny, occupying an idyllic setting against a pastoral backdrop of field and river.

There was no one there of the living variety. All was quiet. Peaceful, even. Absolutely no sign of anything untoward. It was Jed who led them to Eliza's grave, running straight to it, Ruby marvelling over that as she and the others followed.

Eliza Brooks, it read. *An angel amongst angels. 1958-1970*

Rather than hurry to find Danny's grave, they simply stood there, all four of them and Jed, as much out of respect as for any paranormal matter. After a while, Corinna spoke.

"I'm not sensing anything, are you?"

"If I am, it's residual," Ruby replied.

"Such an outpouring of grief," murmured Ness, clearly moved by it.

Theo nodded. "Awful. Just awful. And as we know, that depth of emotion takes time to dissipate. A long, long time. But yes, I think Ruby's right. What I'm sensing here could be residual rather than intelligent. If the poor mite lingered, she's gone now. Thankfully." Addressing the grave, she added, "Rest in peace, dear child, in love and in light."

It had been such a fine day, but now it began to drizzle, the kind of rain that didn't saturate your clothes but sat beadlike on the surface.

Ruby turned to see that Jed had bolted, was sitting in the distance by another grave.

"Jed's found Danny now," she said, and they duly moved over to his memorial.

The epitaph on his headstone was slightly more agonised: *Taken too soon!* Anger clear in those carved words, bitterness throbbing like a vein.

Lee was right when he'd warned Ness – and, via her, the rest of them – that to rake all this up again with any members of Eliza's and Danny's immediate families, if they were still alive, would be insensitive. The only possible way to justify it was to find irrefutable evidence of who the murderer was and then take that to the police. A murderer who was also in need of help. Despite what she'd said earlier about feeling sorry for perpetrators as well as victims, right now any sympathies eluded her. To kill children… It was monstrous.

Each lost again in their own thoughts, Ruby's reverie was disturbed when Jed started barking. Immediately Corinna yelled out and lurched forward slightly.

"Crin?" Ruby said, puzzled.

"Someone pushed me," she explained.

"What? Who?"

All four of the team swung around to see who. The churchyard was still empty, as was the horizon, not even a lone dog walker to punctuate it.

"You sure you didn't trip?" Ness ventured.

"No! I'm totally – ow! Someone just pinched me too!

Hard!"

Ness looked at Theo, who was looking at Ruby.

"Anything?" Ness said.

Jed shot off. In pursuit of something?

"There!" said Theo as they all peered in Jed's direction. "These old eyes are still good for something. Can you see it? A shadow. A moving shadow."

"Eliza or Danny?" Corinna asked, her mouth open slightly, chest heaving.

"I really don't think so," Ness said. "Churchyards are such peaceful places. Until they're not. Oh good grief, look at the church."

They did. There were shadows all around it, creeping up the walls, blacker than the dusk that had fallen so far and therefore perfectly visible. The church was *alive* with shadows, those that had seemingly risen from the ground to writhe and sway there, menacing shadows, ones that reached out, that *knew* they could be seen, not asking for help but mocking them.

"What do we do?" asked Corinna, still breathy. "There's a lot to tackle there."

"Tackle?" Ness questioned. "Yes, I suppose you're right. That's exactly what they want us to do. Tackle them. Get physical, even, as one just did with you, Corinna."

Theo stood firm. "Brace yourselves," she said, pulling herself up to her full height. "Wrap white light around you, imagining it as a shield, impenetrable. As much as I'd like to just walk away and leave them to it, I don't think they're going to let us."

The four were towards the rear of the cemetery, a good few metres from the gate. They did as Theo instructed, putting all barriers in place, protection against a possible onslaught, Jed still running around and barking, doing his utmost to keep more mischievous entities at bay, those that had broken away from the main body of darkness.

"What are they?" Corinna whispered, baffled by it. "Spirits?"

Ness shook her head. "I don't think so. Although…there may be spirits in amongst them. Those that embrace more *base* activities, shall we say, in death as they did in life."

"For real?" Corinna took a step forwards as if fascinated.

"DON'T!" Theo told her. "We stand together, side by side, as though we're one. We've encountered their type before, haven't we, Ness? Do you remember? At Thorpe Morton. They're base, just as Ness said, and really rather merciless. Cold, cold things."

"Shit," murmured Ruby, who'd also encountered this kind of thing too. It came in so many guises, sometimes obvious, sometimes cunning.

She'd been standing next to Theo when she'd sworn, prompting Theo to grab her hand. "Don't worry, we shall overcome," the older woman whispered. "We always do."

True. They did. Or at least they thought so.

"Do you really think they mean us harm?" said Ruby, watching as more shadows around the church broke away, becoming taller and wider, bolder too, inching towards them, forming a front line of their own, a formidable barrier that they'd have to penetrate, the hedge surrounding them too high to negotiate. She and Corinna might stand a chance of scrambling over it, but Theo, never. "God, this place seemed so serene when we first got here. What happened?"

"The light failing, that's what happened," Ness replied, gazing straight ahead, watching at the display going on. "It's ancient land we're standing on. The church dates back several centuries to a time even more brutal than now. Hard to believe, I know, but...despite being alleged holy ground, something must have happened here, something bad, extremely negative – a slaughter, maybe, giving rise to this, what's in front of us. And once these bastards are here..."

"They hang around," Ruby said, her voice low and solemn. "I know."

Ness glanced at her, worry and concern etched on her face, but not fear. Something that bolstered Ruby.

"You okay?" Ness asked.

Ruby nodded. "Fine."

"Corinna?"

"Yeah, I'm good. But what about the interred? Eliza...Danny..."

"They're gone," Theo told her, her voice quite firm. "You know that, their spirits, at least. I can sense nothing intelligent here at all, only...these *things*. They hide in daylight and swarm at night. Multiplying like a virus. Goddamn it, look! They're doing just that."

"We have to be quick," Ness said. "Approach and walk straight through them."

"But they can get physical!" Corinna said. "They just did!"

"The light will protect us," Theo reiterated. "Don't doubt it."

"I'm not, it's just—"

"The wall's coming closer," Ness interrupted, and if Ruby wasn't mistaken, nervousness had at last crept into her voice.

"Fuck," she whispered in response, staring at it. *Jed? Jed, where are you?*

She could no longer hear him barking. Had the darkness consumed him somehow? Her breath was becoming ragged, no matter how hard she tried to disguise it. This was just a simple country churchyard, surrounded by the beautiful South Downs, in which people would come to walk and picnic, to soak up the beauty. A good place. It was. But just as bad things happened to good people, the same applied to land. It could become tainted. You'd never see it by day. This energy hid, but as dusk fell, there was everything to play for, the darkness of the night sky an ally. She'd bet if any local kids from the surrounding villages came here after dusk for thrills, they'd leave pretty damn quickly, not able to see, perhaps, but able to sense their own rising fear well enough. They'd scarper. In her mind's eye she could see how it would play out: the cold dread that would start in the pits of their stomachs, quickly spreading to their extremities, feet that had run through the gate now grinding to a halt, excited laughter evaporating. *This is no place to be*, they would think, and they'd be right. It wasn't. She was sad for anyone who'd been buried here but had to remember Theo's words. It was only their mortal remains, not what had animated them. The likes of Eliza and Danny and so many others were hopefully safe on the other side. But she, Corinna, Theo and Ness were on this side, and far from safe.

"'Though I walk through the valley of the shadow of death, I will fear no evil. For you are with me. Your rod and your staff, they comfort me.'"

Theo was quoting Psalm 23. Religious words when none of them adhered to a religion, but good words nonetheless, words that over time had become infused with power.

"Eliza and Danny might not have lingered," Theo continued, "but we have, for far too long. It's growing cold, too cold for my liking. We can't risk it paralysing us. By God, I swear it's warmer in Scotland! Now come on, best foot forward. I want no hesitation. None whatsoever. As Ness said, we breach the wall, walk through it, show them who's boss."

The four did as Theo said, all clasping hands now, one wall pitted against another, neither made of anything except determination. For that was the thing. The darkness was just as determined as the light, thinking it could overcome the light, always trying.

Theo was right about it being unnaturally cold. The energy against them trying to penetrate the barrier they'd erected, burrowing for gaps to worm its way through in an attempt, as Theo had said, to paralyse them. Just as Ruby had felt a spark of anger when standing by Danny's graveside, it erupted again, for all the times she'd done this before, now, and would do it again in the future. Fighting. All the damned time.

"That's good, that's fine," Theo told her, sensing how Ruby was feeling. "If it's anger that gives you what you need to do this, then let it flow. Anger can be negative, but, by God, harness it in the correct manner and you get results from it."

"Don't you just get so sick of it, though?" Ruby said as they drew nearer still, her tone seething, her teeth gritted so hard her jaw ached. "Of shit like this being part of our remit."

"Yes. But it *is* part of our remit. We're not on that higher plane yet."

"Come on, everyone, focus," murmured Ness. "We're almost at clashing point. Let's all recite Psalm 23. Corinna, Ruby, Theo. We all have to say it."

They did, voices in perfect pitch with each other, the words emboldening Ruby further, as if she were growing in stature also, becoming taller, wider, filling from head to toe with light, dazzling both within and without, her heart bursting with the power of invincibility. Yes! Yes! Yes! It was all going great guns, that dark wall before them not as bold now, stalling, even shrinking. She picked up pace, her colleagues matching her step for step effortlessly, intuitively, positivity flooding the atmosphere. Not just happy, Ruby was rapturous. Whatever had been allowed to flourish here, unchecked, had met its match. Finally.

All going so, so well, the team closing the gap further, intending to smash right through the wall of dark energy and scatter it to the four winds, end the choke hold it had on this land and restore it to the sanctuary it was intended to be.

Another Psychic Surveys triumph.

Within reach.

Until Ruby heard Jed howl in pain.

Chapter Seven

"Jed? Jed, what is it, boy?"

"Ruby, what are you doing?" Theo said. "Take my hand again. Now!"

Ness also warned her. "Ruby, don't break the chain."

"But Jed…" she replied, knowing it was no use explaining further, that they hadn't heard him, didn't know the pain he was in, what this dark matter was inflicting. Torturing him. Torturing *her* to hear it. There was no way she could ignore it.

Still separate from the others, she moved forward. The last time she'd seen him, he'd been chasing something. Whatever had attacked Corinna, maybe? Something akin to an imp. Had it lured him away, deliberately, then attacked him too?

"Jed!" she started shouting. "Jed! Jed! Jed!"

Her voice seemed to bounce back, slamming against her with all the force of a wind tunnel, but with a sardonic tone creeping in. The darkness… It was as though she'd been blinded by it, as though it were coagulating all around her.

With no sign of Jed and her hands outstretched, she started calling for the others too. Where were they? Why had they disappeared?

Her heart was racing, her breath ragged. Despite the icy

chill – the coldness of dark matter solidifying – beads of perspiration erupted on her forehead.

Calm down, Ruby, you have to calm down. Had to remember all she'd been taught, by Theo, by Ness, and by her grandmother Sarah, at her knee as a child. *Draw on the light. Believe in the light. It will protect you.* Hard to think of the light, though, in this.

Not for you, Ruby! You're practiced. You know how to do this.

And she *would* have to do it, before it was too late, because already the cold was like needles against her skin, pricking at it, probing, desperate to penetrate, to delve deep inside, find the very heart of her and stop it from taking another beat.

What happened here, in the past, to invite this in?

From silence, nothing other than her own breathing, an explosion of sound erupted. There was jeering and hollering. Cries of pain and despair – that despair all too human. Laughter of the cruelest kind. Holy land. Sacred. For centuries and centuries. And yet something *un*holy had happened, far, far back in time. A persecution.

Another cry. This one so high-pitched that Ruby was forced to raise her hands and block her ears. A woman responsible. An echo but full of terrified emotion, forced to replay down the centuries, the years, because such pain, such fear had *fed* this other energy, kept it growing like some sort of mould, full of spores, populating, dominating.

Persecution. That was exactly what had happened here. A woman or a group of women, gentle women, most likely, the healers of old who knew how to harness the power of nature, using herbs as medicines. Branded witches.

Of all English counties, Sussex had had the most tolerant approach to those considered witches, most avoiding the attention of the witchfinders elsewhere and the abominable treatment that had followed. But there were always exceptions, pockets of persecution that would spring up, those led by the delusion of superstition, wrongs inflicted that went unrecorded, even unnoticed by the community at large, or ignored.

"There are no witches!" Ruby shouted, a furious indignation rising in her. For what she surmised, it *had* happened. "The only evil was those that thought so, who abused the light, hid behind it, took God's name in vain."

More cries, more screams. A confession.

Ruby strained to hear. What was someone saying? *I am a witch. I am a witch. I am a witch. I AM A WITCH!*

"NO!" Ruby screamed just as loudly. "It's torture that makes a witch, nothing else!"

The light – she'd harness it now, believe in the power of it. What was here tonight had reined too long. It had to be banished.

She closed her eyes, refused to stare into the darkness any longer, an abyss which was crawling, it seemed, with things that had never lived, never been dead either, but still they existed – a by-product of human behaviour and thoughts, the very worst of both. With an effort that was indeed superhuman, she brought her breath back under control – no way you could panic if you were breathing nice and slowly, another invaluable lesson – but what she couldn't help were the shivers that coursed through her, each one violent.

Elysium fields, a golden patchwork, think of them. The sun shining down on you and it's warm there, so warm. Jed's there too. Right beside you. Always. Your protector.

It was a wonderful vision, prompted by her own imagination or another protector – Sarah. The voice in her head stating those words had sounded like her grandmother's, full of a warmth that indeed flooded her limbs, diminishing the cold. God, she missed her gran! The silvery softness of her eyes, her smile. She missed her wise ways too. Sarah had taken care of her, seen her into adulthood, tried to shield her from the other side of the coin. 'Believe only in the light,' she'd say. 'That's all there is for you, Ruby, all that matters.' Not true, though. Not entirely. Because with the light came darkness. The two entwined. Conflict also. Ruby had chosen her side, and there were some who might consider her wise too. Michelle, for example. And yet in days long gone, she, Sarah, Theo, Ness and Corinna would have likely been persecuted for being witches too.

Walk in the fields, Ruby. Walk in the fields…

Ah, there they were in her mind, those fields, resplendent. The sun a burning bright orb in the sky, fierce, and yet its rays would never harm you, never redden your skin. The cold retreated further, she was certain of it, as she walked through long stems of wheat and barley which parted to make way for her, swaying in the breeze but gently, for this was a gentle world, the world she suspected Jed inhabited when he wasn't with her. Why, oh why would he ever leave it? Put himself in the way of such danger. He should stay put.

That's not his role, not his destiny.

Who was talking to her now? A mere echo, a whisper barely caught.

"What is his role, then?" she asked. "What is he?"

He's safe, the voice responded.

"Untouchable?"

Of course.

"Then where is he?"

This Elysium, this paradise, it would be complete if he were here, bounding towards her, eyes full of mischief and tail wagging.

Here he's something else.

"What? Tell me, please."

Such mysteries. Such wonder. She knew Jed was something other than a dog. Besides her, Jessica was the only one who could see him. Whom he'd saved, once upon a time, bringing her back from the brink of abject despair. She'd thought she was unlovable for all the acts she'd committed in her past, the grief she'd heaped upon her family, but if Jed loved her, something as pure as him, then she was worthy of redemption. Yes, he'd saved her, no mean feat for someone as damaged as Jessica, but would he save Ruby now, for she couldn't wander forever in these fields. She had to return, help her colleagues.

"Jed! Where are you?"

Something black. On the horizon and coming towards her. Jed? Not in any danger after all. Safe, as the voice promised. Here, in his heaven. "Oh, Jed!"

Coming closer. She'd see him soon, this beautiful bundle of fur as she knew him, that had come into her life so suddenly, so unexpectedly.

She lifted both hands and waved. As she did, she noticed the barley and wheat grow more frenzied. A breeze, perhaps? An *agitation*? If so, of what sort?

"Jed, is it you? Shit, Jed, what have they done with you?"

Closer still, wider, bigger — too big for the Labrador that Jed was. A wall of darkness.

"Shit," Ruby repeated, lowering her hands before taking a step backwards instead of forwards, watching helplessly as, just like it had done in the churchyard, the darkness closed the gap between them, *gliding* towards her, almost gracefully, almost beautiful in its own way, something that *yearned* for her, that wanted her to meet it halfway and meld with it, become as one. Indeed, it wasn't as solid as she'd thought. She could spy a gap within it, one which was a perfect fit. There was another voice. Definitely not Sarah's.

You fit, Ruby! You do! There'd be no more struggling, then, don't you see?

No more struggling... Now, wouldn't that be something?

Wouldn't it indeed! Step closer, Ruby. Come on!

Barking. *Frantic* barking. And somehow she understood it, the message that barking was trying to impart. *Wake up! Wake up now. The dream is over.*

She blinked.

Dream? Is that what she'd fallen into? One that had started off so sweetly.

Wake up!

That had offered false sanctuary.

WAKE UP!

If she'd been asleep, she wasn't lying down. She was upright, and at her feet was something continuously clawing at her, butting its head against her legs, over and over.

"Jed!" she said on realising it was him, dropping quickly to her knees, wishing she could take him in her arms, embrace him, but just so thankful he was unharmed. Why, oh why did she insist on doubting it, though, for the dark wouldn't dare touch something as light-filled as him. "Where are the others?" she asked.

Raising her head, she looked all around her. The darkness was still there, but it was clearing, being beaten back by her colleagues, who stood not four deep but three. Nonetheless, they were arm in arm and united, projecting white light, a magnificent wave that would engulf her as well as anything that stood in its way.

Back on her feet, Jed remaining by her side, she added to that wave. Maybe Jed did too, because he was staring straight ahead, his gaze focused, intent.

Unholy land, that's what this was. And it wasn't fair. Not on Eliza, Danny or any of the others. Whatever priest presided here might think he was in touch with the light, but about the darkness he had no clue, not real darkness. Ignorance was bliss, but it was also dangerous when it allowed something as poisonous as this to flourish.

"Ruby, you all right?"

It was Ness shouting over to her.

"It's all good," Ruby called back, a smile playing upon her lips at her choice of words. *All good. It really is.* And good was stronger than evil because evil sprang from selfishness, love from self*less*ness, an altogether much purer place.

"Let's get this thing over and done with, then." That was Theo – magnificent, pink-haired Theo. "It really can be so tiresome."

Again, all four focused – all *five* of them with Jed – the tidal wave of light growing higher and higher, reaching far and wide, beyond the church boundaries, soaking ground that had been parched for far too long, devouring what negative energy dared to remain. There was more wailing, more screaming, but this time the kind that was bliss to the ears. Something dying that had no place here or anywhere.

"Hold strong!" Theo said again, familiar words, ones Ruby had heard her speak countless times. Words she clung to. *Hold strong.*

They could do this. They *were* doing it. Carrying out work that should have been the work of priests, countless priests who'd been in charge of this church and grounds since the time of the persecution but who'd preferred to hurry from the church once dusk had fallen, cancelling evensong. Over and over. Their work a mere performance.

There was a blinding flash. One which Ruby had to protect her eyes from. This kind of light wasn't for them to see. One day, perhaps, but not yet, the strongest light of all.

It was done. There was darkness still, but the darkness of a spring evening, only that, the moon providing a bright glow alongside the countless stars that surrounded it. *Never complete darkness*, Ruby reminded herself. *No matter what you might think.*

Such thoughts, such an awareness, was interrupted, her colleagues having rushed over to her side, surrounding her, each of them hugging because this, what they had done, was joyous; they had *neutralised* the land. Made it safe again, a haven. And all in pursuit of two children and a murderer – the former found, the latter still a mystery.

Theo was huffing and puffing in true Theo style.

Ness reached out to her. "You okay?"

She nodded. "I am indeed. But you know what would make me feel even better?"

"A G and T?" suggested Corinna as Ruby glanced around, noticing Jed had disappeared again, needed elsewhere, perhaps. Some other emergency.

"Exactly. Is there a pub nearby? We'll have a drink and a debrief before heading home. We've earned it, don't you think?" As Theo headed off towards the gate, glancing only briefly at Eliza's headstone, Ruby couldn't help but laugh as she heard her continue to mutter, "Good Lord, this job'll make alcoholics of us yet!"

Chapter Eight

It was late when Ruby eventually got home – nearly midnight. What a night it had been! What a place St Martin's was. Yet until the next morning, Ruby slept surprisingly well. So too did the rest of her household. As for what had happened to Jed the previous evening, that squeal she'd heard, that cry of pain, Ness had a theory.

"Mimicry," she'd said in the pub afterwards. "Something designed to fool you, to weaken you and, in turn, us."

Theo had agreed, whilst knocking back raspberry-flavoured double gins with her tonic in a glass that was more like a goldfish bowl. "Dark matter is both a dullard and fiendishly clever. A real paradox. Hard to understand. And yet here's the thing…it understands us." She lifted a hand to tap at her heart. "It seems to know our deepest fears, our weaknesses, as if somehow – bear with me here – it's connected to the grid too, the whole, just as we are. In the end, even non-spirit entities must go to the light, albeit kicking and screaming. Not to be annihilated, as we think, but to evolve alongside us."

"Wow," Corinna said on the tide of a deep sigh. "Heavy, man."

"Very," said Ness, who, in contrast to Theo, had opted for plain Gordon's in a tall glass, and a single shot at that.

"And whilst we exist on this plain rather than some higher one, in dealing with them, we must also deal with ourselves, grow stronger."

"Seems to be the only way to fight it," Theo surmised.

"Again and again and again," Ruby murmured.

"That's right," Theo answered as dryly. "Acceptance, though, can be a wonderful thing. After Blakemort, we said we'd never go in search of the darkness, and we don't, we really don't, but keeping it simple isn't always possible. Regarding Jed, where's he now?"

"Gone, to wherever. He was fine, though. I think I got a glimpse of those Elysium fields he runs in. Although…"

"Although what?" asked Ness.

"They weren't heavenly for long. The darkness managed to penetrate there too."

"Just another form of mimicry," Ness reminded her. "Twisting and turning everything."

Ruby had nodded. "Yeah, yeah, probably. Great place, though, before it turned sour."

With a new day dawning, Ruby yawned widely, enjoying the peace as she lay in bed, Cash and Hendrix still sleeping while she pondered the daily schedule. Psychic Surveys had a house call this morning to an address in Brighton, another where the residents insisted psychic activity was taking place. She and Corinna were to investigate primarily, Ness busy with a private client, working on chakra energy, and Theo enjoying a visit from her youngest son, Ewan, his wife and their children. Hopefully the case today would be of the routine type, not too much drama – she'd had enough of that lately. Then, all being well, she was meeting Michelle and Leo again for more tea in the park, a picnic rug laid on the ground this time so that both babies could crawl, although in that respect, Leo was more advanced, Hendrix preferring to sit there, pointing to things and grunting. Ah well, compare despair. It'd be lovely regardless. She was looking forward to it, to something normal. Yet as Cash stirred, reaching over to pull her closer, she had to admit that being outside of normal had been pretty mind-blowing lately.

The day progressed, the house that she and Corinna visited having no sense of anything grounded at all, Ruby having to deliver the usual advice, that it'd be worth getting pipes checked to explain the rattling and thumping. The residents of Southdown Road, a rather attractive Victorian terrace in Brighton's prestigious Fiveways area, looked – as many did when she told them this news – disappointed rather than relieved.

"Where can we get a second opinion?" Mr Back asked, his wife, Suzy, looking surly.

It was a good question, one that Ruby and Corinna didn't have the perfect answer to. There were various psychics in Sussex, but none who did what they did. Most of them, that the team knew of, liked to keep themselves to themselves and would only help if pressed. One of Ruby's dreams when she'd first started her business had been to have a network of team members all over the UK, freelance as Ness, Theo and Corinna were but all working under the umbrella of Psychic Surveys. That plan had worked for a while. They'd had some contacts in Scotland, for example, who'd carried out domestic spiritual clearances on their behalf but with varying success. What transpired more often than not was actually a hindrance rather than a help – those who weren't happy with services rendered put in complaints to Ruby, which she then had to find a way of dealing with. Eventually, she'd put a stop to it, just as she'd put a stop to her dream of having a high street presence at street level rather than in an attic. Maybe she'd try again in the future, but for now, with a young family to look after, keeping it simple worked for her. Regarding second opinions, it was Corinna who stepped in.

"Google *Brighton psychics*," she said, "or there are guidelines on the Net how to cleanse your home yourself using crystals and sage, that kind of thing."

"A DIY job?" Suzy said, a tad horrified.

"Your home isn't haunted," Ruby reiterated. "We can sense nothing here. I really think an electrician or a plumber—"

"Fine, whatever," Suzy continued, stepping closer to the door in the hallway where all four were standing – a clear invitation for Ruby and Corinna to leave. "We'll sort it out ourselves. It's true, isn't it, that old saying, if you want a job done properly…"

Ruby and Corinna took the hint and left. If anything changed, the Backs could always give the team another call. But that was the thing: *nothing* would change. If your house wasn't haunted, it wasn't haunted. One less stress to deal with, surely? What *needed* to change was for the Backs to get their kicks elsewhere and, of course, their plumbing sorted. Having returned to Lewes, Corinna and Ruby also said their goodbyes, Corinna heading off for an afternoon shift at the pub where she worked part-time in Ringmer, whilst Ruby headed home to pick up Hendrix before meeting Michelle.

She arrived at the park to find Michelle already there, sitting on a red tartan picnic blanket with Leo, who held in his hands a toy, which he was passing from hand to hand –

his dexterity skills something admirable too. As Ruby approached, Michelle looked up, her smile, Ruby noticed, not quite as bright as usual. She seemed…preoccupied.

Nonetheless, she was the first to say hello, shunting up to make room on the blanket so that Ruby could sit down with Hendrix. As she did so, Hendrix clung monkey-like to her, refusing steadfastly to be placed beside Leo or practise any crawling manoeuvres.

Ruby shot Michelle a rueful smile. "Sorry. I think he must be teething or something. He's been like this all morning."

"Oh right, yeah," Michelle said, "teething can be a…*challenging* time, and I don't mean just for him."

Ruby nodded and thought it ironic that she could thwart the darkness, but when it came to soothing a fretful baby, she was all at sea.

"Keep you up last night too, did he?"

"Last night?" Ruby asked.

"You look tired."

"Oh, I see." She laughed, jiggled Hendrix some more, then hugged him close. "I'm always tired. Hazard of the job."

"Which job?"

Ruby stilled, as did Hendrix. Michelle's voice had grown even more serious. Gazing directly at her, Ruby noticed *she* looked tired, Michelle.

"Michelle? Are you okay?"

Immediately, Michelle adopted a wide smile, but unlike all the times she'd smiled before, it didn't reach her eyes. "I'm fine, really. It's just…it's nothing."

As Ruby grabbed a bottle of milk for Hendrix from her bag and placed the teat in his mouth – anything to soothe him – she continued to probe. When Michelle had said nothing was wrong, she was clearly lying.

Under further questioning, Michelle reached out for Leo, brought him closer and hugged him. The total opposite to Ruby and Hendrix, it was the mother in need of comfort.

"I'm being silly. I know I am."

"About what?" said Ruby.

"It's nothing. It's not true. It can't be."

Alarm bells rang inside Ruby's head. What was she denying?

Hendrix thankfully going into a milk coma, his eyelids closing and his mouth releasing the teat to form a perfect oval instead, Ruby reached out. "Whatever's bothering you, you can tell me. No way I'll think you're being silly. I don't take that kind of attitude."

Michelle had been gazing down at her son, who was also drifting towards sleep, but now she turned to Ruby instead.

"She's at home today. My mum's looking after her."

"Who is? Willow?"

"Yes. She said she wasn't feeling well this morning." Michelle swallowed hard. "It's happening more and more, not feeling well, you know, skipping school. Everything that's been going on, I've brushed it aside, but it's getting harder to cope with, to ignore."

Not only were the alarm bells still ringing, Ruby's skin tingled despite the warmth of yet another glorious spring day – one that should have been idyllic, two young mothers meeting in the park, their babies sleeping, providing a real chance for a catch-up.

There was *still* a real chance for a catch-up, but Ruby

suspected it was to be in a wholly unexpected way.

"What is it that you want to ignore about Willow?"

Michelle swallowed again, took a deep breath that was ragged.

"Hard to explain," she finally answered. "Would you – could you – come back home with me to meet her? I think I need your opinion on the matter. Please."

* * *

There was a gravitas to this situation that couldn't be denied. Whatever was wrong with Willow, whatever Michelle was trying to hide, it was clearly causing both mother and child distress – whether Michelle's partner or anyone else was aware of the problem, Ruby didn't know, not yet, but she guessed she'd find out. Soon.

Conveniently, Sun Street was on the way to Michelle's house, so after a quick phone call with Cash – who agreed to look after Hendrix for an hour or two, having made better advancement on the IT project he was working on than expected – she dropped the baby off home, and they continued onwards. After crossing the river, past the Tesco and Aldi superstores, they headed upwards into the Malling area, Michelle's home just across the road from South Malling Primary School, which Willow attended – usually.

On an embankment, Michelle's house was a normal three-bedroom, mid-terrace. Opening the door, Michelle entered first, telling Ruby to wait a minute whilst she parked up the buggy in the hallway, Leo still out for the count. She then called out.

"Mum, we're home. I've brought a friend back with

me, Ruby." She then gestured for Ruby to follow her through to the kitchen. "They'll be in there."

Michelle's mum – slightly rotund and her red hair, if bright once, now faded – was standing at the counter, chopping vegetables. The child was at the table, pieces of paper scattered in front of her. Both glanced up as they entered.

Willow was just like her mother, auburn-haired and green-eyed. She was eight, Michelle had told her, almost nine, but she looked both older and younger. Younger in that she was delicate in stature, perhaps slightly shorter for her age than she should be. Older because of her eyes – they were simply too knowledgeable. Ruby hated to think it, but there was a slyness there too. When Michelle had first spoken of Willow, she'd told Ruby what a good girl she was, never a day's trouble. Was that the truth?

Michelle addressed her daughter. "Willow, darling, this is Ruby. Remember me telling you all about her? She's come to say hello."

Ruby couldn't help but start at that. Michelle had told Willow all about her? Why? For what purpose? She'd thought their friendship a naturally evolving thing, two women with babies finding common ground, but perhaps it was more contrived than that, on Michelle's part, at least. As keen as she was to help, Ruby's heart sank. Could it be – was it possible – that Michelle had *sought* her out? Forged this friendship for a reason and then, just as the darkness did, bided her time, waiting to strike? *My daughter needs help.* Lewes was a small place, and Ruby was known around here. Not by every resident, of course, but she had a reputation. *They* did, the Psychic Surveys team.

Willow looked at Ruby, then returned to the pile of

paper in front of her, picked up a pencil and began to draw. Ruby was also introduced to Michelle's mum, Katharine, who said hello but quickly – too quickly – returning to her culinary chores.

Ruby saw it then, Michelle's sheepishness.

Thrilled, that's what she'd been to have formed this friendship with Michelle, something normal and down-to-earth, the first of many friendships like it. Now she felt used. Michelle swallowed, as if able to read Ruby's thoughts, then reached out.

"I know what this looks like. And…and…it's not true, not entirely."

In the hallway, in his buggy, Leo started crying.

"It's okay, don't worry," Katharine said. "I'll see to him."

Wiping her hands on her apron and with her head down, she practically scurried from the kitchen, clearly glad she'd escaped what was becoming an increasingly awkward situation. The pair didn't return, had perhaps gone into the living room instead.

"What's going on?" Ruby said to Michelle, keeping her voice low for Willow's sake, who seemed absorbed in what she was doing anyway. "Be honest with me."

"When we first met at the pool, I recognised you. Straightaway. Saw it as a sign."

"A sign of what?"

"That you were the one who was going to help us understand this"—with her eyes she gestured towards her daughter—"whatever *this* is. I'd been researching, you see, about those that could help, you know, psychic people. And your name, your company, kept coming up. I read all the testimonials on your website, studied the photograph of you and your team, was trying to summon up the courage to get in touch, and then…there you were. In Leo's swimming class, with Hendrix. And that's when I knew I had to do something about it, that it was like…I don't mean to sound over-the-top here, but fated. So I came over, introduced myself, started talking to you."

Ruby was the one who swallowed now, bizarrely also having to fight back tears. "Why didn't you just come clean? After the lesson, I mean. Say that you knew who I was and that you needed help? I'm used to that kind of approach. I wouldn't have been angry."

"That's exactly what I was going to do," Michelle declared, "but…we got talking about other stuff. You know…baby stuff. And…I couldn't do it, tell you about—" she lowered her voice to a whisper "—*her*. Plus, I was confused, wondered if I was getting myself into a state for nothing. Tim keeps telling me not to worry about it, that it's a phase, it'll pass, but it's not. If anything, it's getting more intense." She took a deep breath before continuing. "She writes, Ruby. Strange stuff, stuff way too advanced for her age, that doesn't make sense, like…I don't know, she's writing what someone's telling her to. That's how it seems. And when she's writing like this, there's no way you can distract her."

Not once during this whispered exchange did Willow look up to see what was happening, what the adults were talking about now, always so secretive. Based on what she was doing, the scattered paper before her, her trancelike state, Ruby thought she knew what Michelle was getting at even if Michelle didn't – automatic writing. The child was being used as a conduit, those in the spirit world who hadn't yet passed trying to communicate. That was the basis of the concept, at least. But you had to be careful with such a skill, drown out the darker voices, the mimics, what was disturbed, or non-spirit, and let only the genuine ones through. A child wouldn't necessarily know how to do that. This *family* wouldn't.

Ruby leant forward slightly. "How long has this been going on?"

"She's always been…different," Michelle said. "When she was younger, she used to talk about a different place, a different mummy. Used to upset me, to be honest. Far as I know, no one else's child did such a thing. Although, if they did, would they shout about it? And then, as she grew older, if I'd lost something, say an earring or a ring, she'd find it even though I'd been searching for days. I'd ask her how she always knew where things disappeared to, and she'd shrug, tell me she'd been told where by them, the others."

"The others?"

"Spirits, maybe? Back then, though, I just thought it was pure luck. That's the thing, I've dismissed so much, put it down to a child's vivid imagination or just another stroke of luck. You deal with the paranormal, Ruby. You know it exists. You accept that. But me, well, I didn't want it to be a part of my life. To…disrupt it. But it has, because it's led to this, to worse things. Most of the stuff she's written, I've destroyed. I didn't want Tim to know how much she's written and, lately, what kind of stuff. Oh, Ruby, I'm sorry. I feel like I've sprung this on you. I have. I know it. But recently, very recently, it's become so much darker, and I'm scared. I want it sorted out. She and Leo have different fathers, but what if this ability is inherited from me? Shit, Ruby, I'm really sorry to drag you into it like this."

Tears sprang from Michelle's eyes, Ruby moving closer to rub her arm, offer some kind of comfort. It was clear to see she was genuinely distressed about this ability of her daughter's. Fearful that she'd, what...*inflicted* it upon Willow and possibly Leo? As hurt as Ruby was, even perhaps a little angry – was any part of their friendship genuine? – she had to help, find out what was happening. But how? Automatic writing wasn't something she had a lot of experience with. It was a new aspect of the paranormal for her.

"It's okay, it's all right. Of course I'll help," she said, crushing any adverse feelings. "Now, why don't you take me over to Willow and introduce us properly."

Chapter Nine

Ruby felt cold. Unnerved too from what she'd experienced at Michelle's house, *frightened*. If she was to deal with Willow, it would have to be a team effort. *If.* The word kept repeating in her head. A word she had to dismiss. She couldn't turn her back on someone in need; that wasn't her style. But encountering Willow again – just a little girl, Ruby reminded herself, an *innocent* little girl being used as a conduit, as she'd already surmised – then maximum protection would have to be put in place. The energy she was channelling was, as Theo had said it could be, fiendishly clever.

She was home now in the kitchen, having a cup of tea, sugar in it when she'd weaned herself off, trying to gather some much-needed warmth. She needed the warmth of the atmosphere in her home too, the security of it. Cash and Hendrix were also in the kitchen, Cash cooking and Hendrix in his highchair gnawing at a rusk, and yet still the coldness wouldn't abate, reminding her of all she'd experienced at St Martin's churchyard. Hard to think that that kind of energy could ever be a part of the light eventually.

Just as Cash always did, he'd asked if she was okay when she got home and what the urgency had been with Michelle. And she'd told him – the bare bones of it.

"Oh, it was about her older daughter, Willow," she'd said. "She writes some weird stuff sometimes, and she wondered if I could help, whether it was this practice known as automatic writing, where a spirit's hand guides your hand. That kind of thing."

"And was it?"

"Well…yeah. Maybe. I'll have to get the team on it. These practices aren't as well defined as we'd like. You know what it's like with the paranormal, always loads of grey areas, always loads of anomalies."

This grey area, though, to do with Willow, it was as murky as it was possible to be.

And potentially very dangerous.

Michelle had indeed taken Ruby over to Willow and introduced her properly, and then the pair had sat down with Willow at the table, Ruby closest to her.

"So, you like drawing?" she'd said, trying to start a conversation with the child.

Willow had duly nodded. "And writing."

"You like writing too? Writing…lots and lots?"

Again, Willow nodded, smirked even, that sly quality of hers coming through.

"I also like writing and drawing," Ruby had said, persevering, "although I don't have much time for either at the moment. I've got a baby, Leo's friend. His name's Hendrix."

Willow didn't look up this time. She simply carried on doing what she was doing, colouring in a picture she'd drawn of a cat and a dog snuggled together. An innocent picture, cute. The cat was ginger and the dog black. A bit Jed-like, actually.

Still with thoughts of Jed in her mind, Ruby pointed to the picture, to the dog in particular. "I think you should colour his eyes brown. My dog's eyes are brown."

Willow then looked directly at Ruby and said, "You haven't got a dog."

Simple words, innocent, surely, and in a way she was right. Ruby didn't have a *live* dog, but it was in that moment that whatever unease she'd felt previously increased.

The child returned to her drawing, took a blue felt-tip pen and coloured the dog's eyes – deliberately defiant.

Ruby glanced at Michelle, who tried so hard to smile. *She's a good kid.* Clearly, she wanted very much to believe that.

"Can you…um…show me what else you've been drawing?" Ruby continued. "What you've been writing too?"

There were other pieces of paper, previously scattered all over the table, but at some point, likely when Michelle and Ruby had been talking, the child had collected them and placed them in a pile, all beneath her current drawing, pressing down on them with more and more pressure. When the child didn't respond, Ruby dared to reach out, and that's when Willow had grabbed her hand, as cold to the touch as Ruby felt now, sending shivers coursing down her spine. And she'd spoken again.

"You want to know how I can do what I do, don't you? You're that lady she told me about, and she told Daddy about, although Daddy just laughed, told Mummy she was being silly. *Very, very* silly." God, her voice! It sliced through Ruby's nerves. Just what had she got herself into here? *Unwittingly* into. "But if you want, if you really want, I can show you exactly what I do. Like this."

The girl had then closed her eyes, Ruby's own eyes growing wider as she'd watched her. Beside her she could sense Michelle stiffen, her breath becoming a little heavier.

With her eyes still closed, Willow wrote all over the drawing she'd been working on, the cat and the dog with blue eyes, effectively defacing it. Not intelligible words at first, more like markings. Again, Ruby looked at Michelle, only for a second, and only to gauge her further reaction, her expression containing so much fear and helplessness. Turning her attention to Willow again, she saw the markings were making sense, words forming at last, and leant forward to read: *Hello. Bin. Long. Too. Long. Hello! Hello! Liar. No. Dog. No Father. You. Say. Have! Have! Have! Hello! Bin. Long.*

In the safety and comfort of her own kitchen, Spotify playing one of Cash's rather eclectic playlists, and Cash crooning along – even Hendrix swaying occasionally in his high chair, jiggling his little body from side to side – Ruby had to stifle a cry. She could tell Cash anything, but she didn't want to tell him this, invite the memory of it into her house, or any thoughts of the father she'd once wanted to find.

Willow had written those words, and when she had, she'd not only held Ruby's hand, she'd clutched it, tighter and tighter, Ruby fearing she'd break her bones if she didn't stop.

Her heart beating as fast then as it was now, she'd tried to extricate herself from the child's grip – she couldn't. Not initially. And still Willow was writing blind.

Say Hello! Say It! Only. Polite. You. Taught. That? Or. Dragged. Up. By Her. Bitch. She is! No. Manners. Scared? Say It! Hello! Hello! Say It! Say. Say. Say!

If Willow's strength was preternatural, then, finally, Ruby's was too. Fear needled at her skin like a witch pricker of old, giving her the impetus she needed. She *tore* her hand from Willow's and stood abruptly up, her chair scraping against the tiled floor.

Her eyes opening wide, Willow looked up at her, that coldness that had been in her eyes replaced by confusion as her mouth erupted in an ear-piercing wail.

"I'm sorry, so sorry," Ruby said, not rushing for the front door – it was too far away – but out into the garden, the French doors already thankfully open.

She was aware of movement behind her, Willow's grandmother drawn by the commotion into the kitchen. There was Michelle too, appealing for calm, for everyone to just stop and take a breath, promising Willow everything would be all right.

Ruby simply stood there in the garden, the warmth from the spring sun having no effect on her whatsoever, shivering as tears formed in her eyes and thinking that Michelle was wrong to promise Willow such a thing. Right now, there was no way of telling.

Once things had indeed calmed inside, Michelle joined her in the garden.

"I'm sorry," she kept saying. "I don't know what all that was about. That's the thing, what she writes makes no sense to me, and yet… Oh, Ruby, I'm sorry if I've been out of order, I didn't mean to be. I want us to continue being friends. I really like you, but I also need help. *We* do, me and Willow. I'm not going to deny it anymore and bury my head in the sand like Tim does, and Mum. They both say don't stress about it, but, Ruby—" a sob caught in her throat, clearly wanting to escape "—as I've said, it's getting worse. What she wrote just now, it means nothing to me, but it does to you, doesn't it?"

Ruby couldn't speak, her voice something shrivelled.

"Ruby?"

She had to find an answer, say something, at least. *Act normal.*

"Ruby, please, you're scaring me. What's wrong with my little girl?"

"Nothing," she said at last. "Nothing…that we can't help her with."

The relief on Michelle's face! "You'll do it? You'll help? Oh, thank you! Thank you! I don't mind…you know…if she's a little like you. That's fine. Just that…whatever she is, it doesn't overwhelm her, because that's what I feel's happening here. Whatever ability she has, whoever she got it from, it's taking her over. And I can't have that, Ruby. I can't."

Despite how bleak she'd been feeling, Ruby had then comforted Michelle, putting her arms around her, and Michelle clung to her, desperate for some reassurance.

"We can help," she'd reiterated. *We.* The team. Not just her. As she'd already decided. How, though, had Willow known about Ruby's father? No way she could have.

In the kitchen, Cash was now plating up, Ruby's tummy, despite everything, grumbling.

"Here we go," he said, two plates in his hands piled high with food and delivered to the table with such flourish before he doubled back for another bowl, this one a plainer, mashed-up version for Hendrix, who kicked excitedly and even brought his hands together in a clap on seeing it. Jerk chicken for the adults, pureed chicken, vegetables and mash for the baby.

As she ate, something in her was restored. Some kind of faith. It *would* be all right. The darkness couldn't touch her, not while she walked in the light, or strived to. These two, they provided so much of it, the balance she craved. She recalled Michelle's words from earlier: *I don't mind, you know, if she's a little like you.* A little what? Weird? A misfit? An outcast? And yet Cash, a normal person, loved her just as much as she loved him. A man who, even now, was lifting his head and grinning at her.

"Good, isn't it? The jerk chicken. My best effort so far, I think."

"It's amazing," Ruby replied. "Thank you. Thank you so much."

As Cash continued to devour his plate of food, Ruby returned to hers.

Whatever ability she has, whoever she got it from, it's taking her over. And I can't have that, Ruby. I won't.

Ruby mustn't let it overwhelm her either.

The child needed help; her family did. After dinner, Ruby would text the rest of the team, knowing full well that whatever plans they had for the following day, they'd drop them in order to deal with this. They had to tread carefully when a child was involved, but if nothing else, they could teach her about the light and how to use it to protect herself.

Maybe that would do the trick. It might be enough.

As Ruby continued to eat, as she and Cash chatted about more everyday matters, as the baby gurgled, enjoying getting as much mash over his face and fingers as in his mouth, she could only pray it'd be enough, trying to suppress the suspicion that whatever Willow was channelling, it would kick right back, put up a fight. A particularly vicious one.

Chapter Ten

The next morning, in the cramped confines of Ruby's attic office in Sun Street, along with the rest of her colleagues, Theo sat and listened to all that Ruby had to say about Michelle and her daughter Willow. When Ruby had finished, there was a brief silence, all of them processing the information. Before speaking, Theo took a deep breath.

"As you say, dear girl, Willow's channelling something, some kind of energy that's found her. Clearly, she's a psychic in training. A conduit."

Ruby looked at her, Theo noting the naked fear in her eyes and wishing she could chase it away. "But, Theo, how did she know? About…him? Was it…? Do you think…?"

"That it actually was him?" Theo said. This wasn't a time to beat about the bush but to lay bare their thoughts, try to navigate a way through them so they could reach some kind of clarity, form a plan of action. "It's more likely that whatever energy was feeding off her was feeding off you too, detecting what's in your mind and throwing it back."

"You think it's definitely a bad energy?" Corinna asked.

Ruby glanced at her before answering. "That thing with Jed, with his eyes, it was, like…eerie, you know? Like…oh, how can I describe it? So defiant, the way she coloured them blue instead of brown, an insult, even, mocking him. I was just glad Jed wasn't there to witness it. He'd have been most annoyed." She smiled at this, but ruefully, Theo admiring her for trying to inject some light into what was indeed a disturbing situation.

Before she could stop herself, Theo yawned, prompting Ness to ask if she was okay.

"Oh, stop, please. I'm just tired from our rather epic battle the other day. Aren't you?"

Ness shrugged. "I'm okay, considering. But yes, you're right, it was on the epic side."

"Just a tad," Theo continued. "As I was saying, if your father is on your mind—"

Immediately, Ruby denied it. "I hardly ever think of him! That's what's so strange."

Theo, however, wasn't buying it. "Ruby, I wish that were true, but I rather suspect it isn't. He…" She hesitated for a moment, recalling meeting him at Cromer – a maximum-security mental health facility on the edge of the Brookbridge Estate near Horam – his intensity, his insight. "He may not be at the forefront of your mind, but this kind of dark energy digs deep. Plays on our weaknesses. You know that."

"He is *not* my weakness." Again, Ruby said it through gritted teeth, and Theo empathised. She did. Hated that Ruby's family history was so chequered. With a sigh, she returned the conversation to Willow. "So, Michelle wants us to get involved?"

"Definitely," Ruby said.

"As it's a child, we have to tread very carefully," Ness said, continuing to fret. "It's a case that could turn against us in more ways than one."

"True," Theo said, also concerned about that. "And I think that going to her home en masse, the four of us, might prove a little scary. Perhaps…two of us go initially."

Regarding Theo's point, Ruby sighed. "Yeah, you're right. I hadn't thought of that."

"Whoever goes," Ness continued, "there needs to be someone independent of us, an official, and independent of the Bayliss family too to witness, just in case."

"Who?" asked Corinna.

"Lee," Ness suggested. "I know he and I are linked, but as a police officer, he can remain objective should anything kick off, ensure no lines are crossed. We'll need to do some paperwork too with Michelle, that she insists upon us and not the social services."

"I'd like to go with you, Ruby," Theo said.

"Or you and Ness could go?" Ruby ventured. "Along with Lee, of course."

"But you're the link," Theo countered. "I'm sorry about what happened before. I know it's troubling you, but you're the one the family are familiar with. We'll go along, you and I, with Lee if he's able to, and we'll see how we get on, take it from there. You don't have to hold her hand again, Ruby. She can hold mine instead."

Ness frowned. "Are you sure it's best only two of us go? I'm rather thinking not."

"I'm only talking initially, Ness," Theo replied. "it may well need all of us there eventually. This case certainly sounds like an interesting one, so I'd definitely like to give it a shot. Plus"—Theo smiled as she played her trump card—"look at me. What do you see? I'm the archetypal granny. Less – don't get me wrong when I say this, Ness – austere. And my hair," she added, pointing to her coiffeur, "what little girl doesn't love the colour pink?"

Having secured a plan, Theo continued. "So, conduits. What do we know about them?"

"As we've already discussed," Ness said, "a conduit is someone who channels energy, an energy that can also feed off the energy of others, as seems to have happened between Willow and Ruby. A conduit can also feed back their own energy to the person they're in physical contact with." Ness settled into her chair as she got to grips with the subject. "The conduit can also use other people's energy to enhance his or her power, connecting two people mentally. One other thing to note is that being a conduit can wear down a person physically. Ruby, you've said Willow's been having more and more days off school?"

"Uh-huh."

"Little wonder. She must be exhausted. It sounds as if she's channelling on a regular basis, at least recently."

"So how can we stop it?" Corinna asked. "Deny her pen and paper? Something as simple as that? I know she's at school, so that's not always going to be possible, but when she's home, at least? Take away the tools of communication."

"We can advise on various steps such as those," Theo agreed, "and, as already said, other methods of protection, the kind we use, if we can get her to comply, that is. As we're fond of an adage around here, you can lead a horse to water, but you can't make it drink."

"We can only do our best," Ness pointed out.

"Which we will," murmured Ruby.

"Definitely," added Corinna.

"You say she goes into a kind of trance when she's writing?" Ness checked. "Correct?"

"According to Michelle," Ruby said. "She seemed to whilst I was there as well."

"Other than what she wrote when you were there, what else has she been writing?"

"Before I left, I had a look at what else. Michelle's mother, Katharine, she'd removed Willow from the kitchen by that time, taken her and her brother, Leo, out for some fresh air. So yeah, I took a look at what's been written recently, and the best I can say is it was random. There were various words and sentences, some that fit together and some that didn't. No particular words recurring like they did with me."

"So could it be," Theo said, playing with the possibility in her head, "that the process becomes more refined when holding on to your hand? More…targeted?"

Ruby shrugged. "Possibly."

"As I've said, interesting."

"You know," Ness interjected, "right now, it seems she's tuning in to the darker stuff, along with that which exists in the psyche of others. But if we can cause it to divert to the angelic rather than the demonic, and divert it permanently, it'd be a wonderful gift."

As much as Theo agreed, another question weighed on her mind. "Despite Michelle's fears that Willow inherited this from her, she doesn't appear to have a psychic bone in her body, does she, Ruby? So, what about Willow's father? He's not Leo's father, is he?"

"They're two different fathers," Ruby confirmed. "Michelle got pregnant when she was nineteen and had Willow when she was twenty. I don't have all the information to hand regarding who her biological father is, though. Not yet. Sorry."

"It's no problem. We can find out when we visit. So…how soon does she want us?"

"As soon as possible. Whenever Lee can make it, basically. When it fits his schedule and when all paperwork's been completed. Ness, about Lee, can you let us know?"

"Of course," she said, retrieving her phone from her bag, then rising from her chair to exit the room. "I'll try and get in touch with him now."

She was back in just a few minutes.

"Any joy?" asked Theo.

"Funnily enough," Ness answered, "he's free right now."

* * *

The visit started off well. Michelle agreed to sign the papers Psychic Surveys had brought with them, and the little girl, Willow, was proving very sweet, Theo thought. Her hunch was right, as the child took to her almost straightaway, chatting animatedly as they sat around the kitchen table. It was just her, Ruby, Lee, Willow and Michelle in the house. Tim was working and then going straight from work to meet some friends, and Katharine, the grandmother, had taken Leo back to her house, which was only a short drive away. Everything was bobbing along swimmingly, the atmosphere relaxed, jovial even, cups of tea placed on the table in front of them, and Willow showing Theo not her writing, not yet, but some pictures she'd drawn, innocent pictures, they appeared to be. Exactly the kind Theo's own grandchildren would draw – animals, houses, mummy, daddy, baby, that kind of thing

– and Theo exclaimed enthusiastically over every one.

Gaining Willow's trust was the aim. According to Ruby, the child hadn't acted like this before, not when Ruby had been there alone. And still the girl regarded Ruby suspiciously, Theo had to admit, green eyes flecked with amber narrowing slightly whenever turned in her direction. Theo wondered whether she should be more concerned about this? Just what was her problem with Ruby, and if the child herself didn't have a problem, then what was it that did? They could only press on. This was a preliminary meeting, allowing Theo to get to grips with the situation too. Get a take on it. She rather suspected it would take session after session to get to the bottom of it properly and equip the girl with the tools she needed, just as she herself had been equipped when younger.

As Theo continued to chat with Willow, as Ruby sipped her tea, as Michelle and Lee looked on from the sidelines, a part of her brain couldn't help but reminisce. Her guide, her mentor when young, the one her parents had put in place for her, Margaret Cuttress, she'd considered an angel on earth, a lifesaver, someone who had understood what Theo was going through even though she wasn't psychic herself. Who'd helped her more than she could've ever known. Was it now time to give back? Oh, it was true Theo had helped many, but here, in the kitchen of the Bayliss house, it reminded her of how she'd been all those years ago, so innocent, so trusting, yet deep down so damned frightened and bewildered.

If Willow was frightened or bewildered, she was hiding it well. She must be, though. Ruby had said she'd been missing school lately, pleading illness. So there it was, right there, signs of her being confused by it all, feeling more and more like an oddball, a misfit, as those with abilities were prone to feel – initially, anyway. On the contrary, Willow should be proud of her gift, if it *was* a gift, and that's what Theo hoped to instil in her and, as Ness had said, get her to channel something more positive.

"Another cup?" Michelle rose from her chair, clearly desperate to do something other than sit there, trying not to stare.

Lee nodded at the offer, a regular tea monster, but both Theo and Ruby declined. It was time to focus, to approach further the heart of the matter.

The child was sitting in between Ruby and Theo, although turned more in Theo's direction, with her back practically to Ruby. That had to be rectified, evened out.

"Why don't you sit up straight, now?" Theo suggested, her voice gentle but firm, going so far as to take hold of the child's shoulders and assist her in doing so.

There was hesitance, a force that rebelled. Theo could feel it well enough, something inside the child that didn't like being told what to do. Although not strictly given to labels, the team had nonetheless dubbed her a conduit, having to find some way to describe her, if only for convenience's sake. Were they right in that? She was a conduit but also something else? Like that other child, the one that had appeared to Theo, possessed?

Quite suddenly, Willow gave in and sat more front facing. Theo should have been glad about that, a small triumph, but she was confused. The child had complied with her wishes, but only when her thoughts had strayed to the other issue dominating her mind… Could it be that Willow was able to read minds? Something Theo knew was perfectly possible because she was able to do it too, with some people, at least. Not with Willow, though. She was a closed book. There'd be no probing inside her head, unless…

Another plan formed. One which Theo ran with.

"Your drawings are so lovely," she continued to enthuse. "You really are quite the talent, aren't you? The colours you use are so vivid, but…I'd love to see some of your writing now. *We* would, Ruby and I. Is that all right, Willow? Under that pile there, is that where you keep what you've written before? Would it be okay if I just—" reaching out, Theo brought the pile a little closer "—took a quick peek?"

Willow didn't object, but she stiffened, almost as much as Ruby, who was struggling, Theo knew, to maintain a cool, calm exterior. Theo moved the top sheet to reveal another drawing, the one Ruby had told them about, with the ginger cat and the dog so like Jed but with blue eyes. Beneath that were pages with the writing that Ruby had also mentioned, aimed at her, *defiling* her: *Hello. Bin. Long. Too. Long. Hello! Hello! Liar. No. Dog. No Father. You. Say. Have! Have! Have! Hello! Bin. Long.*

Even Theo gulped to see it, how hard the words had been scored. Placing those sheets aside, she looked at other pages, other words, seemingly random: *There. Who. Me. Who. Hello! House. Cat. Dog. Hello. There? Find. See. Can. Find. Me. Can. Can? Hello! Here.*

Words plucked from where – her subconscious? Automatic writing could be just that, the product of the subconscious, nothing more, that which had accumulated, then was stored away in deep, dark recesses. Words that could be construed as innocent were it not for the fact that with Ruby, she'd read her mind, reached into it. A talent indeed!

Michelle had returned to the table with Lee's mug of tea, placing it before him.

"There," she said on seeing what Theo was reading. "Those words. What do they mean? Willow"—briefly she glanced at her daughter and smiled—"she won't talk about it, not to me. But you might talk to these nice ladies, mightn't you? They've come to help, Willow. So, as we've discussed, there's no need to be worried. You know Mummy only ever wants what's best for you." A crack in her voice forced her to stop talking, to turn away instead, returning to the counter to no doubt wipe surreptitiously at her eyes.

Distressing. For all concerned. *A dark situation.* Those were the words that flashed in Theo's mind, words she refused to entertain. The light they'd brought with them could overpower the dark, therefore it was far from a dark situation. Especially when a child's well-being was at stake. They'd get this under control.

She had to focus, bring the shutters down in her mind, seal them with light so that what they were about to do would give them an insight into Willow, not vice versa. She took in the words again, those that kept repeating: *Can. Find. Me. Can. Can? Hello! Here.*

A conduit. Being used. By whom or what?

Carefully, gently, she placed a fresh piece of paper in front of Willow, reached out for a pen and brought that closer too.

"Here's what I'd like you to do," she said, adopting her best grandmotherly tone and smile, her blue eyes with a twinkle in them, she knew it. "I'd like you to write something for me, Willow. That…*special* writing you do."

The girl gazed back at her, so trusting and just so damned young, her skin perfectly plump, a smattering of freckles across her nose. "I held her hand last time," she responded, not mentioning Ruby by name, just gesturing towards her with her head.

"Would you like to hold my hand?" Theo offered, still smiling.

The girl nodded. "Hers again too."

Theo frowned, and she could see Ruby doing the same. "But…how will you be able to write if you hold both our hands?"

Willow reached out, took Theo's hand, her fingers cold, Theo noticed, clutching tight, and then, without looking at Ruby but gazing straight ahead, she took Ruby's hand also, Ruby's breath growing more rapid, Theo willing her silently to keep calm.

"Willow?" Theo prompted.

The girl smiled, as softly and gently as Theo had, but there was something about it, something…sly. Was that the word? Disingenuous.

"I'll show you how," Willow whispered as the world went black.

Chapter Eleven

"Theo? Theo, where are you? What's happening?"

Ruby was trembling, her chest heaving too as she struggled for breath.

One minute they were sitting around a kitchen table in a house in the Malling area of Lewes, the next there was this – total darkness. As if she'd been struck blind.

"Theo, where've you gone?" she called again.

She had to remain calm; she knew that, had seen the look Theo had given her just before all this had happened, urging her to do exactly that. Then Willow had reached out, taken her hand, her grip as strong as before, as cold.

What the hell had happened from thereon in? Had she been…transported? Where? The in-between was somewhere she'd been before, only once or twice, but she hadn't lingered – she'd soon been expelled from it, thankfully. Would the same happen this time? She wouldn't be kept prisoner, surely? By whom? The child? Was Willow really that powerful?

Breathe, Ruby, for God's sake, breathe! This'll pass; you know it will. It may not even be real. It could be an illusion the child had somehow created. The paranormal was such a vast subject, one that only ever expanded. Ruby had learnt over the years that if you could think it, you could bring it into being, manifest it, if you had the will to. But she hadn't manifested this, such a bleak place, such...*nothingness.* She'd been placed here, by her, by Willow. *I'll show you how,* she'd said, just before the world was extinguished.

One deep breath followed another, becoming deeper, less frantic. No sign of Theo, but that didn't mean she wasn't here. After all, she'd also taken the child's hand. Concern for her colleague at last gave her the courage to put one leg in front of the other. Pitch black, but what was beneath her feet, a ground of some description, felt solid enough. As she continued to take steps, she couldn't rid herself of the awful feeling that somewhere there was a precipice and just one more step would send her plummeting over it.

Not real. This experience. Cerebral. It had to be. Her physical body was still at the kitchen table, sitting beside Willow, holding on to her hand, but her mind...it had indeed been transported elsewhere, by a child whom Michelle had every right to be worried about. Heck, Ruby was worried if she could do stuff like this! If you were gifted, you had to be careful, show restraint. Something Willow didn't yet know.

As Ruby continued to walk blindly onwards, she wondered how long this experience would last. Even if seconds, it could seem like aeons. In a place like this, time meant nothing; it was irrelevant. Oh, where was Theo? Here or in a separate hell?

"Theo." Her voice had reduced to a whisper. "Where are you? Answer me." *If you can.*

The darkness was so disorientating; she turned one way and then another, wasn't sure if she was doubling back on herself or not. As well as confusion and frustration, she felt anger. She didn't need this crap! She'd thought she'd protected herself well enough, but clearly not; Willow had somehow got around that protection. Regarding conduits, even experienced psychics like them didn't know what was being channelled half the time.

She hoped it was only seconds passing, no more than that. She ached for Hendrix, hated to be parted from him like this. It was no use. She had to stop drifting along, stand still and project white light, the only way to combat this.

That plan put into action, she drew on all she'd been taught as a child herself, drawing light straight from Source, against which the darkness could not thrive. Usually, it was so easy to summon, to feel the warmth of it, but this time, no matter how hard she tried, her mind remained as black as her surroundings. As empty.

What the heck? Try harder!

She pushed her shoulders back, straightened her spine and tried again – the light was there, always, even in a place like this. She tilted her head back, certain she'd detect a glow in the distance that would only grow in strength. Still nothing. Not yet. But no need to panic. That was one thing she mustn't do, give way to the emotions broiling in the pit of her stomach, every bit as cold as Willow's touch, all the baggage she dragged around, day in, day out, whether she acknowledged it or not, that existed even so.

She tried to ignore such negativity. *Knew* to ignore it. Her task here was to bring the light in, as they'd done at the churchyard a few days ago.

Not you, Ruby! It was Theo, Ness and Corinna who did that. They blasted it apart. You…well, you got stuck!

Oh, what a place this was, full of cold hard truths! And

yet she was sweating, beads of moisture on her forehead and dripping down her back, her chest heaving again.

Get yourself under control!

Not just a request, it was a command she gave herself. But that other thought, the one that had preceded it, continued to wreak havoc. She *had* got stuck in it; it was true, chased Jed into the darkness because she'd thought he'd been harmed in some way. *You idiot, Ruby.* The darkness couldn't harm something like Jed! The yelp she'd thought she'd heard had been meant to weaken her. And it had worked. Now here she was again. Why? Because she wasn't like Jed, nowhere near as pure or as good? Because she *did* belong?

The light…where was it? In every dark place, in the darkness of every human, there was a crack of some sort where the light could penetrate. So why not here?

She closed her eyes. The darkness became even more intense. But at least it was *her* darkness, not this fabrication courtesy of Willow. On another deep breath, she took a step forward, then another. If she couldn't see the light, she imagined being drawn towards it instead and that suddenly, and magnificently, it would appear, a great column of it right in front of her. It would beat back this warped reality until the world she knew materialised again, her eyes snapping open to find she was still at the kitchen table, that Michelle and Lee were there, Theo, of course, and the garden in all its spring glory just beyond the French doors. The beauty of it dazzling compared to this.

This was a stark place. Lonely.

"Theo," she said again, having to force her mouth to open, getting too used to the silence, maybe even fearing to break it. "Theo. Theo. Theo." Her name like a mantra now.

Could it be that she wasn't here? That this was a show put on solely for Ruby? The child had made it obvious she didn't like her, had shown none of the friendliness towards her that she'd shown towards Theo. She'd smiled at Theo, many times, chatted happily with her, shown her all the drawings she'd been doing, *benign* drawings. During all that time, she'd as good as kept her back to Ruby, ignored her. Even before, when she and Theo had first walked into the kitchen, Willow once again sitting at the table there, the child hadn't bothered to glance her way. Was she now experiencing some kind of punishment designed just for her? Why? If it was, though, there was hope. Theo wouldn't let it continue. The second she realised what was happening, she'd break the hold Willow had over Ruby. Michelle would too, and Lee. Springboard her out of this.

So what was taking them so long?

Seconds, she reminded herself. That was likely all that had passed on the outside. Each one a lifetime in a place like this. Therein lay the hell of it.

Immediately, she reprimanded herself. *Don't breathe life into thoughts like that!* But what was the alternative? To not think at all? Become like this space she was suspended in, empty too? A vessel. Just until whatever was happening was over?

She came to another halt. As nothing else was working, perhaps that's *exactly* what she should do. Be still, be silent. Emotion*less*. Play the waiting game.

Easy to do. In theory. In practice, though…

The mind was so hard to control! Rather than seek to emulate such stillness, it took advantage of it, reared up and ran riot. All kinds of thoughts and memories entered her head, cramming the space there, dredged up from the depths, those that she had long buried or tried to, all soaked in fear and more fear. Such faithful companions.

Thoughts about…him. How she'd longed for him, shaped him in her mind, forced him to manifest. And he had – or so she'd thought – a quiet man, a man with another family, who'd seemed ready to welcome her, and she had so wanted that, a chance to be normal, not psychic, fatherless Ruby, whose mother had been little more than a shell for most of Ruby's childhood, whose grandmother had tried so hard to shield her from all that was coming, what was clearly inevitable. One of two men could be her father, her mother had finally revealed – not the benign man, as it turned out, someone so gloriously pedestrian and run-of-the-mill, but another that was far from it, a dark shadow of a man her mother had spent one night with and then ran from, as fast and as far as she could. Too late, though, for he'd planted a seed that would grow to become a child of the light…and the dark.

This dark, right here.

She couldn't take another step. All she could do was hunker down, her arms wrapped around herself, trying to find comfort from such a pitiful hug, to make herself smaller, to hide. From what? There was nothing here, only herself – and her memories, of course. Of meeting her true father, a patient at a maximum-security mental health facility. His face…she could see herself in it, beyond that hideous smile of his, the one that stretched Joker-like from ear to ear, and in eyes that glittered with nothing but danger. A man who knew what Ruby's mother, Jessica, was. She'd told him that night, when Gran had always warned her, warned *them*, to be wary, just until they'd got the measure of the person. Jessica, though, had been drunk, upset after breaking up with the ordinary man – he'd been married and had gone back to his wife – and this new man, this stranger, he'd been so persuasive. *Tell me*, he'd said. Ruby could imagine it exactly, hear in the silence the liquid molasses of his voice: *I want to know all about you.*

He'd *craved* the knowledge Jessica had, her talent, because he was obsessed, not with the light but the darkness, the occult, the power he thought it could give him. Desired it as the power*less* often do, choosing to worship the wrong deity, the god of false promises. A devout man. He was that, all right. And Jessica, once she'd sobered and realised what she'd done, the mistake she'd made, had fled. Held the memory of him as a secret all these years. Until Ruby had pushed and pushed and pushed…

Be careful what you wish for…

She'd often thought those words since meeting him, which were now being engraved upon her mind as if…as if…she was not the only one here after all. As if someone else was also privy to such private thoughts.

Willow?

What was better? What was worse? To be alone or have her here, tormenting her?

Hell.

Another word formed in her mind, forcing her to open her eyes, to see the same wall of black in front of her, the word engraved on that too.

What was it that Theo had said when the child had taken both their hands? *How will you be able to write if you hold both our hands?* And Willow had replied, *I'll show you how.*

She didn't need pen or paper, something so primitive.

"Willow." Ruby's voice was pitiful as she said her name. She had to inject some strength into it, some authority. "Willow! Whatever you're doing, I want you to stop. Let go of my hand, of the hold you have on me. Willow, this is wrong. Stop it! Now."

Instantly, the word *hell* vanished. Was that a good sign? Did it mean she was listening?

God, Ruby wanted to escape this place.

Escape. Yourself.

She gasped as the words appeared. A childish scrawl.

What did they even mean?

You. Know.

She shook her head. Refused to acknowledge, to entertain them.

The words repeated themselves, *screamed* at her, *YOU KNOW!*

"Stop it, Willow. You don't know me at all. You know *nothing* about me."

The words vanished. There was darkness again, so much darkness. She couldn't stand how much there was of it, a maddening amount.

Laughter.

Ruby swung her head from side to side. Whose laughter? From being hunkered, she stood up, squared her shoulders, tried once more to summon the light, cursed again when she failed. There wasn't even a chink here, no way to infiltrate.

Two realisations came to her: she herself had been responsible for the laughter, no mirth attached to it, though, no joy. And she knew exactly what this place was.

She was inside herself. Locked up in a prison of her worst fears, the ones she'd told no one about, could hardly even admit to herself.

That she was the product of madness.

And because of that, was there madness in her too? Was it another attachment, content to bide its time, safe in the knowledge its day would come?

Madness wasn't only in her father but also in her grandfather, Edward Middleton – something she'd only recently learned via a diary found in the family home – and in her great-grandmother Rosamund's father, William Howard. So much madness.

Ready to eat you alive, from the inside out.

Those were her words this time. Nothing to do with Willow.

But Willow was listening.

Willow was also laughing.

Ruby clamped her hands against her own mouth.

As she'd said, so much madness. Hames, Middleton and Howard were just those she knew about. What about family that went back further? What gems existed there?

She wouldn't give in to this, to memories that crucified her, that would accelerate the madness, if it was even in her at all. *It's not! It isn't! Willow, get me out of here!*

More laughter from Willow, filled with malice. Whatever the child was channelling, Ruby could channel something stronger. She mustn't forget that. It was all too easy to focus on the negative, the lure of it always so strong.

So…tempting.

That was Willow – reading her mind again, connected way too deeply.

"Just…fuck off, will you? Leave me and the child alone."

TEMPTED!

Had her own words, her anger, riled her opponent somehow?

"No!" she said, noticing how the darkness tried to swallow her words. "You don't tempt me. In fact, you know what? I think you're pathetic, trying to scare me like this, to turn me against myself. I can break out of here on my own, sever this connection." She looked down at her hands, *empty* hands – in this place, at least, but not in reality. In reality, Willow was doing what she'd done before, gripping tighter and tighter, crushing her.

A small smile played around Ruby's lips. "What if you can't, though? Crush me? Does that make you feel frightened too?"

More words were scrawled in front of her, the only thing bright around here. No use ignoring them. Even if she closed her eyes, she'd see the same thing.

She gritted her teeth. What did Willow have to say this time?

The same words she'd written before, when she and Ruby had been in the kitchen, were now ten feet tall, filling every bit of the space in front of Ruby.

Father. Have! Have! Have!

More words added.

Coming. You.

Ruby shook her head, denied it.

Coming!

You!

"No," she said. "No. No. NO!"

Free.

Ruby swallowed. Free? What the hell did that mean?

He is not free, she tried to say. *He isn't.*

As she stared at the wall, she willed the words to disappear, for the light to power its way in at last, break the sickening neon of them, destroy the threat.

When that didn't happen, when the words kept on coming, flashing repeatedly one after the other, she heard another sound. Not laughter, not this time, no matter how mirthless, but screaming instead, and full of agony – her own or his?

I'm. Free.
I. Am.
Coming.
For. You.

Chapter Twelve

At last, there was light.

Ruby lifted her hands – *both* hands – to her face to try to blot it out, sure it would sear the retinas of her eyes after so long in the darkness.

So long?

When she was sure she could focus, she looked around her. Nothing had changed. Absolutely nothing. Michelle and Lee were at the table, making a show of minding their own business, chatting to each other in hushed tones about everyday subjects, where they might go for a holiday this year, the promise of a good summer to come. Swiftly turning her head, she saw Willow was sitting innocently between her and Theo, her hands on the table in front of her, and that Theo was eyeing them both curiously.

Willow suddenly laughed. A sweet sound, not malicious at all.

"Oh," she said, "I can't show you like that after all."

As she continued to sit there, the smile on her face turned sly.

You fucking liar!

"Ruby!" Theo's voice held a mixture of softness and sternness. From staring at the child, Ruby lifted her head and saw the reproach in her colleague's eyes but also the understanding. Despite that, she felt another burst of anger: Was nothing sacred? Her own mind? Theo had just tapped into it too, read her thoughts, the fury behind them.

Theo stood up. "I think…" she said, "as lovely as this visit has been, meeting you, Willow, and your mother too, we need to go and return, perhaps, at a later date." As if answering her own question, she nodded. "Yes, yes, we'll do that. Definitely. We'll gather our thoughts, then return. Michelle, would you mind?" Theo indicated for Michelle, Lee and Ruby to follow her into the hallway, the child continuing to sit at the kitchen table, rocking slightly from side to side now, humming a tune under her breath.

Ruby stood up too, as did Michelle and Lee, Ruby for her part having to prevent any more traitorous thoughts from entering her head, from reaching out, even, with her free hands and shaking the child, screaming at her, *What do you mean he's free? My father? He's not. He's locked up, he's behind bars, with no sign he'll ever be leaving. So what do you mean? What could you possibly mean?* She had to work hard to restrain herself, to remind herself too that Willow *didn't* know. That none of this was her fault. She was a child. Just a child being used. A child who now looked straight at her, albeit briefly. Even so, Ruby caught the amusement in her eyes, the continued taunting. *A child*, Ruby kept repeating, forcing those words to the forefront of her mind when others seemed more urgent, *a conduit. She needs help. We will help her.*

And yet all she wanted to do right now was bolt, put as much distance between herself and Willow as was humanly possible and never return.

They reached the hallway, and Theo was talking, addressing them all.

"…she's a very talented child…unusual. But, Michelle, the reason you've called us in, myself and Ruby, is because you're worried about her."

Michelle shrugged, with something like hope on her face, glancing only briefly at Ruby before her eyes settled on Theo. "I mean…all that, in there, it all seemed relatively normal, didn't it? Maybe what's been happening is a phase after all. I really thought she'd play to the gallery today, but…she didn't. She was just, like, happy to chat mostly."

Ruby could have choked. The child *had* played to the gallery, spectacularly! Albeit a gallery of one.

"Mum!" Willow's voice penetrated the air between them. "Mum, I'm hungry!"

Michelle, her eyes on Ruby this time, shrugged again. "Kids, eh? Always hungry."

Ruby couldn't form a response.

"Best you see to her," Theo answered instead, the perfect picture of calm professionalism, "and we'll make a date to come back soon."

Ruby couldn't help but interject this time. "If we think it's necessary."

Perhaps only Ruby could tell Theo's laughter was forced. "Oh, I think one or two more visits might be just as well. But go, Michelle, feed your child. We'll be in touch."

Michelle nodded, but her eyes were still on Ruby. Seeking what? Her approval? Her consent?

When Ruby continued to stand there, mute, Michelle forced the issue by addressing her directly. "Is that okay?" she said. "I'll see you soon, in this capacity and…as friends, with Leo and Hendrix?"

Ruby had to at least nod, muttering a response before turning and heading further down the hallway to the front door. "Of course."

Outside the house, Ruby, Theo and Lee stood on the garden path that meandered up to the pavement.

"All okay, Ruby?" said Lee, a slight frown on his handsome but lived-in face.

"Fine." Ruby's voice was tight, even to her own ears. "Thanks so much for coming to the house with us, Lee, taking time out of your day. We really appreciate it."

"No problem. Always best to err on the safe side when there's a child involved." He raised an eyebrow at this before adding, "A living child, I mean."

Ruby nodded. "Absolutely."

After checking his watch, Lee said his goodbyes and walked off to where his car was parked. Following in his footsteps, Ruby steeled herself.

"Right, okay," Theo was muttering, for once keeping effortless pace with her, "we won't do this here. We'll wait until we're back in the car."

"Whatever," Ruby replied, her tone surly, she knew. Of course she'd have to explain what had happened, but she didn't want to, wanted to push it back down inside her, box it up and put a bloody great padlock on that box – imprison it. *Like he should be. Like he is!*

Shit! Her bottom lip was wobbling. She walked faster, just wanting some time alone, not to dissolve like this in front of Theo, her colleague and one of her best friends, not just a friend but part of her family. Even so…she'd had enough of the darkness, of fighting it, of *being* it, having it pump through her veins, a bona fide part of her DNA.

She didn't realise she'd practically broken into a run

until a voice boomed behind her, one with all the authority she'd tried to muster when addressing Willow earlier.

"Ruby, for God's sake, stop!"

Having reached her car, she did stop, leaning forward to rest her forehead against the edge of the roof, her shoulders heaving because of the sobs that burst from her. Double shit! If Michelle should be looking out the window, seeing this…

Theo was clearly thinking along the same lines.

"Open the door, Ruby," was her second command, "and get inside. Quickly."

Again, Ruby obeyed whilst Theo made her way round to the passenger side, both of them climbing into the Ford and pulling the doors shut.

For a while, both just sat there, Ruby trying to force back the tide of grief and shock that had consumed her. When Theo spoke again, her voice was far gentler.

"Do you feel you can drive?"

Ruby shook her head.

"Okay, fine, no worries. Just so you know, no one's peering through the windows at us. I think I know what happened. Willow took you to a dark place."

Ruby nodded.

"A place that's…personal to you?"

"Yes," Ruby managed.

"Or that she thinks is personal to you."

Ruby turned to Theo, wiping at her eyes and sniffing hard. "What do you mean?"

How sincere Theo's blue eyes were as she reached out to take Ruby by the hand, her touch altogether warmer than Willow's, such comfort in it. "Darling, she *doesn't* know you, but…she can read you. Not Willow, though, as we must keep reminding ourselves, whatever she's channelling, an energy of some sort that's…"

"Malevolent," Ruby said when Theo faltered.

Theo didn't deny it. "Yes, malevolent. Oh dear, oh dear, that poor child."

Ruby's hackles rose again. "Theo, she's…dangerous. For me, at least, because you didn't experience anything like that, did you? She was nice to you. She left you alone!"

"Ruby! She's just a child! Why do you keep forgetting? And remember your training too. All you've learnt to date. She's being used. Another one."

"Another one? Like the girl who came to you, 'something rotten' inside her?"

Theo released Ruby's arm, hugged herself instead. "Let's…stick to this case for the moment, to the facts. Where is it you think she took you?"

Ruby wasn't sure she could answer, but Theo's stare pierced her.

"Inside myself, of course," she said at last. "And…it was awful. One minute it was empty, the next…full of horror. Full of…"

"Go on," said Theo, as much dismay in her voice as Ruby heard in her own.

Ruby took a deep breath. "*Him*," she said.

"Your father?"

She nodded as Theo contemplated this.

"In what way was it full of him?"

"There was darkness," Ruby explained, "total blackness. And then…and then there was writing in front of me, *her* writing, Willow's. At first, anyway."

Theo had shuffled in her seat to peer closer at Ruby, scrutinising her.

"Ruby, carry on."

She had to take another deep breath.

"But right at the end, before I broke the hold, the writing changed." She closed her eyes, then swiftly opened them, afraid of the darkness again and what she might see in it, another scrawl that in its way was as childish as Willow's, that same haphazard quality to it. If written on paper, it would have ruined the table beneath. "Oh, Theo, why is it that the darkness clings so hard to me? At St Martin's I lost my way too. I got…fooled."

"But we were there to guide you through it, as we always do."

Ruby couldn't help the word that left her mouth. "Always?"

Theo clearly knew full well what she meant by that, that she was so much older than Ruby, than Ness and Corinna too – she *wouldn't* be there always, not physically.

"Yes, Ruby, always," Theo insisted. "Somehow and in some form. We've all been lost in the darkness. It happens to everyone at some point."

Ruby remembered what Theo had said before. "The darkness is an integral part of us."

"But we still have to fight it."

"We do." Her voice sounded so small again, so defeated.

"So, what did this…*other* writing say?"

"Terrible words. Like…the worst. Shit! It can't be true. It can't be!"

"Ruby, just tell me. A problem shared is a problem halved. The same goes for fears – they're worse when they're kept inside. When they're left to…rankle."

"Rankle? That's what this one's been doing. And it took

the darkness to show me. Okay, all right, I'll tell you what the writing said. But, Theo, it isn't true, okay?"

"Just tell me."

"The words said…*he* said…he was free. And that…that he's coming for me."

Chapter Thirteen

In the confines of the car, in the ensuing silence, Ruby's phone rang, causing both women to jolt.

"It's my mobile," Ruby said, gesturing towards her bag, which she'd chucked in the footwell just before Theo had got in the car too.

"We can leave it."

"Better not," Ruby said, reaching over to grab it.

"Ruby!" The warning was clear in Theo's voice. She wanted to discuss more what had just been said, the *possibility*, whereas Ruby didn't; she welcomed distraction. Glancing at the caller ID, she also dared to glance at Theo. "It's Ness," she said, answering.

"Hi there," Ness said. "Sorry to disturb you if you're busy—"

"We're not. We've finished at Michelle's." Swallowing, she added, "For now."

"Lee was okay?"

"Lee was great. We're grateful to him for being there."

"No problem. You know he likes to help if he can. Right, back to business. The reason I'm calling you is precisely because of that, business. I've had a call, an emergency call."

"Okay, hit me with the details," Ruby said, ignoring the exasperated sigh from Theo, who was nonetheless busy fastening her seatbelt.

"You've not got far to go, actually. The house in question is just down the road from you, towards Ringmer. About a ten-minute drive max. I'll send you details. Theo still with you?"

"Uh-huh," Ruby replied.

"Oh good, good. I'll send her details, then, as you're likely driving. I've got Corinna with me. We're almost there, actually, so if you leave now, we should arrive at the same time."

Putting the phone in its cradle on loudspeaker, Ruby, now feeling better able to drive, fired up the engine and also fastened her own seatbelt. "When you say an emergency…"

"Ah yes, this couple, the Greens, they sound fairly youngish to me, possibly in their twenties or thirties. They've just bought this cottage overlooking the fields between Lewes and Ringmer. The house itself is fine; they feel safe in it. It's what's outside the house that's causing concern. And it's drawing closer. *Dangerously* closer."

"Whoa," said Ruby. "Sounds ominous. This something, have they described it?"

"It's Mrs Green who mainly sees it. She described it as shadowy and humanlike, possibly a man. She spotted it when they first moved in, but only in the distance. Dismissed it at first as a curious neighbour, something like that. A dog walker, perhaps, who just liked to…stand and stare. But it isn't a dog walker, it isn't a neighbour, it's something…other. And as they've said, it's drawing closer."

"Will we be able to see it during the day?" Ruby queried.

"Apparently, yes. It doesn't only appear at night."

"And it's still shadowy, even in the light?"

"They said it's like their eyes refuse to focus properly. So yes, whatever distance it is, it remains shadowy."

Ruby pulled out onto the street, glad to put some distance between her and the Bayliss house at last, and what it contained.

"Tell me, Ness," she said, just before ending the call. "Are there any children involved?"

"Children? No. Not that I'm aware of."

"Thank fuck for that. See you in ten."

* * *

As Ruby got out of the car outside the address Ness had given them, the only thing that came bounding over the fields was Jed, heading straight for her, his tail wagging.

"Jed's here!" she told the others, both elated about that…and worried. She sometimes used Jed as her barometer. The times he appeared to her were quite random, but always, always, he was there when needed. The case of the leering shadow man, as she'd already mentally termed it, was it going to be a tricky one? So much so that they'd need Jed's help? Although concerned, she smiled as she greeted him. "So, what's brought you here this time, eh, boy? Thought you'd be at home with Cash and Hendrix. The pair of them must be having their afternoon nap right about now, and I know you love a nap too, curling up with them. So why have you put yourself out? What's about to happen?"

Then, greeting Ness and Corinna, she steeled herself. Again.

"Okay," said Ness, rubbing her hands together, anticipating the excitement of a new case, "you need any more details, or shall we head inside?"

"Let's head inside," Ruby said as Corinna swung around to observe the field that the house – Carters Rest – overlooked. A beautiful stretch of green, currently lying fallow.

"Not a bad place to haunt," she commented wryly.

"It's not haunting the field, though, is it?" Ness pointed out. "It's haunting the Greens."

"Shadow people," Theo sighed. "Awkward sods."

"Maybe. Maybe not," Ruby replied. She'd rather deal with a shadow person than any other matter that had cropped up today.

"Come on"—Ness strode towards the house—"they're expecting us."

"You said this was an emergency," Ruby said as they all duly followed her. "Why?"

"Why? Because Siobhan Green is about to have a breakdown, that's why. It was her husband that called me, Dom, and he sounds pretty much at the end of his tether too, but Siobhan swears to God she won't spend another night under this roof if we can't stop what's happening. As I've told you, the shadow man's drawing very close. She's thinks he'll be in the living room next!"

The door opened before the team could reach it, Jed keeping to the rear of them and, like Corinna, scanning all around him, as if expecting whatever was allegedly haunting this house to jump out from behind a bush and ensnare him. *Just you try*, thought Ruby, glad that something of her fighting spirit was returning.

A woman and a man greeted them, Siobhan and Dom

Green, presumably, and, as Ness had said, a young couple around the same age as Ruby, in their late twenties. Ruby's gaze immediately travelled to Siobhan; she looked exhausted, pale skin accentuating the darkness of the circles under her eyes. Her shoulder-length hair, the same brown as Ruby's, was limp, and as she addressed the team, she held on to her husband's arm, fingernails seemingly digging into the skin there.

"Thank you for coming to see us," she said. "For taking us seriously."

"That's our job," Ness assured her. "To take this kind of thing seriously."

"Good, good, because it is," Siobhan insisted. "It's…ruining our lives. And we thought…we thought we'd be so happy here, didn't we, Dom? Our first home together."

Dom – only slightly taller than Siobhan, dark haired and dark eyed too – gently but firmly released his wife's clutch and stepped forward with his hand outstretched to greet them all. "Thanks for coming," he said, echoing his wife. "We're really very grateful, just so relieved that there are people that deal with this sort of thing. Kettle's boiled. Come inside and have a coffee or tea, and we can tell you more about it."

It was the usual process, or the start of it, anyway – discussion over a hot drink and then a plan of action – but as they filed in, two things disrupted proceedings: Jed started barking, *maniacally* barking, and Siobhan started pointing and screaming.

"There!" she said. "Just behind you. Oh God, it's there again."

Ruby swung around to the field that they'd just been

admiring, as did Ness, Theo and Corinna. Ruby could see nothing, although she stared hard and squinted.

"I don't think—" she began, but as Siobhan and Dom shrank back into the cottage, Jed started acting all sheepdog like, herding the team further inside too, only stopping his incessant barking when the front door had been slammed shut.

Siobhan was sobbing uncontrollably, Ruby confused but also sorry for her. After all, it hadn't been so long since she'd been doing the same.

Ness hurried over to Siobhan and began comforting her, as did Dom, although he was also pretty shaken, in need of comfort himself.

"Did you see it too?" Ness asked Dom.

He shook his head. "Sometimes, it's like…I kind of catch sight of it, just out the corner of my eye, you know, that kind of thing, but not this time. This time…I don't know, it happened too fast, I suppose. Did any of you see it? You followed us in and slammed the door, so…"

"That was my fault," Ruby said, also drawing closer. "I…um…just got this feeling we should be inside, try to understand this thing before we confront it."

"Understand it?" Siobhan managed at last. "I don't want to understand it! I just want it gone! That's why we called you."

"And we'll do our best regarding that," Ruby promised, Corinna nodding avidly behind her before Theo took the reins.

"I'm parched," she said. "Let's go through to the kitchen and have that cup of tea you promised us, and then, Siobhan, Dom, you can tell us everything we need to know."

For a moment both husband and wife looked uncertain, Ruby, although not able to read thoughts, knowing exactly what was on their minds: *Are we mad for doing this? For believing something's out there? For getting these people involved too? Their kind. Perhaps if we ignore it, it'll all go away. All we want is a normal life.*

They turned, though, eventually, and led the way into the kitchen, which was a good-sized room with aged oak beams. Faux, Ruby suspected, as this house was relatively modern, built in the thirties or forties. There was also an Aga, pillar-box red and gleaming, plus an old oak table and a Welsh dresser, everything striving to give it a more convincing aura. Whatever they did for a living, they earnt well to afford all this so young.

Dom indicated for them all to sit down, including his wife, then set about filling a teapot and bringing it over to the table, along with milk and sugar. Cups were already laid out.

"Please, help yourselves, unless anyone wants coffee," he said.

They went straight for the tea, a simple everyday prop that was always the quickest way to calm a situation.

As she drank, Ruby searched for Jed. Where was he? He'd followed them into the house but not the kitchen. Was he waiting by the front door still? She could hardly get up to check, not yet, at any rate. Just what had been out there?

As Siobhan and Dom told the team what they'd already told Ness, Ruby also plumbed the depths of her mind regarding what she knew about shadow people. So many religions, legends and belief systems bowed down to the concept of such beings, figures that materialised out of nowhere to stalk you – their intention to frighten you, to feed off your fear and thus grow in substance. They were also considered to be an omen of the worst kind. People claimed to see them preceding the death of someone close to them. Is that what was happening here? Were Siobhan or Dom or someone close to them in mortal danger? In the past, Ruby had studied various clips on social media – YouTube, TikTok and the like – that claimed to have caught shadow people on camera, shapes that roamed at will, particularly under the cover of darkness, which offered them a camouflage of sorts. To some, though, the light of day was not a deterrent. They'd grown bolder than that.

"The thing is," Theo was saying, "and I'm sure you realise this, but if this figure is, as you say, something shadowy that stalks you, there's sometimes a normal rather than paranormal explanation. How well do you both sleep?"

Siobhan and Dom – neither of which had touched their tea – simultaneously frowned.

"Okay," Dom answered, "on the whole."

"Siobhan," Theo persisted, "what about you?"

"I…lately, not that well, I suppose."

"But which came first, the shadow man or the lack of sleep?"

Again, Siobhan seemed confused, unsure of what to say. "I've never slept well," she finally admitted. "It's just…I'm more of a catnapper. That's what my mum used to say. It used to drive her potty when I was a kid. I could be up at all hours. But that's got nothing to do with this. I've never seen a…shadow person, is it? Not until I moved here."

Ness gave a sincere nod. "My colleague is right in that

studies have shown sleep-deprived people can experience this kind of phenomenon, the result of an overstressed brain playing tricks on them."

Siobhan, though, refused to accept this theory. "In that case, as I've said, wouldn't I have seen them before whilst I was growing up? And also, if I'm going to see shadows, why not…I don't know, shadow cats or shadow dogs or shadow cars, even? That wouldn't be so scary. A shadow person *is* scary. Particularly this one. He's terrifying."

"He?" Theo questioned.

"Yes, it's a shadow man, I'm sure of it. And he means us harm. Shit! We've only just moved in here, and now we're going to have to move out again. It's a nightmare!"

"Now, now," Ness soothed, "it may not come to that. We may be able to solve this mystery, nullify it. Do you know anything about the history of this place?"

"It was built in 1932," Dom said, confirming Ruby's previous thoughts, "and nothing weird has happened here, no deaths recorded. We had that checked out. It's been a normal family home. The last owners, the Dobsons, were here for thirty years and only moved out because they were getting old and wanted something smaller and closer to shops, that kind of thing. We met them. They were, like…really ordinary, you know?"

"Okay, good," Ness said before a brief pause. "I really am sorry to have to say this, but…have either of you taken hallucinogenic drugs? I don't mean recently, but ever."

Ruby waited as avidly as the rest of them for the answer – Ness had asked a tough question, but a necessary one.

"No," Dom replied. It had taken a few moments for him to answer, but when he did, he was adamant. "Sometimes a bit of weed, you know, when I was a bit younger, in my teens, but even then, only a handful of times. I was just never that into it."

"Siobhan?" Ness said.

"I hate drugs," she said, her bottom lip trembling again. "My older brother…he's an addict. Heroin. *Was* an addict, I should say. He died four years ago." Before anyone could respond, offer their sympathies, perhaps, Siobhan rushed on. "When he was alive, he made our life a living hell, me and my mum's. She was a single parent, so it wasn't as if life wasn't tough enough already. So…yeah, I detest drugs, and Dom doesn't do it anymore. Sometimes…" She swallowed hard before continuing. "Sometimes, I think he's the reason my sleep continued to be erratic – my brother, I mean, because…we were always so scared, wondering when he was going to turn up at the house and in what state. He'd get violent, you know, start smashing things, especially if Mum refused to give him what he wanted, which was money, of course, for more bloody drugs. God, the names he called her! You've never heard such language. Look, I don't want you to feel sorry for me, okay? I can see that you do, and I don't want it. And I don't regret his death either. When the news came, I welcomed it."

Before anyone could comment, the sound of Jed barking furiously again – he had indeed remained in the hallway – brought Ruby to her feet.

"What is it?" asked Ness, Theo also climbing to her feet, Corinna once again scanning all around them, trying hard to conceal any show of nervousness.

Siobhan's hand grabbed for Dom's arm again. "Oh no, God, don't say it. It's him, isn't it? It's my brother. He's the one haunting me!"

"We mustn't jump to conclusions," Theo began as Ruby started moving towards the hallway and the front door. "Ruby?" she asked, Ruby giving one simple reply.

"Jed's barking."

"Jed?" Dom tried to rise to his feet too, but his wife refused to let him.

"They can deal with it!" she said, her breath continually catching in her throat. "Because…because…if it is my brother, I can't."

Theo, Ness and Corinna duly followed Ruby, Ness advising the couple it was actually best to stay put, that they would see what the matter was and be back within minutes.

Jed was in the hallway. Ruby could see him, but he'd stopped barking and was staring at the front door instead, his head cocked to one side as if in confusion.

"Ruby?" Theo said again. "Is Jed still barking?"

"He's stopped," Ruby informed them. "He's just…looking at the door now."

"Do you think it is her brother?" Corinna asked. "Back for revenge?"

"Revenge?" Ness questioned. "What for?"

"Because of what she said, that she welcomed his death."

"With bloody good reason," Theo muttered, "if he was making their life hell."

"That's what I mean," Corinna replied. "He did then, and he still wants to."

Ness interjected. "Like Theo said, we mustn't jump to conclusions."

"But there's no history here," Corinna continued.

Theo looked at her. "Darling, there's history

everywhere."

"Whatever's happened, it's all quiet now," Ruby said. "We'd best get back—"

A scream.

Glass imploding.

Jed not in front of but behind them, running into the kitchen.

"Shit!" said Ruby, barely glancing at her colleagues before she also turned and ran.

Chapter Fourteen

Siobhan might have been screaming, but by the time Ruby reached the kitchen, she was silent, although her mouth hung open still, her eyes bulging as one hand lifted to point at the window, the glass shards now littering the floor, the glint of them lethal.

Beside her, Dom too was trembling. "What the fuck? My windows! What's going on here?"

Ruby and the team stopped just before the mess of glass, trying to work out the same thing. A shadow. Was it there at the window? Something…hazy.

Jed was barking as Ruby peered harder. Something *was* there, but it was hard to make out what, exactly, to get a handle on it. Whatever it was, a shadow person, a shadow *man*, it knew how to cloak itself.

"What do you see?" Ruby kept her voice low as she asked the others.

"Likely the same as you, nothing at all," Theo said. "Almost."

"There is something there," Ness replied, although she was squinting too.

"Definitely," murmured Corinna.

Staring at them, just as they were staring at it. No… Ruby frowned. Staring *beyond* them, to where Siobhan stood with Dom.

A second window imploded, causing more screams, this time from all of them, hands flying up to protect faces.

"Get out!" Ruby screamed. "Everyone, get out of here and into the hallway."

They all did as they were told, moving away from the windows, only Jed staying put, barking and growling, doing his best to act as a deterrent. But would it work? Ruby could swear she heard the door to the garden rattle too. Whatever was outside, as Siobhan had previously pointed out to Ness, was determined to enter. But why now? Was their presence there, their energy, lending it strength?

As all six stood huddled in the hallway, as far from any windows as it was possible to get, Ruby worked hard to get the situation under control. Siobhan was shuddering; she was crying, muttering all the while, "No one would believe me, Dom. I don't think even you believed me, not deep down, but see? This is real. Something's out there. My brother. It's him. It makes sense now. He's coming for me. Oh shit, he's coming for me."

Her words made Ruby shudder too. They were so similar to what she'd heard only this morning at the Bayliss house. Could it be… Hope flared. That selfish hope when something terrible was happening to someone else instead of you. Was Willow predicting *this*, rather than anything to do with Ruby? Somehow she knew about Siobhan's brother, had foreseen it – a dark energy that had broken free of his earthly body and was coming for his sister, like Corinna had said, hellbent on revenge. *Welcome my death, do you? I'll welcome yours!* If he could utter words, then maybe, just maybe, those would be the ones. Terrible to hope for such a thing, to deflect, but…

Theo was glaring at her, knew exactly what she was thinking, and Ruby's cheeks burned because of it. She gave a gulp before changing tack. "Siobhan, Dom, stay here. We're going back into the kitchen to see what's going on."

Siobhan immediately reached out and clutched Ruby's arm as she had clutched Dom's, nails digging into flesh. "Don't let him come in! Don't let him get me!"

Terror. It was there in her eyes. Not just that but a deep pool of grief that Ruby identified with only too well, a sadness that knew no bounds. Shame flared in Ruby, that she could ever wish this on someone else, even for a moment, all to save her own skin.

She reached out too and took Siobhan's arms as doors rattled louder in the kitchen, made the woman focus on her and only her, stared into her eyes and connected.

"We are here to help you," she said, "and we will. Whatever this is, *whoever*, we will protect you. But you have to help us with that aim."

"How?" It was one word but laced with so much desperation.

"You have to let him go."

"What? How?"

"If this is your brother, and it may well be, because it makes sense, let him go."

Immediately, Siobhan protested. "I have… I told you. I…*hated* him."

"There's a fine line between love and hate," Ruby reminded her. "Both are powerful."

Dom had closed the gap between them and reached out too to gently rub at Siobhan's back. Clearly, those words resonated with him also.

More tears sprang from Siobhan's eyes.

"Mum…he persecuted her, persecuted us both. As for Dad"—her mouth twisted into a grimace of further hatred—"he bailed out, didn't he? When the going got tough, the coward got going. Left us to it. Headed for Spain with a new woman. Left us at his mercy."

"Whose mercy?"

"My brother's!"

"I want you to say his name."

Siobhan shook her head, dark hair like a curtain swishing just as the sound of a third window imploding reached their ears.

"No," she said. "I can't."

"Siobhan," Ruby pleaded this time, "give us something to work with here. We're going back into the kitchen to confront him, and we need a name. Come on, please."

That kitchen door. He'd break it down soon with the might of his rage.

"Siobhan—"

"Darren! There! I've said it. His name was Darren, okay? Now fucking get rid of him!"

Ruby let her go, turned around and joined Theo, Ness and Corinna as they filed back into the kitchen, ready to face a shadow man who might or might not be Darren.

Whatever, whomever, he was, he hadn't entered the house yet, likely thanks to Jed, who was standing at the latest blown window, continuing to growl and bark. There was only one more window to go, which all the team stood well away from, but speed was of the essence here. They had to diffuse the situation and fast.

Anger.

There was so much of it. Something palpable that you felt you could reach out and grab. The anger of the shadow man and Siobhan had combined to become something not just potent but explosive.

You couldn't choose your family; it was either fate or just a lottery. Some families loved each other, others tore each other apart. Family rows were always difficult, and now here they were, caught in the middle of one, in the crossfire. If the shadow man was Darren, he was vengeful indeed, his rage manifesting from beyond the grave, somebody who'd made his family's life hell, but perhaps they'd made his life hell too in their own way.

Ness started the address.

"Darren, is that you out there, trying to enter this property? Either way, we'd like you to calm down. We're not here to cause further distress. All we want is to help. I'm Ness, and this is Theo, Ruby and Corinna. We've come here with good intent. Only that. You're distressed and, in turn, distressing the occupants of this house. Please allow us to help you."

The glass in the only intact window rattled in its frame.

"Darren," Theo said this time, having adopted her no-nonsense voice, "this behaviour will get you nowhere. You are not coming in here. I repeat, you are not welcome. We're sorry you feel such rage. It must be awful for you, truly terrible, but it's your choice to be so full of hatred, no one else's. And look at what it's done, what it's turned you into, something dark, something that hurts, when it doesn't have to be that way, not anymore. You could be full of light and love and laughter instead. *Healed.*"

Still the glass rattled. Still Jed growled.

Theo dared to step forward. "Darren, we know life was difficult for you—"

"Life was difficult for *you*?" Faster than a striking viper,

Siobhan entered the room. "Oh my God! No one forced you to take drugs, did they? To be as evil as you were. You know what I think, Darren, what I told Mum? That you were born evil!"

"Siobhan!" Dom had followed her and was now trying to calm her, looking shocked, truly shocked, not only by the state of the kitchen but his partner's words too. Perhaps she'd never said out loud what she really thought. If so, there was no stopping her now.

"You were!" she screeched. "You were! When we were little, when Mum wasn't looking, you used to pinch me, try and find all sorts ways to make me cry. You used to *love* it when I cried. But Mum…she'd never believe me when I told her what you used to do. Sometimes—" a ragged sob escaped her "—she used to believe you over me, and again I'd see it in your eyes, how it delighted you. I think…I think she always loved you more than me – her precious boy – right until the day you threatened her. Nothing to do with drugs that time, it was before all that. You'd just grown bigger, into even more of a bully. You threatened to hit her, and you meant it. I could see it, and so could she. You were barely eleven, and the violence in you was like a cancer that just kept on growing."

"Twins."

Ruby realised Ness had whispered something but had to step closer in order to hear it. "What did you say?" she whispered back as the drama continued to unfold.

"They were twins," Ness said, stark realisation on her face. "That's why the bond's so intense."

The glass in the fourth kitchen window finally shattered, all having to huddle together to protect themselves. What was next? Ruby wondered. Would the crockery start being hurled around the room, pots and pans? She'd seen that happen before in 44 Gilmore Street. It took an enormous amount of energy on behalf of the spirit – or Siobhan – because the window that had just shattered, she didn't think the shadow man was responsible, not this time, not something deceased but very much alive.

The team sprang into action. Corinna and Theo went to stand in front of the rattling door, Darren still determined to enter the house, the only sanctuary his sister had. Jed also stood there, on guard. As they'd done in the churchyard, they sent out light to force the darkness to retreat. Sent out love and understanding too, for this was not soulless energy this time, that which had formed from thoughts alone; Darren had been human once. And no one was born evil. If evil had got a grip, it had done so on the human journey, because of paths that should never have been chosen. It was a sound belief, and yet Ruby sympathised with Siobhan, knew how hard it was to believe it and how easy to let the doubts come creeping in...

"Ruby, come on," Ness said, perhaps reading her thoughts like Theo and taking her arm, the two of them heading for Siobhan and Dom instead.

Dom was the archetypal rabbit caught in the headlights. He didn't know what to do, where to turn, how to deal with events that had gone from suspected sightings to this – utter paranormal catastrophe. As much as it had taken Ruby and the team by surprise too, they had to find a way to deal with it.

The key was Siobhan – right now as dark as her brother, a mere shadow of herself.

As she was still hunched over, Ruby took her by the arms and shook her gently, willed her to look up, to open her eyes. She refused, tried to curl tighter into a ball.

Ruby then glanced at Ness, saw the message in her eyes: *Encourage her to say more.*

A risky procedure, one that could make matters even worse. If one of them should get hit by something…some of those pans looked heavy, Le Creuset-style ones. Even so, they couldn't just up and leave, not when everything was coming to a head.

"Siobhan," Ruby said. "Siobhan, listen to me. Tell me more about Darren, tell me *everything*. Let it all out. Don't bottle it up anymore, don't judge yourself either or your feelings about it all. Just…tell me."

At last Siobhan's head came up, her eyes open now and staring again into Ruby's, such…surprise in them, Ruby noticed. Had no one ever said this to her before? Not her mum, or Dom or any of her friends? Quite the contrary, had she been encouraged to say nothing, to just…forget it? The shadow man – Darren – he might not even be real, hence why it was only really Siobhan that could see him. Her brother might well and truly be in the light, having passed with no problem, despite his earthly woes. Most did. It was Siobhan, who'd started this journey with him in their mother's womb, who couldn't let go.

"Tell me," Ruby repeated, knowing that Siobhan saw it, the understanding in her eyes.

Such vitriol spewed from her mouth, such…filth. So much so that Dom took a step back, tried to distance himself from his wife. Ness saw what he'd done and went over, took his arm and led him quietly from the room. She would no doubt try to explain what was happening here –

that the evil in Siobhan's brother had wormed its way into her by proxy. She'd imbibed it too, the lesson, at least, the essence of it. And she had to dispel it, all that she'd lived with for so many years, had tried to hide from everyone including herself, vomit it up into words – end the possession she'd allowed to take hold, one that grief and disappointment had sculptured for her.

Hatred had a rich vocabulary, and all of it was being used here, thrown into Ruby's face as tears poured from Siobhan's eyes.

"Bastard. Fucker. Cunt. Do you know how many times I wished him dead? Do you? Thousands and thousands and thousands of times! I used to lie in bed and imagine his death – never an easy one, oh no. It'd be a slow death, the worst. He'd be writhing on his own bed, thrashing, begging for mercy, and I'd stand by and I'd watch him and do nothing. Fuck all!"

Most would flinch, like Dom, but Ruby held firm. Nodding her head, encouraging Siobhan further. Nothing was off-limits here. The darkness needed to rise and rise wholly. Only then could the light swallow it whole.

But what a process. A hard and time-consuming process.

The door behind Ruby was rattling harder. Soon it would burst open, Jed becoming more agitated than ever. *Have faith.* She did. In her colleagues for being able to hold back what sought greater dominance, and in Siobhan for wanting to fight against it too – at last.

As the tirade against Darren ended, the tears came, the vessel emptying.

Ruby reached out and hugged her, Siobhan clinging to her, not as an adult but as a child might, something scared and bewildered and just so, so hurt. If only people realised the damage they could inflict, Ruby thought, the repercussions.

Another realisation dawned. Siobhan wasn't an empty vessel. Far from it.

"You're pregnant," Ruby whispered into her ear.

Siobhan froze in Ruby's arms. "What? How… Nobody knows yet. Just me. Not Dom…"

"I won't tell him. Don't worry." Ruby laughed a little before continuing to whisper. "That's one thing that's not in my job description. But that's why all this has got so much worse. You're pregnant, and you think…you think…" She moved her head a few inches back from Siobhan's so she could press this point home. "This child, if it's a boy, will be nothing like Darren, okay? He's not just you, he's a part of Dom too, and you're both good people. Anger…can be destructive, but tell me, do you feel angry anymore?"

Siobhan looked beyond Ruby, towards the door which was still rattling, Theo, Corinna and Jed having to focus still, and from the hallway low voices as Ness spoke to Dom.

Siobhan blinked hard. "It's so hard to forget. I…he… It's so hard."

How could Ruby argue? She knew it was. Miracles could happen, but they weren't always instant; they required time and dedication. She could feel her own eyes water, her own lack of forgiveness, the fear that persisted despite knowing how to dispel it.

"Siobhan—"

Inexplicably – *immediately* – Siobhan's whole expression brightened. "Look!" she said. "Oh my God, look over there!"

Ruby turned to where Siobhan was pointing, her eyes widening too.

Through the kitchen window closest to the sink, a white cat was climbing in.

"She'll hurt her paws," Ruby said, making to rise, but Siobhan stayed her.

"She won't. She's fine."

It was Siobhan who went towards the cat, the cat training her gaze on the woman and making a beeline for her too. Siobhan bent and picked her up, the door not rattling anymore, no sign of a shadow man, of anything other than a beautiful spring day.

Corinna and Theo were facing Siobhan too, Ness and Dom also back in the room, watching as Siobhan continued to fuss over the cat, the cat fussing right back, licking at Siobhan's face and purring, Siobhan laughing in delight. She was like a child again, thought Ruby, a *happy* child, the way a child should be.

Jed ran up to them, wagging his tail approvingly.

A white cat…a black dog…

"I wonder who she belongs to," Siobhan murmured, her nose touching the cat's nose, healing something in her, just as the baby would. All in good time. A family, the four of them, in which only love would reign.

Ruby drew closer, as did her colleagues and Dom, all of them drawn to Siobhan and the snowy white cat, whose purr was, by now, deafening.

"I think she's yours," Ruby said and then amended that. "She's *definitely* yours."

Chapter Fifteen

As the team left the Greens' house, there was another phone call, Corinna answering it this time. As all looked at her expectantly, she raised her eyebrows.

"Okay, right, some ghostly activity, like you say, but you're not scared. You wouldn't call it an emergency. So…you're happy to wait until tomorrow? It's just we've had a really full-on day. We need to head home, rest up. Oh no…no…nothing like that, nothing fearsome, just…busy, that's all. Oh yep, sure, there certainly is a lot of demand for our services." Corinna laughed, obviously in response to something. "Definitely something in the water," she added. Asking the potential client to email over details and setting a date for an initial survey the next morning, she then said, "See you then," and finished the call.

Theo's shoulders slumped with relief. "So," she said, "for today we can just go home, eh? Put our feet up, zone out."

Corinna nodded. "We sure can. Well…you can. I've got a shift at the pub this evening. Still, Presley'll be there," she said, referring to her boyfriend, Cash's brother, "propping up the bar, but I can always rope him in to lend a hand if we get busy."

Theo smiled indulgently. "You youngsters, so full of

energy."

"You are too," Corinna insisted. "You knock most of my friends out the ballpark."

Theo could see Ruby also smile at this exchange. Even Ness – God bless her soul – managed a hint of a grin. What they'd just done, scrub that, *achieved*, was yet again something enormous, all of them feeling the high from it but also drained – a curious feeling, really, elation mixed with exhaustion. She couldn't see Jed, Ruby's familiar, as she liked to call him, but if she could, she'd imagine the little rascal was as pleased as punch with himself too, chasing his tail and hopping from foot to foot. That little white cat…what a darling creature! Where had it come from? Was it similar to Jed? Another familiar? Ruby seemed to think so; Ruby seemed to *know*, which was good enough for her.

So sweet how it had climbed in through the window to crunch its way unharmed over broken glass and into Siobhan's arms, Siobhan waiting for it, *needing* it. An adult survivor of childhood trauma. Theo hoped that whatever the cat was, it would bring her all the healing she needed. There was a journey ahead of her still for certain, but she could embark on it with renewed hope, Dom by her side, because despite what had happened earlier when hatred had poured so colourfully from her mouth, when she'd later stood there with the cat in her arms, there was only love in his eyes, one that would endure.

A happy conclusion. If only everyone could be that lucky.

The team peeled off from each other. Corinna and Ness in one car, Ruby and Theo in another. Good. That would give Theo an opportunity to discuss the idea forming in her head, one that Ruby might…or might not…go for.

In the Ford, Ruby was more upbeat, having stowed away what had happened with Willow earlier, if only temporarily. Shame, then, that it had to be dragged up again.

Theo waited until they were parked outside her own house before doing so, the journey there mostly a silent one, exhaustion most likely the reason behind that – dealing with such anger always took it out of them. It was like a poison. *Something rotten.*

This idea of hers was potentially dangerous, just as the situation in the Greens' household had been, but it could also lead to resolution. What truly mattered was protecting the child – the conduit, Willow. Making sure she didn't come to any harm. A long shot, but nothing ventured, nothing gained. She could but ask.

Ruby yawned, eliciting more sympathy from Theo. Should she do this? Or wait? Thoughts of another child, one who perhaps could wait no longer, spurred her on.

"Ruby, I hate to bring this up again, but…what happened with Willow, we have to deal with it."

Ruby turned to her, the strain of the day evident on her face. So young, and yet she'd experienced so much. The light shone brightly in her, spectacularly at times, but sometimes those who burnt brightly were the first to burn themselves out.

"I know we do," Ruby responded, "brief Ness and Corinna too, but tonight…"

"Yes, yes, of course, tonight you have to return home. Your family needs you. But what I'm about to say, to suggest, really, there's no need to give me an answer straightaway. Take some time to mull it over, the possibility."

Despite herself, Ruby was clearly curious. "Theo, what is it?"

"Willow took you into the darkest reaches of yourself." Theo lifted her hand, tapped at her head with it. "In here. The mind."

"The mind *and* the heart," Ruby amended. "I can't go there again—"

"I know that. I realise that. I'm not asking you to. What I want is for Willow to do the same with me, to take me into the darkest reaches of *my* mind and heart."

Ruby was aghast, as well she might be. "Theo? What the hell—"

"Hear me out. In no way would I endanger Willow. It could all be done in a very controlled manner. You know what she's capable of. If I show any signs of distress, you could intervene, sever the connection."

"Me? But…Theo…your heart… What if…"

"What if it causes a heart attack? Is that what you're worried about? It won't. Ruby, I'm on medication. *Good* medication. Oh, I know I have to lose weight still, darn it, and I've been trying, but it refuses to shift. My metabolism's a stubborn old thing, good for nothing, practically. But…" Now she was the one to falter. "I can't forget about her."

"Who? The child with no name? The murderer?"

"Yes."

"You think you can connect with her via Willow?"

Theo nodded. "I haven't seen her in years, but she's deep inside me still, the memory of her. And maybe that's enough. Maybe if Willow can take me that far inside myself, to where the memory's fresh rather than old, where it's vivid rather than irritatingly vague, I can connect again and coax her forwards, bring her out from where she's been hiding."

"But can't you do that anyway? Can't…we help you do that? The team?"

"I don't think so," Theo answered. "And I don't seem to be able to do it on my own. It's like…I need the kind of help only Willow is capable of. The girl's hiding, as I've said, but what happened in the newsagent's…that book… God, the times I've been in there! That book could have been on the shelves for years, yet nothing like this has happened before. But now it has. I not only knock it off the shelf, but when I pick it up, I open it at the precise spot of those two murders, Eliza's and Danny's, the only murders in that entire book that could fit the timeframe – and, believe me, I've checked several times over. Ruby, you know that feeling you get when you put two and two together and it makes four, when you know you're right, that you simply can't be wrong? It's like…I don't know… a blinding flash, isn't it? That certainty." Lifting a hand, she indicated the heavens above. "The Fates are coming together, conspiring. They use us as something of a conduit too because now's the time for resolution. Not everything can remain a mystery forever."

It was a passionate speech Theo had just given, more of an outburst, really, but she wasn't sorry for it. Those words that had just left her mouth – *not everything can remain a mystery forever* – felt right too. The dead, as much as the living, had to move on eventually. Only then could bigger parts of the design fall into place, the cogs shifting into next gear.

It was a speech that rendered Ruby mute, for a short

while, anyway. Eventually, she took a breath and responded. "Theo, I understand…I do…but…not that way, not Willow."

"A few moments is all I need."

Ruby shook her head. "It won't work, not with you. It didn't before. You held her hand, the same as me, and you experienced nothing of the sort."

"Didn't you put all your barriers in place?"

"Yes!"

"Ruby?"

Ruby's shoulders slumped. "Willow unsettles me. I think…I think she sensed that."

"Whatever's taking advantage of her ability is what's unsettling you," Theo reminded her. "Tell me the truth, your father has been on your mind a lot lately, hasn't he?"

"No…yes… Oh, Theo, it's having a child, *adding* to your family. Somehow it brings all that other stuff to the surface."

Theo nodded. "Yes indeed. The past informing the future."

Ruby nodded too. "In a way. Ties. Connections. That kind of thing. Doesn't matter if those ties and connections are unwanted. And I don't want it, Theo. None of it!"

"Why?"

Ruby looked astounded. "Why?"

Theo held her ground. "Yes, Ruby, tell me why. What do you think those words scrawled in your mind really mean?"

"It's obvious, isn't it?" When Theo remained silent, she added, "What I'm scared of most is…is… Theo, we have to help Willow, not use her too."

So Ruby wasn't going to voice her deepest fear. As

frustrated as Theo felt about that, she told herself she should also respect it. Just one last push…

"I don't mean to use her, but if we can help her *and* the other child, then it truly will be an achievement."

"What…would you do? Take her hand again? Let your barriers down?"

"I'd seek," Theo said, "just as whatever's using Willow seeks. I'd need seconds, probably, just like it was seconds for you. And then…"

"What?"

"Then I think we help shut that energy down in Willow, try to turn off the tap. It'll never be angelic, as Ness so heroically thinks. We take the child under our wing and teach her how to do that, all the tricks of the trade, as I've said. But before that, just for those few seconds, give me a chance to reach out, to find the other one and save her as well."

"Theo—"

"I've told you, you don't have to give me an answer now. Just think about it. One thing – although all the team is in attendance, we don't tell them about my plan. You know how Ness fusses. It won't work if we do. And this is my chance, maybe the only one I have."

Immediately, Ruby shook her head, brown hair moving against her shoulders. "No, no, no. That's a bad idea. Honesty is the best policy with us, you know that."

"I do, yes. Except it's not always that cut and dried, is it? Look, I've been around the block a good few times now. I know what I'm doing. We don't tell them that part of the plan, but they're there, and if anything goes wrong, *then* you tell them, bring me back."

"I don't know," Ruby reiterated, "I…"

"Trust me. Please."

"Of course I trust you! It's just…I don't know if I can see Willow again, or Michelle." Again, there was that crack in Ruby's voice, Theo's own heart cracking a little to hear it. She knew how much Ruby craved normality sometimes, had clearly thought she'd had that in her friendship with Michelle, only for it to prove the opposite. One day she'd understand more fully that normality didn't exist, not for people like them, maybe not even for Willow, despite their best efforts – the prospect of which was also heartbreaking. Then again – another thing she usually expounded – normality didn't always live up to the hype.

"Whether you go near Willow again or not," Theo assured her, "is your choice entirely. If you decide not to, then myself, Ness and Corinna will take care of it, and I'll have to tell them my plan, suffer Ness's objections. The thing is, though, she's your client, and Michelle's your friend. We'll need your blessing to proceed – regarding *all* of it."

Before Ruby could reply, Theo reached for the car door and opened it, huffing and puffing as she got out of the car. Wretched things, she needed a crane with some of them.

"Want any help?" Ruby said, having also opened her car door, intending, it seemed, to rush round and haul her out of the Ford if needs be.

"No, no, no," Theo insisted, "almost there."

"Theo!" The frustration was clear in Ruby's voice.

"Oh, stop fussing," Theo returned. "You're as bad as the other two, you really are."

"Because we care about you, that's why."

Fully on the pavement, Theo stooped slightly as she

turned back around to face Ruby.

"I know you do, and I can't deny…it's getting harder and harder just to do the simple things. This getting-old business—"

"It's not for the fainthearted, I know."

"Glad to see that saying of mine has sunk in, at least," Theo replied, her smile wider.

"Theo, you've taught me so much. You know how grateful I am to you."

"Sweetheart, *I'm* grateful to *you*. For having found you in this life, part of my soul circle."

"Like calls to like, huh?"

"It does. And with you, with Ness and Corinna too, for the very best of reasons."

Before she straightened, heading inside to the kitchen for a restorative cup of Darjeeling, she tried her luck one more time.

"Let me know about this Willow business…about my idea. Sleep on it, Ruby. Okay?"

Chapter Sixteen

Sleep on it, Theo had said, Ruby tossing and turning in bed later that night. If only she could sleep! What a blessing that would be. When she'd got home, it was to find Hendrix kicking off big-time and Cash, usually so calm, so laid-back, flustered.

"Thank God, Ruby!" he'd said, handing the baby straight over before she could even kick off her shoes. "It's been a crap day!"

Ruby wanted to retaliate, to say, *Hang on, I've had quite a day too. Give me a minute, will you? A chance to breathe*, when something really very unexpected happened. The moment her baby was in her arms was the moment he calmed, all crying abruptly ceasing. She was stunned. She was…elated. It was Cash who normally had the magic touch, not her, something they joked about. Not only did Hendrix cease crying, but he started gurgling, as if…just so pleased to see her. Although she loved to work, *had* to, maybe there was something to it, absence making the heart grow fonder. He'd gurgled and, with one chubby hand, also reached up to touch her cheek, Ruby catching that hand gently in her mouth and kissing it, then kissing his face, laughing too as Cash stalked off, back to the front room where his workstation was, closing the door on them.

Even her husband's grumpiness couldn't dent the mood

she'd found herself in, courtesy of her own child, and the evening had passed with the two of them glued to each other's side, Cash finally cheering up and joining them for some splashy fun at bath time, all three of them drenched by the time Hendrix was placed onto a soft white towel.

Once he was in bed and the pair of them had also dried off and were downstairs, having a glass of wine with dinner, Cash finally asked about her day.

"You know what?" she said, giving his hand a quick squeeze. "I don't really want to talk about it. Not yet. It was…interesting. By and large, successful. But all I want right now is this, what we've got here. You, me and Hendrix, and Jed when he decides to turn up." Over the dinner table, she'd leant closer, giving him that look he loved. "I really, *really* want you."

Their ensuing closeness later that evening had been just the balm she'd needed, and him too, most likely, because as tired as he'd been, as stressed when she'd first got home, by God, he'd rallied to the cause, making her have to stifle her screams on occasion.

Best friends and passionate lovers – it never ceased to amaze her they were both.

He'd slept afterwards, Ruby fully expecting to do the same, and yet here she was, once again heading towards the witching hour – 3:00 a.m. – and still wide awake.

The witching hour…

She really wanted to sleep, wondering if it was possible to force it.

She could try, hope for the best.

Her eyes already shut, she screwed them tighter, emptied her mind of all the racing thoughts, the memories of the day, both good and…not so good. Drifted…

A snort startled her. Not courtesy of Cash but her own, both annoying and hopeful – annoying because it had woken her, hopeful because the technique she was adopting was working. Later, when the day dawned, it'd be her turn to look after Hendrix so that Cash could get some much-needed work in. Normally, she'd plan to do something like meet Michelle, and it was likely that Michelle would indeed call her, if only to discuss further what to do about Willow. There was also that job Corinna had pencilled in, although Ness or Theo could accompany Corinna on that to do the initial survey. Instead of meeting anyone, what she could do was spend the day alone with Hendrix. Maybe it would be like the evening that had just passed – special.

Another snort. But this one sounded distant. Perhaps her, perhaps Cash.

So special…being with Hendrix, *just* him. Mother and baby. Such a bond.

Unbreakable…

She was drifting again. Dreaming of someone special. Someone close to her. Her baby, of course, Hendrix. The bond with him was unbreakable. An unconditional bond. The parental love of a child, no matter who they were, whatever they did. But what about the reverse? Would a child love their parents with no conditions attached? Deep down?

She was drifting further, as though caught on a gentle tide. So, so relaxed.

Her mother. Jessica. Ruby loved her. Absolutely. Despite everything that had happened between them. So, yes, it did work the other way around.

Also, their bond had strengthened in recent years now

that Jessica was in recovery, was stronger, braver.

You have to be brave.

Ruby was nodding, although likely only her dream self, feeling really very, very happy. Jessica *was* brave, and Ruby considered herself to be brave also. Certainly Cash was for taking her on! A normal person who'd welcomed someone way beyond normal into his life. He was as much a rock as Ness, Theo and Corinna, like Jed, a guiding light.

Lucky. And content. After such a day too. A strange day, full of contrasts. *Remember the good, Ruby, only the good, and go deeper into sleep…*

Funny how something so restorative as sleep, so needed by the body to function, involved the darkness too. Odd world. A world at odds with itself. This dreamlike state a nightly voyage into another realm, one so willingly and innocently taken.

"Ruby! Ruby!"

Was that someone calling her? Who?

"Hello," she called out. She was still dreaming, right?

"Ruby!"

That voice again. Hard to tell who it was, neither male nor female. It just…was.

"Who's there? I can't see you. Cash?"

For the first time, she noticed what was around her – nothing. Just darkness. A void. Familiar, although she couldn't fathom in what way. Perhaps…she should go deeper still, to a place where no dreams existed, where there were no strange voices.

Always trying to reach out.

To get some kind of response…

As though someone had poured icy water down her back, a coldness seized her.

She'd wanted to sleep, that was all she asked, but sleep was too much like that other darkness she'd been plunged into courtesy of that child – what was her name? An unusual name, pretty – a place where a friend of hers wanted to go too. Why? She couldn't remember the reason now, found it hard to think at all, her mind foggy.

"Ruby!"

Such amusement in that voice now. *Grim* amusement.

She didn't want to call out again. Didn't want to know who it was.

She'd definitely go deeper. All the way down. Hide there.

Again, she was successful in forcing it. It was as though she were…falling, but slowly, even gracefully, arms and legs spread out, her hair fanned all around her. It was quiet again. Peaceful. She could rest at last. Face yet another hectic day rejuvenated.

Nothing.

No one.

Oblivion.

Exactly what she wanted.

"RUBY!"

The voice screamed for her this time, pulling her from slumber, waking her.

She *was* awake, wasn't she?

She was certain she was sitting up in bed and looking all around. If she was awake, though, she couldn't see Cash, the bed, or the glow of impending dawn from beneath the curtains. And yet…she was absolutely sure she was awake, that the dream had ended.

"Ruby."

It was more whispery this time, coming from where,

beside her? From in front?

The baby monitor was to her right, wasn't it? Although in this darkness, she couldn't see it. Why on earth was it so dark? As black as pitch.

Another whisper.

"Ruby. Coming. You."

She froze again. Icy cold…again.

Somehow, she forced her mouth to open. "Who is it? Who are you?"

There was a static sizzle, as if it was indeed the baby monitor. Some interference, maybe, before more words broke through, not whispered this time but *rasped*.

"Coming. You. And. Him. The baby. Both."

Hendrix?

She forced life back into her limbs, air into her lungs, climbed upwards through layer after gauzy layer towards consciousness until she was absolutely awake, could see again, could hear everything, not just a voice but Cash's snoring, the ticking of the alarm clock, the monitor there on the bedside table, the white outline of it – the baby screaming.

"Shit!" she said, leaping out of bed, rushing forwards the instant her feet met the hardwood floor, half slipping but quickly righting herself, determined to reach her child before something else did. In the time it took to reach him, she was more scared than she'd ever been. Had that voice been a dream or more than that? Impossible to detect what was true and what wasn't, or know whether she was creating something out of nothing, letting fear take over, ruining any peace of mind, any happiness. If she wasn't responsible, though, then it was Hames…incarcerated but somehow free, because no matter what you did to the person, the mind could still roam, could reach out. Attack.

As fast as she was running, so was someone else. Cash was hot on her heels.

On reaching the door to Hendrix's room, she thrust it open, certain she'd see a black shape hovering over him, another shadow man, this one truly seeking revenge.

As Cash crashed into the back of her – his fear, his confusion something palpable too – she saw what was really there, and the relief was so great that laughter bubbled upwards.

"Ruby, what is it? What's the matter? Something wrong with Hendrix?"

She had to calm her hysteria, gather herself enough to answer. The baby having woken, he had screamed, but only for milk, most likely, that screaming having died down on seeing them, knowing his needs would be met.

"Nothing's wrong," she said eventually. "I just…I got a shock, that's all, when he started yelling. I was in such a deep sleep."

"Yeah, me too." Cash yawned. "Oh well, I'm awake now. Shall I get his milk?"

Her gaze still on Hendrix, she accepted his offer. "You do that, and I'll feed him."

"Fair exchange," said Cash, padding from the room.

Not her father standing there, glowering, full of dark intent, but something else instead, full of *promise – I'll keep him safe, don't worry. Nothing gets through me.*

It was Jed by his bedside, guarding. Looking as fine and as mighty as ever. A dog but also so much more. There when she needed him, always. When *Hendrix* needed him too. A dog that – incredibly – Hendrix was looking right at, she'd swear it – his giggle rattling around the room, chasing away any gloom that lingered.

Whatever was going on in her mind, whether it was her own fears spinning out of control or something more real than that, Hendrix was safe. Like Theo, like so many others, she had unfinished business to tend to – one day. But today was not it. She might even get to choose when. Holding the power over it in that regard.

She certainly felt buoyed with confidence as she drew closer to the cot, as Jed jumped up to greet her, causing the baby to giggle again, to clap his chubby fists in delight.

Ruby picked Hendrix up and breathed in his sweet smell, felt such warmth when, only recently, warmth was a memory too distant to recall.

The strong must carry the weak, and the hope-filled those whom hope had deserted.

Right now, they had other children to help. Two of them.

As she rocked Hendrix – hearing Cash hurry back up the stairs, a warm bottle of milk in hand that she took from him, watching him give Hendrix a peck on the cheek before he returned to bed – and as she fed the baby his milk, she considered Theo's request, just as Theo had asked her to do. Finally, she decided what her answer would be.

Chapter Seventeen

Ruby was going to do it, ring Michelle and request another meeting, and attend as well. All the team would be there, but, as Theo had asked, only two of them would know the full plan. If Theo believed this to be her last chance to reach the unnamed girl, Ruby couldn't deny her. And it would only take seconds, she reminded herself, just that.

In the end, with Ruby busy with Hendrix, feeding and dressing him, it was Michelle who phoned her, Ruby hesitating when she saw the caller ID, realising just how much she'd been putting off the task. Or perhaps, as she quickly corrected herself on answering the phone, gathering the strength to deal with the situation.

"Hi," Michelle said, obvious relief in her voice that Ruby had picked up.

"Hi, Michelle. How are you?" Ruby winced at the flatness in her voice. "How's Willow?" she added more brightly.

"Ruby, I... First, I want to say again, thank you so much for helping me with this, whatever *this* is. Tim, well...he's insisting everything's all right now, and I thought so too. After your visit yesterday, Willow seemed back to her normal self. But then..."

"Then what?" Ruby prompted, curious despite herself.

"She's been very quiet today so far. And when I went to

wake her this morning, when I kissed her forehead, she flinched." There was a slight pause before Michelle added, "Actually flinched. As if…as if my touch repulsed her. It really, really upset me. I mean, I don't know, Ruby, but does she resent me for trying to help her?"

"No," Ruby replied instantly, "of course not. You're her mother." What she didn't say was that whatever Willow was channelling might be the thing that resented her, resented them all for interfering with its diabolical plans.

"It's just it's every mother's worst fear, isn't it, that their child ends up hating them?"

"Willow does not hate you," Ruby reiterated. "Don't even think it. Michelle, listen to what I've just said, to my exact words: *don't even think it.* Okay?"

There was a brief silence before Michelle commented again. "You will come over again, won't you? To help her? You won't just…abandon us?"

Ruby swallowed, clutching the mobile to her ear that little bit tighter. "Of course not. It's our job to help." *As you well know.* "I'll phone the rest of my team right away, and we'll set up a time to visit again that's convenient for everyone."

"Any time's convenient with me," Michelle assured her. "Willow's off school again today, flat out refused to go, caused such a fuss when I tried to make her. I just…couldn't seem to fight against it. It's like…I don't have the energy for it. I…I'm so tired."

She didn't need to finish the sentence or make further excuses. If she was being drained of energy, if there was disagreement between her and Tim regarding how they should deal with Willow, then, once again, it could all be down to what Willow was channelling. Ruby frowned.

Fathers. That was a key issue here as well.

"Michelle, you've told me that Willow has a different father to Leo and that you're worried she might have inherited this ability, so do you think…is it possible—"

"That she inherited it from him?"

"Yes," Ruby replied. "Exactly that."

"Not to my knowledge. I wasn't with him for long, a little over six months, and I've had nothing to do with him since. When I told him I was pregnant with Willow, as you know, he didn't hang around." Her voice cracked slightly as she added, "He said I'd trapped him."

"So, he doesn't pay maintenance or anything?"

"No. I could go after him, you know, via the CMS, but…Tim said we don't need him in our lives, that we're a family now, and he'd take care of us."

"What's Willow's dad's name?"

There was a brief silence on the phone. "Do you really need to know that?"

"It's just, sometimes a psychic gift *is* inherited, and if it's not from you…"

"I really don't think Shaun was like that. He was into football, beer…girls, that kind of thing. A player, and selfish and immature, as it turned out. I was an idiot for loving him."

"Shaun?" Ruby prompted.

"Shaun Murphy," Michelle said at last.

"Irish?"

"Oh yeah. He might not have been psychic, but he had the charm of the Irish, all right."

* * *

Several phone calls all begging to be made and a baby on her hip to jiggle. Ruby sighed as she FaceTimed the team, told them she'd spoken to Michelle and that Michelle was happy for them all to come over and see Willow. Ness was feeling unwell with a slight stomach bug, and so an appointment was made for the following day to convene at the Bayliss house – Ruby's third visit. Ruby also told them Willow's father's name, that his current whereabouts were unknown to Michelle, as they'd lost contact, but no doubt he could be found easily enough. "He used to live in Lewes, so could be he hasn't gone far."

"Would you like me to try and find him?" Ness asked, her pixelated face pale indeed.

"Would you mind?"

"Not at all. It'll give me something to do whilst stuck at home."

Corinna and Theo went off to see the client Corinna had taken a booking from previously, Corinna promising feedback on the case as soon as they'd visited.

"But it sounds fairly straightforward," she said, "a cold spot in one of the bedrooms, some shuffling at night, that kind of thing."

"Same old, same old," Theo said, smiling.

"For us," Ness reminded her a little tersely, "not for some."

"Muggles," Theo replied undaunted, having adopted the *Harry Potter* term for the non-psychic.

The normal, Ruby was going to say but didn't. No point in adding fuel to the fire. Sometimes she'd give anything to be a muggle, if just for a day.

"Okay, all right," said Theo. "Anything else on the agenda for today?"

Ruby shook her head. "Don't think so."

"You sure?"

Ruby shrugged. "For me, it's just childcare and then more childcare."

"Good luck with that, then," Theo returned, before her pixelated eyes fell on Ruby in particular and she added in a more sombre tone, "Good luck with everything."

As the team logged out, Ruby frowned. She was awestruck, because there *was* something else on the agenda today, at least for her, something she'd tend to just as soon as Hendrix was having his nap, and Theo, she had known. She'd plucked what Ruby intended to do from her mind as easily as some people plucked berries from a bush, despite the fact she'd put boundaries up to prevent her from doing so. Ah, this stuff, the mystery of it, it could drive you mad sometimes…send you…right off a cliff.

Her entire body jolted.

Why'd she just thought that? Not only thought it but visualised it too, that cliff edge, hurtling towards it at speed, filled with some sort of desperation.

She shook her head, tried to dispel the vision. The mind was so wayward when it wanted to be. Gazing over at her baby, she could see he was tiring. He'd been fed, milked up, played with and now was rubbing at his eyes and grizzling.

This was it. She felt good today, strong, so should seize her chance. This was her opportunity to do what she had to, confront the question that was begging for attention.

With the baby in her arms, she left the kitchen, stopping off in the front room briefly so that Cash could pop a kiss on his forehead, and headed upstairs. As she placed him in his cot, she looked around her. "Keep an eye on him, Jed. Okay?"

Straightaway, he materialised by the cot, his tail wagging as he gave a woof.

"Best guard dog ever," she murmured, remembering when she'd first met him, the people who had called her because they could hear a dog barking in their house although they didn't own one. And there he was, Jed, in another room, in another house, long ago, guarding something too, although she knew not what. The people had only recently moved in, so it was someone from the past, someone that Jed had...*died* guarding? "Or have you always been like this?" she said. "Here in spirit only?"

Stop stalling, Ruby.

Again, she was guilty of doing that, chatting to the dog and allowing other thoughts to occupy her mind, anticipating that Hendrix wouldn't settle, that she'd have to pick him up and take him back downstairs. But lo and behold! He was already asleep.

Ruby, you can do this. You have to.

Planting a kiss on the same spot Cash had, smiling as Hendrix snuffled slightly, she left him and Jed to it, climbed further to the attic office to focus. Sitting at her desk, for a while all she did was stare at what lay upon it: her computer, notepads and pens, plus an assortment of crystals, the highly protective ones, including tourmaline, labradorite, obsidian and jet, such beautiful, shining pieces. She had crystals all over the house, plenty of amethysts and quartz too, but here in her office, it was always the heavy-duty ones, industrial strength, as the team called them. Her hands were shaking, as well they might. Her breath also slightly ragged. She wished she were wearing her tourmaline necklace, an inheritance from her great-grandmother Rosamund, but as Hendrix had a habit of grabbing it, she'd stowed it away safely in a jewellery box, not wanting it to get damaged.

Although the house was full, her husband, child and Jed occupying the floors below, for a moment, and quite overwhelmingly, she felt alone in the world. The light shone brightly enough through the dormer window, a carpet of radiance right there in front of her, dust motes performing a graceful dance in its spotlight, yet she felt stuck in the darkness still.

If she didn't do this, find out, it'd mess with her mind. And she couldn't afford that.

She hit the space bar and watched the screen burst into life, then, bringing up the Google search bar, she typed *Marlowe Hospital, Northumberland.*

The details appeared immediately, including the website address and a phone number.

Her hands already on her mobile, she punched in the number, visualising white light in abundance as she waited for someone to answer.

Would he know she was doing this? Would he…guess? Was he truly reaching out from across the divide, trying to connect with her? Threaten her?

He was talented, this man who'd fathered her. Not naturally talented, though, only able to do these things because he'd opened himself up, *allowed* himself to be used, to become an instrument of the darkness, another conduit, one of the willing.

The call was answered at last.

"Hello, Marlowe Hospital. Do you know the extension you need?"

"Um…no," Ruby said. "I just want to check up on a

patient."

"Check up?" The voice – female – was stern and confused. "On who?"

She took a deep breath. "Hames." Realising her voice was too low, that the receptionist would never be able to hear her, she repeated herself. "Aaron Hames."

There was a slight hesitation on the phone. Did this woman know of him personally? Did *all* the staff at Marlowe know of him, no matter their role? She could imagine it now, the rumours, the whisperings…the fear.

"And who are you in relation to Aaron Hames?"

"His daughter." How it pained her to say it. "Ruby Davis."

"Ah, right." There was definitely a hint of knowledge in the woman's voice – *I know about him, and I know about you too.* Immediately, she reprimanded herself. She mustn't give in to paranoia. "Hold the line, please," the receptionist continued. "I'll put you through to Doctor Andrews. It's him you need to speak to. Extension eight-four-four for future reference."

Ruby didn't make a note of it. Refused to. All she had to do was check one thing. After that, she'd end the call.

Another voice came on the line. "Hello, this is Doctor Andrews. I believe I'm speaking to Ruby Davis, Aaron Hames's daughter?"

God, this was hard! Ruby remembered what she'd told her father that time at Cromer: *Your progeny I may be, but your likeness I am not.* How he'd told her something too: that he'd found her once, he'd come to the house that Ruby had shared with her mother and grandmother in Hastings, Lazuli Cottage. He'd tracked Jessica down, wanting to see her, to use her again, but found a child instead and put two and two together – his likeness in some ways indeed despite her protests. Gran had chased him away, sent the darkness rushing after him too to consume him, and what had he done? He'd turned towards it and opened his arms…so, so willing. Greedy too because he was *addicted* to the darkness. Wanted more and more of it. More and more from *her*.

"Hello? Are you there?"

"Yes!" Ruby replied. "Sorry. Hames's—"

"He's going through one of his more subdued phases. In fact…he's been a model patient since he arrived. We're pleased with how he's responding to medication."

"Pleased?" Fear, colder than ever, gripped Ruby. "But…you're not planning on releasing him, are you?"

"Releasing him?"

"Yes!" she said more forcefully. "He's…dangerous! Mad. Of course he's mad, you know that! You're not going to…free him, surely?"

A slight laugh, one that ignited fury in Ruby, the doctor's nonchalance.

"No, no, no. Of course we don't have plans to release him. But he's able to receive visitors now if you'd like to? He's talked of you often. I'm sure he'd welcome it."

Her voice reduced to a whisper. "He's talked of me?"

"Yes, of course. What a bright girl you are, talented."

"Talented?"

"Mrs Wilkins, would you like to schedule a visit or not?"

A jolt – as if there were wires attached to her head, sending shockwaves from head to toe.

Mrs Wilkins. Why had he called her that? She'd said her name was Ruby Davis to the receptionist, hadn't informed this facility of her new status. And yet somehow the doctor knew, because Hames knew, that was why, because he was indeed reaching out…and, as she'd feared, he'd know about this phone call too.

"No! I do not want to visit him," she said on a further tide of fury. "And don't be fooled by him. He's as far from a model patient as it's possible to get. Don't ever, ever release him!"

Before the doctor could answer, she did as she'd promised herself she would, once she had the information she needed, and ended the call, wanting, in fact, to hurl the phone from her too, as if just by speaking about him to someone on it had led to contamination.

She didn't, though. She placed the phone gently back down on the desk, took deep breaths and focused on the beam of light in front of her, imagining it cleansing the room.

After a few deep breaths, she was calmer, but when the phone rang unexpectedly, she yelped and stared in horror at it.

It was facedown, so she couldn't see the caller ID.

Not Doctor Andrews again, surely, calling her back. *Mrs Wilkins, are you quite all right? You seemed very distressed. Do you have any other concerns I can help you with?*

"NO!" she screamed and then raised her hands to her mouth to stifle herself, fearful of waking the baby below.

The phone stopped ringing. Then promptly rang again.

"Oh, for fuck's sake!" she swore, snatching at it. Not knowing who it was, was worse.

She almost cried with relief when she saw Ness's name there.

"Ness! Ness!" she said on answering. "Oh, thank goodness. Everything okay?"

"Yes, of course," Ness replied. "Is…um…everything okay with you?"

"Yeah! Yeah! It's just…good to hear your voice, that's all."

"We only spoke a short while ago," Ness pointed out.

"I know, I know. Ignore me, I'm being silly. Feeling a bit flustered, actually, what with the baby, et cetera, et cetera. You know what it's like…" She cringed at what she'd said, Ness being childless. *Mad. Completely mad.* Damn it, she had madness on the brain! She stopped and took a second, forced a smile onto her face, tried to feel that smile. "So, what is it? You haven't found out about Shaun Murphy already, have you?"

"Actually, I have," Ness said, a gravitas in her voice that told Ruby whatever it was she'd discovered clearly wasn't good.

"Oh shit. Fire away," Ruby urged.

"Shaun Murphy's dead, Ruby. He committed suicide two years ago."

"*Suicide?*"

"That's right, he—"

"Threw himself off a cliff, didn't he? Beachy Head."

"Well…yes. How did you know?"

"Because…earlier, I think I connected, that's how. Just by thinking about him."

"Do you know why he did it?" Ness asked. "There's no explanation recorded."

Ruby nodded. "You know what? I think I do. Because, like Willow, he was a conduit."

Chapter Eighteen

Another day would pass before Ruby and her team could visit Willow again, due to the extra work that now came with the case. Ruby had sought out Shaun's family, wanting to speak to them, trying to gather as much information about him as she could, and subsequently his daughter, before returning to the Baylisses'. As Theo always said: knowledge was armour. Even the smallest details could prove crucial.

A small family, as it turned out, just his mother, Anne Murphy. She was fairly local, an Uckfield woman, living in a flat close to the high street. Of course, Ruby had to tread tactfully when contacting her. According to Michelle, Shaun had refused to have anything to do with Willow, and therefore it was entirely possible that Anne never knew she had a granddaughter. When she made that initial call, however, Ruby found she did.

'A honey trap,' Anne had called the pregnancy. "That girl tried to pin him down any way she could, but my Shaun, he weren't having none of it. He i'n't gonna be tied down to some needy bitch, and why should he? He wanted to be free. And now he is. He truly is."

"Mrs Murphy—" Ruby said, but the older woman cut straight to the chase.

"So you're asking me about his daughter, this…*alleged*

daughter? Why? And don't bullshit me. Because I'll know if you do."

"You're like him, then?" Ruby said.

"Like him?" Anne wasn't going to make this easy for her.

"Sensitive."

"Sensitive? Oh, is that what you call it? Fey. That's what we call it. And okay, I am like him, or rather he was like me."

"And me," Ruby told her. "I'm fey too."

There was silence on the phone, and then Anne coughed, a hacking sound that forced Ruby to distance her ear from the phone. When Anne spoke again, it was without apology. "I don't like phones. If you want to talk about Shaun, then do it face-to-face. Only you, though, face-to-face and fey woman to fey woman."

Although Ness accompanied Ruby on the drive to Uckfield, insisted upon it, she also agreed to wait in the car. "But if you need help, shout out, and I don't mean verbally."

"I know how you mean," Ruby replied, smiling at her before exiting the car, Jed appearing by her side as she walked up the path but disappearing again before she entered the actual building, letting her know she'd be okay, that she wasn't in danger.

But Anne...Anne was a sad woman, the grief of her past like a shroud around her.

Her flat was small but crammed with belongings and reeked of a lifetime of smoking. There was not one corner that hadn't been stuffed with things, nor was there any space on any shelf. As the woman ushered her to a battered armchair, one that faced where she sat, Ruby looked around, saw the abundance of trinkets and statues, clocks too, so many of them, antique mainly, in various shapes and sizes. Such an odd assortment of furniture, no flow to it, nothing matching: a footstool, a low coffee table, two sideboards, a dresser, all bunched up to one another. What really caught her interest, though, as she knew it would, were the photographs, all of mother and son, of Shaun through the ages. A cute kid who'd grown into a good-looking man, his swarthy looks a magnet, but his eyes…in every picture, even when he was a kid and smiling, were haunted.

Anne took a seat too. "Beautiful, wasn't he?"

Without hesitation, Ruby agreed. "Yes. He really was." A catch for anyone. Anne had clearly been a good-looking woman too; she had dark hair, long once, Ruby imagined, but now almost torturously cropped, and the most piercing violet-flecked eyes, more lines around them than perhaps was normal for her age, which was mid to late fifties, Ruby guessed.

"My pride and my joy, a good boy." Anne continued, stressing the word *good*. "I want you to know that. He loved me, and I loved 'im. We were each other's world."

"It must be so hard for you——"

A flash of temper. "Don't be stupid, girl. Of course it is! It's *agony*! I saw you lookin' round here, at the clutter, but…this stuff is all I've got left. Everything means somethin'. It's got a memory attached. Can you do that? Lay your hand on an object and read it?"

Ruby shook her head. The practice she was talking about was psychometry – the ability to tune in to an object's history just by touching it. "Not usually," she admitted.

"So, in what way are you fey?"

"I…can see the dead on occasion, the grounded. I can communicate with them."

Anne nodded, as if satisfied. "I see. That's a rare talent. Shaun's not here, though. He didn't linger. I'd know it if he had. No, Shaun's gone. He—" she swallowed slightly "—had to escape. I understand that. I'm fey, I've told you, but I can also shut it off, live peacefully enough. He couldn't, though." Before Ruby could interject, Anne hurried on. "I weren't going to have any children. I'd sworn off 'em because the way Shaun was wasn't an isolated incident, not in the Murphy family, and the menfolk, they couldn't deal with it the way the Murphy women could. It…destroyed them. But when I fell pregnant, I couldn't resist, couldn't get rid of it." Tears filled tired eyes. "And I don't regret having him. In with the dark times there was plenty that was good, you know? We'd laugh! Ha! We'd laugh, us two, an' at such stupid things too, but even so. It was the kind of laughter that made your face ache, tears streaming down our cheeks, *happy* tears, mind. Never laughed with anyone like that before, and I won't do so again. Oh no, never. This ability, some people call it a gift. Do you?"

She didn't feel like admitting it, but Ruby nodded. She – *they*, the Psychic Surveys team – did call it that.

From being animated, Anne grew still again. "Some gifts you can do without. Like Willow. Like 'er."

Ruby went in for the kill. "Anne, just what was it that Shaun channelled that was so detrimental to his health?"

"Oh, come on, girl, what do you think he was channelling? Spit it out!"

Ruby shuffled in her seat. "Okay, right, well…if I had

to give it a name, I'd call it the darkness, that or negative energy."

"Negative energy." Anne mused upon that term before leaning forward and holding Ruby's gaze. "Let me tell you this: my child was a force for good, but, yes, negative energy targets those that shine. All it ever wants to do is snuff the light out."

"Because it's afraid of it," Ruby stated.

"Yes! I know that. You know that. But we also know something else. It *doesn't matter* if it's afraid, because it doesn't stop it." There was a pause before Anne's gaze penetrated deeper. "You fight it too, don't you? The darkness?"

"Yes."

"Got children?"

"One. A son."

"Like me, then."

Ruby wanted to scream then, to yell back, *No, not like you. I gave birth to a normal son!* But she just sat there, mute, fighting her continuing paranoia. She had to take this one step at a time. This was about Willow, plus a child whose name they didn't yet know, who'd died a long, long time ago. That was enough to go on with. Hendrix, Aaron Hames, family matters could all be dealt with another day.

"Families, eh?"

"Sorry, what?" Ruby replied, having become distracted.

"They're what life's all about."

"Willow's a part of your family. She's your blood. And…she's fey."

Anne surprised her by contemplating what she'd just said. After a few moments, she spoke again. "As I've said, the women in our family don't tend to suffer so much. It's either milder or we're just more adept at dealin' with it." A burst of bitter laughter escaped her. "God, I make it sound like a bloody disease, don't I? This alleged *gift*. But it is for some. Willow might be a part of my bloodline, but I can't…" A glisten in her eyes replaced laughter. "I can't get involved. All I want is to live out the rest of my natural life here, in this flat, with my memories and my photographs, remembering the good times. I don't want the rest of it, not the end, that terrible call I got when they told me…when they said…"

She couldn't continue, at least not for a while, Ruby's own eyes watering too, the pain of what Anne had endured too awful to contemplate but felt nonetheless, every agonising moment. What had happened to her son could never be allowed to happen to Hendrix. *Pray God he's like Cash,* exactly *like him.* Hendrix also had Jed guarding him. Did Shaun have nothing and no one? Ruby couldn't believe that. He must have done, but perhaps he never thought to look, to ask for help, just too overwhelmed instead. It wasn't a gift, not for him.

"Anne," she said, extending a hand, but Anne flinched, then moved herself out of reach.

"He told that woman he didn't want a child, did you know that? He didn't want a child because he never wanted to risk it. An' she told him she was on the pill, that there'd be no risk. She lied, and this is what happens. Does the child…look like him?"

"She has red hair."

Anne sneered. "Like her, then. He showed me a picture of her once, the woman."

"Her name's Michelle," Ruby said, "and she's nice."

"She's a liar!"

Ruby was about to deny it but found her voice stuck in her throat. Michelle *had* lied, not just to Shaun but to Ruby as well. She had secured her friendship under false pretences. Lured her to Willow, making the child her problem too.

"Anne," she said again, "whatever plagued Shaun, I think it's attached itself to Willow, and she's not like you or like the other women in your family. She's only a child, and she doesn't know how to deal with it, and her family certainly don't. They're growing frightened. If there's anything you can do or say to help us, then, please, don't hold back. Surely…surely not all the men who have this ability in your family succumbed to it? There were those that overcame it? Think, Anne, please."

Anne had lowered her head, but now she raised it, her eyes glittering with grief, with anger and – to Ruby's dismay – with hopelessness.

"*All* the men succumbed," she told her, "those that were fey, eventually, one way or the other and, yes, sometimes the women too. There've been cases of that happenin', way back. No reason it shouldn't happen again. This thing could devour her."

"It won't," Ruby whispered. "It won't."

There was nothing more to say. Anne had come to a halt, and so had she – two fey people at odds with each other, one who, Ruby couldn't help but think, was succumbing to the darkness too despite her protests, losing the battle.

Before leaving, Ruby handed over her business card, imploring Anne to get in touch if she thought of anything that could help Willow.

"Cast a gypsy's spell, is that what you mean?" Anne

sneered again as she indicated for Ruby to put the card down on the coffee table. "No, we're not the ones who curse. We're just the ones who *are* cursed. So bloody many."

Negativity seemed to pool in this tiny flat, creeping forwards from all four cluttered corners, a tide as sticky as the nicotine tar on the walls and the ceiling. There was no fight left in Shaun's mother at all. Just…acceptance.

Ruby rose, and Anne did too, walked her to the front door.

Before leaving, Ruby tried again.

"Take care, Anne, and thank you for seeing me today. Something of Shaun remains, besides yourself – Willow, and she'll lead a happy life, a life full of light, and wherever Shaun is, he can look down and be glad that Michelle gave her life. He'll be proud. I'll make sure of it, Anne. I'm going to help her not just fight this but banish it for good."

Anne didn't reply; she just stared at her for a few seconds before stepping back to close the door, Ruby continuing to stand there after she'd done that, projecting as much light and as much love as she could muster back into the flat, hoping that the darkness would stay in the corners, not come any closer.

She travelled back with Ness to Lewes, en route making the appointment for the team to see Michelle and Willow the next day, the relief that they weren't just abandoning such a strange case evident in Michelle's voice.

"Thank you, Ruby," she said. "Thank you so much."

And then there they were again, at the Baylisses' the following morning, all four of them and Jed too, although he was sitting in the rear garden, watching through the French doors, just…monitoring proceedings. And well he might, because there was indeed danger here, Ruby could sense it, could *see* it as the child in the kitchen turned to her, her gaze as piercing as her grandmother's, a child with such a…rich heritage. *The child of the fey. The child of a liar.* Not her words, not her thoughts. Willow had put them there, or rather the something that was in her.

As Ruby stared back at Willow, she projected her own thoughts.

You're a child, she said and felt a sense of triumph as she saw Willow's body jolt, even if slightly. *An innocent child. There's no place for the darkness in you.*

They had to help her, but first they'd get Willow to help them.

To find another child, innocent or not.

Theo stepped forward, broke the gaze between Ruby and Willow.

"Hello, darling," she said. "How lovely to see you again!"

Chapter Nineteen

A dark place. Bleak. But it wasn't her own bleakness she was wading through this time, it was Theo's. She'd been gone too long, and Ruby was searching for her.

Once again, it had all happened so quickly. They'd entered the kitchen, and, again like before, Willow was at the kitchen table, as was Michelle. Ness was taking the place of Lee, remaining an observer, taking notes, recording everything.

When Theo had greeted Willow, the child had risen, happy again to see her. She'd left the table, a big smile on her face, and ran towards Theo. This was it. Crunch time. Their plan might or might not work, but Theo had reached for her, all boundaries lowered.

At the last minute, though, Willow had bypassed Theo and headed straight for Ruby, the smile all but vanished from her face. Ruby was prepared, the light shining brightly in her soul. The child had reached for her hand and grabbed it, but Theo had darted backwards with an impressive agility given her age and weight and grabbed Willow too – by the hand. The three of them connected once more, and Ness and Corinna, ignorant of this particular part of the plan, had no doubt tried to second-guess all that was going on. Although there'd been a brief moment of personal fear, Ruby realised she was safe, that she could hold out against the child. This wasn't about her, nor Hames, but about two children. Willow and what possessed her. And what had possessed the nameless child too.

What had happened had taken seconds and might be continuing to play out in increments of seconds still, but Ruby was growing impatient, worried, had stepped outside her psyche and into Theo's, chased her into her own darkness, marvelling such a thing was possible but knowing that anything was. Something which Theo maybe relied on.

"Theo?" she said, her voice echoing in this strange place, so alien and yet so familiar. "It's me, Ruby. You're not alone, okay? I'm here with you. And…we have to be quick. Get what you need, the name of the girl or any other detail you think might give us some kind of clue, then break this connection. Theo? Theo!"

Someone else was calling Theo's name as if far away, down the end of a long, long tunnel. Ness, perhaps. Or Corinna. Because they'd be doing just that, questioning everything, maybe even moving towards Willow to force their hands from hers.

Ruby was striding, but she came to a halt, swallowed hard. They should have told the others of Theo's intention. *She* should have. As boss, it was her call. What if they delayed too long in helping them? Rather than a successful outcome, this could be disastrous.

"Theo!" she cried with renewed vigour. "Answer me if you can. I've changed my mind. We shouldn't do this." Play the darkness at its own game.

With no time to linger, she began walking again, the atmosphere thick and as cloying as before, something that parted before you but not willingly; rather, it preferred to entomb you instead. "No chance," Ruby whispered through gritted teeth.

Theo was here, somewhere, and Ruby would find her. She'd continue to part the darkness until Theo came into sight, and then she'd rush to her, tell her there would be better ways to achieve what she wanted – to connect with this girl, the child who'd killed other children, who'd thought there was something rotten inside her, who'd likely had no help in dealing with that, not then, fifty years ago, who'd then died herself. How she'd died, they had no idea. Was she murdered, or was it suicide again? Just so fearful of condemnation. *Am I the devil? Is this hell?* That's what she'd said. What Ruby could *hear. Right now.* Whispered words: *Am I the devil? Am I? Am I? The devil…*

Ruby had chased Theo into her own psyche, trying to find her, to help her, but in truth, she hadn't known what to expect. She'd done this on instinct, without regard for the consequences. And so here she was, truly within her, connecting to memories, to a guilt harboured for far too long, having condemned the child rather than helped her, calling her evil. Theo feared she'd subsequently festered in a low, low place, somewhere her soul could be further tortured. Guilt could torture you, though, and with Theo, it had done.

Theo, if she won't connect, you have to let the guilt go!
"NO!"

The word was violent, like a whip cracking in the darkness, hard and fast.

It was Theo Ruby had heard – the despair in her voice, the guilt only mounting.

She had to find her soon. What was happening here, all

she was experiencing, was too much…too far outside of normal even for her, who was often on the outermost edge.

She picked up speed, her hands in front of her and cutting through the darkness as though she were swimming, not running, in the depths of an ocean yet to be discovered. She didn't care, though, not when Theo's well-being was at stake, but kept on going. She'd find her, save her. In this, she was a warrior. They both were.

"Theo! Theo! Theo!"

Let whatever lurked hear her. Let it quake, continue to hide.

"Theo, I'm here. Don't shut me out. We'll do this together, side by side. We're stronger together. You know that. It's what we've always said. For fuck's sake, Theo!"

There she was! At last. In front of her. Ruby crying out with relief.

"I'm here, Theo," she said again. "Let's do what we need to do, then leave…"

Her voice drifted off as she wondered what was wrong with her. Theo was standing with shoulders slumped and head down, one hand raised to cover her eyes. Not like a warrior at all but someone tired. Already defeated.

"No, no, no, Theo! That's not you. That's not what's happening."

From having felt as though she were running, Ruby slowed, although still continued the illusion of moving. Theo, though, refused to acknowledge her, or maybe she couldn't.

Ruby had to close the gap, get some response from her friend, some agreement that their time here, their purpose, had come to an end – then call out again, this time for Ness and Corinna, who would bring them back into the light. Again, she berated herself. It was such a mistake not to have told them about Theo; she shouldn't have listened. This was Theo's one shot, maybe, but what if it turned out to be a shot too far?

Inches from Theo now, that's all she was, and still there was no reaction.

"Theo?" This time Ruby's voice was gentle, as soothing as Theo's when she was trying to cajole a spirit. There were so many spirits, grounded, trapped, just as she and Theo were trapped right now, but in places as terrible as this? The in-between was a place no one belonged, living or dead. It was a dumping ground for non-spirit only, those that never had a heart or soul in the first place, nothing that could crack open and bleed.

It was as though Theo were set in stone. Immoveable. No heart and soul in her either.

Not true!

Don't give in, Theo, don't despair. You've led a good life. You've saved so many. You saved me many times!

Ruby was only too happy to return the favour.

She reached out, did what Willow had done and took her hand.

This was the way to do it, to truly connect, flesh on flesh, warm flesh.

At least her own was. Theo's was icy cold…and grabby.

As responsive as lightning, Theo's hand held on fast to Ruby's, her head rising just as quickly to stare at her, Ruby gasping as she stared back. The eyes that bored into hers didn't belong to Theo; they were black instead of blue, flat with no sparkle. The face was someone else's too – someone young and childlike, with a child's temper.

"You've led a good life, Theo," the person

masquerading as Theo mocked. "You've saved so many. Well, she didn't save me! She refused to! I begged and begged. I needed her help, cried out, but she turned me away, sent me further into the hell of despair."

No way could Ruby respond. Not when she didn't know what was happening. The child, though, didn't need her response. Froth at her mouth, she continued to expound.

"Is this hell? Is it? Yes! That's exactly where you are and where you'll stay, not with Theo but with me. I can't be alone here. I can't! Not anymore." A childish whine was quickly stifled. "Do you know what hell really is? Not something crawling alive with devils. Oh no, that would be better. That would be company, at least. Hell is a place even the devils have left, where you're alone, completely alone, to think and think and think…"

The girl opened her mouth, wider and wider, Ruby sure the ensuing scream would deafen her, but when she stopped and spoke again, Ruby could hear all too well.

"She wouldn't help me. No one would. And I won't be alone anymore. She's found me, deep inside her, waiting, and she can stay there, and you…you can stay here too. There's something inside me, something…rotten. I'm rotting still. You can both rot with me."

Where was Ness? Where was Corinna? More to the point, where was Theo? Was there a place deeper inside herself than this, somewhere even worse?

If so, that was where Theo had gone. Unable to bear the guilt she'd heaped upon herself. An empath who had gone all the way.

"Not my fault," the girl was wittering now, dribble *and* froth at her mouth, her eyes not on Ruby anymore but on some invisible point in the distance, far, far away, babbling continuously. "Not my fault, not my fault, not my fault…"

Ruby took up the mantra. "Not my fault, not my fault, not my fault…" The two of them fell into perfect rhythm, as though only one voice spoke, no longer two. The same tone, the same whine, the same denial.

Ruby stopped the mantra, took a deep breath and filled her lungs.

"Theo," she said instead, "it's not *your* fault, do you hear? None of this is. You couldn't help at the time, and you know why, because you were too busy trying to get well again. What's that saying? What is it? Something like…you have to draw from the well to nourish yourself first before you can nourish others. That's what you had to do back then, grow as strong as you are today. Theo, come back from wherever you are. Don't go any deeper. If you do…if you do… Theo, listen when I say this, when I scream it out loud, louder than she can: YOU ARE NOT AT FAULT HERE."

Sudden light caused her to raise her hands to shield her eyes. There were voices again, not the voice of the dead child but adults, familiar adults. She'd done it, broken the connection! There should be relief about that, shouldn't there? Theo'd returned, not gone deeper after all. Ruby was back too, where she belonged – in this kitchen, of all places, in the heart of Lewes. But the voices, there was such urgency to them.

"Ambulance…be quick…please…hurry."

"Ruby, are you okay? Ruby, listen to me."

"For God's sake, you must hurry. I…I don't think she's breathing."

Who wasn't breathing? Checking, Ruby breathed in, then exhaled. They weren't talking about her; she was breathing just fine. Theo? Something was wrong with her? Had she not returned after all? Was she…stuck?

Ruby tried to lift her head, to understand the situation further, but was told by…Corinna – that was it, her Titian hair like a curtain falling forward as she knelt beside her – to stay still, that the situation was being dealt with. "…so fast," she was saying, she was whispering. "Oh, Ruby, it all happened so fast."

What had?

There was barking, growling – Jed agitated again – and then another voice joined the tumult, also familiar, a child's voice. Rising so high, it overrode everything.

Not the child she'd just encountered, the child murderer. It was Willow's voice, shouting the same thing as that other one. *Continually* shouting.

"Not my fault! Not my fault! It's not my fault!"

Chapter Twenty

Cautiously optimistic. That's how the doctors felt about Theo's condition, that she was stable...so far. And yet Theo hadn't regained consciousness. For a larger-than-life woman, in the hospital bed, hooked up to all sorts of monitors and machines that bleeped, she was small, frail. Ruby tried to convince herself she looked peaceful, but it wouldn't wash. She didn't. There was a slight downturn of the mouth as though she were grimacing, features rigid instead of relaxed.

She, Ness and Corinna stood around the bed. Family were on their way and would demand an explanation, which Ruby would do her utmost to give, but first she had to explain to Ness and Corinna – had to also find a way to get Theo better, along with the doctors and nurses, because her biggest fear right now was that Theo was stuck in that dark place deep inside herself and that in her desperation to find the girl, she had indeed gone further, risking everything, her life, even. God, the things that guilt made you do! And now here she was, Ruby, guilt-stricken too because she'd condoned this.

"Ness… Corinna…" she began.

Ness had been gazing at Theo, no doubt sending her love and light in abundance, but now she looked at Ruby.

"Not now," she said, "not here. We gather ourselves.

Get our strength back. Wait."

"Wait?" Ruby questioned as Corinna also glanced at Ness.

"Yes, we wait until—" her voice cracked "—I'm able to hear what you have to say."

Ruby nodded. Ness didn't have to go on; Ruby understood. But she was also impatient. Theo had suffered a heart attack despite protesting there was nothing wrong with her, that meds had all her health issues under control. But they didn't. Stress was master of all, it seemed, another thing that bided its time, waiting to strike.

The scene at the Bayliss house, when Ruby had finally come fully round, had been utter carnage: Theo collapsed; Ness on the phone, frantically begging for help; Jed barking; the child screaming and Michelle trying to calm Willow down, her eyes wild as she'd wondered, no doubt, just what the hell had been unleashed, just as Ruby was wondering now. About Willow too, a child from a long line of gifted people – the fey, such a Celtic term, so sweet, so charming, magical even, but nothing could be further from the truth. What Willow was, what she channelled, was none of those things. Darkness had sought out her father and, as far as Ruby knew, Shaun's father, his brother and his cousins too, an attachment of some sort that had plagued the family for generations. Something ingrained, maybe even invited at some point during their history. Then, once it got a stronghold…

Theo's sons arrived, their wives having to stay home with the children, likely telling them Gran was unwell but that she'd rally soon because Gran always did. She had to.

When her eldest, Wayne, rushed straight to Theo's bedside, Ruby, Ness and Corinna stepped back, allowing him his space. Theo's youngest, though, Ewan, approached them.

"I've told her," he said, "so many times I've told her to stop all this." His face was carved with anguish. "That it'll be the end of her. She's just not well enough for it anymore."

Ness replied before Ruby could. "All *this*," she said, "is what your mother is. What she feels she was born to do. She's a woman who knows her own mind."

Harsh words, perhaps, given the situation. Ruby thought Ness might go easier on him, but Ness was proud of what they did, what she herself had *fought* to do against so much prejudice from her own family, the remaining members of which had subsequently disowned her due to it. So, no, perhaps she wouldn't go easy.

Ewan took a step back, although his eyes remained fixed on Ness. Would he argue the point further? Start blaming them? He didn't, perhaps because he dared not. Theo – usually – was formidable, but so was Ness. She'd let no one tell her that what she did for a living was wrong or peculiar or…evil. Not anymore. Theo never had either. She took no nonsense from strangers and certainly not from her sons. Whatever Ewan was going to say, he'd thought better of it. He did what any good son should and turned to his mother, moving to her bedside with his brothers to hold Theo's hands, murmuring to her silly things, playful things, things like 'Oh, come on, Mum, that's enough nonsense now, wake up. It's little Evie's birthday in a couple of weeks. There'll be cake. Chocolate cake. Your favourite. You're not going to want to miss that, are you?' The kind of words Theo would appreciate, that might reach her. She adored her grandchildren. She'd move heaven and earth to be there for Evie's birthday if she could.

The team made to exit. Ruby could call Wayne in the morning, try to explain, in as simple terms as possible, what had happened to cause the heart attack. He had a right to know more. All her sons did. She'd reiterate too what Ness had said, that Theo *lived* for her work, that she performed quiet miracles, many of them, but now it was up to the hospital staff to perform the kind of miracles that they did.

Not a word was said between the three as they left the stark white room behind and stepped into an equally stark corridor, rode the lift down to the ground floor, hurrying through reception and out into the fresh air, Ruby breathing it in.

"Shit," Corinna murmured at last. "Shit, shit, shit. This is all just…shit."

It was only late afternoon, although it felt so much later – like the dead of night itself.

Ruby's eyes filled with tears, which she blinked away. She didn't have time to crumble; she had to remain strong, solve yet another mystery. Two of them, actually, the one surrounding Willow and that of the girl Theo had gone in search of. With her, though, where to start when they didn't even have a name?

Despite her determination to stay strong, tears fell, Corinna also dissolving into a soggy mess, Ruby moving over to her and the pair of them hugging. Ness remained dry-eyed, however, which Ruby was strangely glad about. Maybe because in the face of Ewan she'd been forced to reaffirm her belief in her vocation, when, earlier, by Theo's bedside, that belief had slipped, just a little. Either way, there were no tears in Ness's eyes and no crack in her voice when she spoke.

"Now," she said. "Now's the time to discuss all this. Ruby, Corinna, I'm sorry if you had plans for later today, but cancel them. I'm sure Presley will understand," she said, referring to Corinna's partner, "and, Ruby, I'm sure Cash will as well. Let's head back to mine, right now, and examine all we know. Help Willow but, most of all, help Theo because I know as well as you do, Ruby, it's guilt that's destroyed her. Almost."

* * *

In Ness's kitchen, sitting around the table there, Ruby confessed about the pact she'd made with Theo, who had not just allowed but encouraged Willow to take her deep inside herself – to the darkest places, the places people normally shunned.

Whilst Corinna simply looked aghast, Ness shook her head in a show of despair.

"It'd be an invitation that an energy like that wouldn't be able to resist," she murmured through pursed lips. "What I don't get is why you didn't let Corinna and I in on it."

"Because Theo knew you'd block her, you in particular, Ness. She thought this was her one chance to do what she had to, what she *needed* to. I don't know…she's just so determined. She wants to find this girl and, murderer or not, help her. It's Theo's unfinished business, and she'll deal with it, with or without us."

Ness contemplated those words, her face gradually relaxing, becoming a little less severe. "Yes, yes, I can understand that determination. You know about my twin…"

Corinna, who'd started chewing at her nails, stopped what she was doing and frowned instead. "Your twin…with no name?"

"She *did* have a name. As you also know, I found it out. And I wanted to tell her because…because it upset her so much thinking she didn't. To be nameless was like the greatest insult of all. It was to be too much like them, non-spirit. I banished my twin at an early age – oh, I don't need to go into the nitty-gritty – but then, afterwards, for so many years I searched for her, desperate to tell her what had been written on her birth certificate, the name my parents never, not once, spoke. Like Theo, I also refused to give up. I just kept hoping somehow, someway, I could reach her. To that end, I would have done anything, *anything*. But finally, it was her that found me. I told her who she was, but…it didn't seem so important to her anymore, having a name. She'd grown, you see, whilst in the spirit world, evolved. She knew who she was, something worthwhile. She was *bright* with that knowledge. Rather than a name, she had purpose."

"What was her purpose?" Corinna asked. Yes, she knew all about Ness's twin, as did Ruby and Theo, but on this last point, she clearly wanted elaboration.

"To help people, just as we do. That's what I believe, anyway. Part of an entire army that do that job." She nodded towards Ruby as she continued. "Like Jed, my sister is a guide. Again, as you know, I feared for years that she was growing darker instead of brighter. As a spirit child, she was prone to displays of anger, hurt and bitterness. I focused on that, forgetting at other times how full of fun she was, the girl that only I could see, how sweet and loving. I'd lived, and she'd died. She was alive in the womb, but that was all. There was no gasp of breath on entering the world. She was buried without ceremony, forgotten by those that should have preserved her memory. Unfair. Terribly. A shot at life is a marvellous thing. Oh, I know it can all go so horribly wrong, but overall it's a privilege. There's so much we can learn on this journey, but it isn't the only place to do that, as so many believe. There are other places too. She grew, and she learnt, the right kind of stuff, and she blossomed. All that fear, all the worry that choked me…and now it's gone because I was wrong, because, wonderfully, she *proved* me wrong."

"But this girl," Ruby said, enjoying hearing about Lyndsey but also desperately wanting to focus on the matter in hand, "I don't think she's been in the same place as your sister. I think she went somewhere entirely different."

This time Corinna and Ness sat rapt as Ruby explained all, the girl she'd seen at the heart of Theo, disguised as their friend. It was grotesque, when she thought about it, how the girl had used Theo in that way, *mimicked* her, luring Ruby closer and closer until she was caught in her gaze, eyes as black as tar, something rotten inside.

"And yet Theo was there too," Ruby said, "some semblance of her, in body as well as psychically. At first—" Ruby screwed her eyes shut briefly, trying to recall every detail "—it was like she was made of stone, a statue, frozen in time, like those in Narnia. You remember that book? *The Lion, the Witch and the Wardrobe*? Like them, but maybe…I don't know…she was still at a stage where she could have broken free if she'd wanted to, but she didn't.

She chose not to. Chose to stay, to keep on searching.

"The thing that had hold of her, I now suspect it was whatever Willow channels, nothing to do with that other girl at all, trying to deceive us, mislead us, mimic not just Theo but her as well. It said…it said the worst thing was being alone, totally alone, that hell is where there's nothing to do but sit and contemplate everything that torments you, relive it, over and over, a kind of eternal Groundhog Day. I knew exactly what she meant because that's the kind of place Willow also took me. This place inside." Ruby raised a hand to rub at her chest. "All our memories, all our thoughts, all our feelings, there remains a trace of every one. It's like…we're our very own dumping ground, our own world, our own universe. We're infinitesimal yet infinite too. God, the human being is just so complex. The *spirit* is."

Corinna gulped. "So you think that's where Theo is now? Stuck in a place deep inside herself, searching for the memory of this girl? And Willow in pursuit?"

Ruby nodded. "That's my fear, although I don't know for sure. You broke the physical connection, didn't you, in Michelle's kitchen, snatched our hands out of Willow's, and broke the mental connection too, at least with me. So yeah, I just don't know, and that's not good enough. What if she isn't there by choice anymore?"

"I took her hand again," Ness said. "In the hospital, I mean. Did you, Ruby?"

Ruby had to stop and think. What had happened was all such a blur. Had she taken her hand? Ness said that *she* had. And Corinna had. Corinna wouldn't let go of Theo's hand, not for a long while; she'd clasped it in both of hers. But had Ruby done similar?

"I don't think I did," she said at last. "I think I just stood there like an idiot for most of it, too shocked to move. Why d'you ask?"

"Because I took her hand, and I felt it," Ness answered, swallowing hard.

"Felt what?" Ruby said, impatient for what she was about to say and yet knowing it would confirm her worst fears.

"Nothing, absolutely nothing. There was no connection at all, when always before there's been a glimmer of something, a frisson. Like electricity, we spark off each other."

"Nothing?" Corinna whispered.

"Why would that be?" asked Ruby. "Come on, Ness, why d'you think that was?"

"Because she's cut all connection to us, that's why," Ness said, her face stricken as realisation caught up with her. "Wherever she's gone, she doesn't want us to follow. That loss of connection is a warning, a *dire* warning. If we follow her, we all risk our lives too."

Chapter Twenty-One

Life was a privilege. Ness had said that earlier in the confines of her own house, the three of them, when it should have been four, sitting in her kitchen and ignoring the tea she'd made, discussing what had transpired. Had it really only been a few hours ago they'd done that? It felt like days had passed. What a strange thing time was; it went so slowly sometimes, yet other times it got stuck on fast-forward. Time was a thing that could deceive you, throw you off balance, as well as guide you.

At Ness's earlier, time had indeed passed quickly, growing dark and all of them continuing to sit there, contemplating how to move forward regarding recent happenings. The way ahead was not presenting itself clearly, was as murky as when Ruby had been in the in-between too. One thing was clear, though – they wouldn't heed Theo's warning. If she was trapped, they wouldn't leave her there. But how to reach her when she'd cut them off?

Of course Willow also had to be dealt with. All three of them had left the Baylisses' in such a hurry, such a flurry of confusion, following the ambulance from Lewes to the hospital in Brighton, with nothing but concern for Theo on their minds. Now, though, it was time to shift that focus, at least temporarily and no matter how late it was getting.

Ruby phoned Michelle, all three of them on edge as the line rang and rang and rang.

"She's not answering," Ruby said at last, ending the call but trying again and getting the same result.

"Text her," Corinna urged. "We need to speak to her, see how Willow is."

"Okay." Ruby was on it already, and the text was sent.

Again, the three of them waited expectantly. Sent on WhatsApp, grey ticks turned blue.

"She's read it," Ruby said. "She'll reply soon."

But she didn't, despite Ruby truly believing she would. Surely she was frantic about all that had happened, wanting to know how Theo was and what to do about Willow?

Another message was sent: *Michelle, the doctors said Theo's stable, but so far she hasn't regained consciousness. We're so worried about her, also about Willow. How is she? She must be so distressed. I'm sure you are too. Call me, please. ASAP.*

That text wasn't read this time, the ticks remaining grey. From staring at her phone, Ruby eyed the others.

"Do you think…do you think she's ghosting me?"

"Ghosting?" queried Ness.

"Ignoring her," Corinna explained. "Michelle is just going to cut off all contact, make like Ruby doesn't exist."

"Oh, I see," said Ness, sighing.

Willow was key in all this, wasn't she? It was because of Willow that Theo was in the state she was, because of the child's terrible ability to plunge you into the furthest reaches of yourself, the places you normally ghosted too. Could she do it again? Ruby wondered. Could Willow be brought to the hospital to take hold of Theo's hand, and Ruby's also so that Ruby could return to Theo's psyche and continue to chase her down?

Right now, that seemed like the only solution.

She yawned, couldn't help herself. It was so late. They had to get some rest. As much as Ruby wanted to go to Michelle's right now and bang on the door there, demand that this plan be put into action immediately, she agreed with Ness and Corinna that doing so would only make things worse. It could make Michelle afraid of them. Willow was her child, a child she'd brought into the world via deceit, maybe, but she loved her, and a mother who loved her child would do anything to protect them. She'd already illustrated that by deliberately befriending Ruby, bringing her into the picture and pleading for help, only for it to lead to further chaos and confusion. Ruby couldn't be angry at Michelle for her actions, though. In her situation maybe she'd have done the same. So why was Michelle now burying her head in the sand? She couldn't ignore Ruby for long.

She'd head over to Michelle's first thing in the morning, and it had been agreed she'd go alone, Ness and Corinna on standby, though.

The night had come and gone, and morning had broken. It was another pleasant spring day, not a cloud in the cobalt sky.

All night Ruby had slept close to Cash, he just as upset about Theo as she, just as fretful. She'd closed her eyes and again forced sleep to come, wondering if she could connect with Theo that way, reach her somehow, keeping her at the forefront of her mind, opening herself up to that possibility. But there'd been no dreams, none she could recall on waking, something aching in her to realise it, and silently cursing too. Dream connection was a valid tool for the psychic, but it had eluded her, eluded *them*, Ness and Corinna also, who later revealed they'd tried the same technique, also unsuccessfully.

At the Baylisses', no one answered the banging on the door or the ringing of the doorbell, Ruby unable to peer through the windows to detect movement inside because Michelle had kept the curtains shut, ghosting her as suspected.

On the doorstep, she texted again, begging Michelle to respond. *This is urgent! Willow needs help. So does Theo.*

No use. Ruby wished she could break the door down and remove all barriers – well and truly – barge in there and grab the woman by the shoulders, tell her they needed Willow, that she was the only way back to Theo. She could get them to where they needed to be – Ruby, at least – and once there, Theo could be persuaded back.

But the barriers remained, on all levels.

Meeting up with an equally frustrated Ness and Corinna in the attic office of Ruby's home shortly after, all three sat in silence until Corinna piped up. "St Martin's, where those murdered children are buried. We can go back there."

Ruby's frown deepened. "Why? We've been there, checked for their presence."

"We've removed the darkness that contaminated the land," Ness also said.

Corinna grew more animated. "Exactly! We removed it. Left it benign again."

"They're not there," Ruby reiterated. "There was no connection."

Corinna wouldn't be swayed. "They may have been hiding. Hear me out. If you were still grounded and there was just so much…darkness still, so much terror, instead of going to the light, wouldn't you make yourself smaller, try not to get noticed? But once the darkness was gone…once you *trusted* that, you might come out of hiding? Be braver?"

Ruby calculated. "It's been a while since we've been there. What if—"

"Do it," Ness said, already out of her seat and moving towards the door, just so desperate for a lead like the rest of them. "Ruby, okay to take your car?"

They entered the churchyard roughly half an hour later, Ruby having put her foot down on the way, darting in and out of traffic. All this pursuit of children was making her miss her own so much – but Cash understood. He'd roped in his mother too to look after Hendrix. 'Do what you have to,' he'd said. 'Hendrix is being spoilt rotten by his nana. He's loving this time with her. She's no replacement for you, I'm not saying that, but…we have to get Theo back. God knows how all this works, but pull out all the stops, make that happen.'

God…he'd been absent from the grounds of St Martin's for quite some time. But now he was back, and the birds were calling out to one another, rabbits also darting in and out of bushes, and spring flowers – yellow, the most cheerful colour of all – had bloomed fully. There was even the sound of chatter, that of a young couple exploring the grounds, who lifted their hands in greeting to the team on their way out of the churchyard.

"Such a lovely place," one said.

"So peaceful," the second added.

Ruby waved back. "Yes, yes, it is," she replied, adding under her breath, "for now."

Peaceful it might be, but it was still the burial place of two murdered children and of others who'd had their lives cut short, in amongst those who had expired naturally, having reached a ripe old age, a 'good innings', as some people called it. Plus, spirits that lingered often returned to more familiar places rather than a burial ground, one with more memories attached. The children *should* have flown, but if not, if they were here, the last place they'd ever been with their family standing by the graveside, mourning them…it could prove useful. Might they know the identity of their attacker? The reasons behind it?

The three went in different directions, Ness returning to the site of Danny Bailey's grave, Ruby at Eliza Brooks's, and Corinna midway between the two. Each focusing on the space around them, they tuned in. *Knock, knock. Anyone there? Danny? Eliza?*

Ruby tried to build a picture of the little girl. Although Sally's book contained some photographs of the victims she'd documented, there'd been none of these two. No visual representation found either during their research at The Keep – research which had, admittedly, been cut short because they'd rushed off here to St Martin's as soon as they'd found out the location of the children's burial site. Since then, they'd been too preoccupied with Willow to follow it up further. Standing there, the children's names and fates were once again all the information they had to go on.

Did you have blond hair, Eliza, or dark? Did you like to wear dresses, or were you a tomboy? I used to be a tomboy, you know? Knocking around in jeans and baseball boots, hair all scruffy. What kind of music did you like? She tried to recall some seventies bands, the kind a twelve-year-old might idolize. *The Who? The Doors? Um…T-Rex and David Bowie? Okay, okay, let's try this. What food did you like? Ice cream? Chips? Fish fingers? Pizza? Oh, I know – Angel Delight. Eliza, if you're here, let me know. If you were hiding before…*

A frisson of something…a presence…one that sent her hopes soaring.

Eliza?

She lifted her head, could see Corinna staring at her, perhaps sensing something too. As for Ness, her head was lowered, one hand on Danny's headstone, almost caressing it.

Eliza, please, if you are still here, there's no need to hide anymore. The darkness is gone. We've removed it. It won't come back, I promise. Come out of hiding and come into the light. Eliza? Listen to me. Trust me. All I want to do is help you.

Not quite true – she wanted information too – but Ruby stifled that thought, her skin still tingling with anticipation because she might be closer to getting it.

Eliza… There was a flash of something in her mind, a sound, that of laughter, light, breezy and carefree. Another burst of laughter from someone different, not as carefree, although whoever emitted it tried hard to make it sound that way to emulate Eliza. A game was being played. Yes, that was it. Hide-and-seek? An age-old game that practically everyone played at some point in their lives, or variations of it. Words now being spoken, distant words. She had to strain hard to hear them, catching them only sporadically.

Hide! Go on…count…ten…then find you.
Again?
One more time… Go.
Home.
Not yet.
You…home?
No! One more game!
My mum…
I want…play!

As vague as the memory presenting itself was, as tenuous, Ruby could detect a change in tone, the one urging Eliza becoming even more insistent.

Go! Hurry! Now. Quick!

A pause, then remnants of more words.

Got…you.
But…
Can't…hide…me.
Let go!
Out…there.
No!
Out…there!
Leave…me.

Briefly Ruby closed her eyes, swallowed hard as she continued to tune in.

Leave…me.
Too…late.
Tell…Mum…she…angry.
Angry? You want…angry?

A torrent of words followed, Ruby still only hearing snatches, but she knew them to be the very worst words. How did a twelve-year-old child know that kind of stuff? She'd told Theo there was something rotten inside her.

Something poisonous. Something she was at the mercy of? Horror had clearly rendered Eliza mute. All Ruby could hear was this other one, her voice much lower than she'd expected, guttural. What was it that Eliza had seen when she'd looked into the face of her supposed friend? Ruby wondered. Something twisted beyond all recognition, becoming hideous?

There was a scream. Eliza's? The attack becoming physical?

Oh, Eliza, I'm sorry. So sorry.

And it was fury again that took another victim in a similar manner a few days later, Danny meeting the same fate. A boy and therefore supposedly stronger, but strange how shock and disbelief could render you defenceless. Blood. A fountain of it. Covering everything. That was right, wasn't it? The girl had presented to Theo drenched in the stuff.

"Eliza," Ruby whispered, "I'm really so sorry for how you suffered. Are you still here? I think now that you are, that you've just shown me what happened, and you're caught up in it still, reliving it." A type of Groundhog Day for her too. "Eliza, come out of hiding."

But she knew it was futile. Eliza would *not* come out of hiding. *Fool me once…*

The day came back into focus, Corinna and Ness each walking towards her, such grief on Ness's face, having perhaps experienced the agony of what Danny had gone through, Corinna also aware on some level, her green eyes clouded.

They stood in silence, listening further to the birdsong, craving the sweetness of its lullaby. Not a bad place to be grounded, not now. Not if the grounded could also hear the trill of the birds. The churchyard was coming back to life. More people would visit, attend mass there, the current priest bemused by the increased numbers but overall just going with the flow, happy to see it, which was good because happiness was needed here. And maybe, eventually, that happiness would draw the children out; they'd remember the happiness they'd once felt too before someone had robbed them of it. That, or finding out about their murderer because maybe, just maybe, they were also desperate for answers, for the reasons. For unfinished business to be solved.

Corinna was the one to break the silence. "What now?"

"What now indeed," Ness murmured.

Ruby thought long and hard before voicing her opinion about what they should do. "Lee said we weren't to get in touch with the murder victims' families, or words to that effect, that it wasn't fair on them to rake it all up."

Ness eyed her. "Uh-huh. That's right. He did."

"Thing is, right now we're fighting blind."

Again, Ness agreed. "Yes. Yes, we are."

"Then we do it. We go back to The Keep and find out more about Eliza and Danny, check to see what family is still alive, parents, brothers, sisters. And we get in contact. We have to if we're ever going to find out the name of their murderer. Once we've done that, we find a way of following Theo into the darkness. With or without Willow."

Chapter Twenty-Two

Eliza had been fair-haired and cherub faced, younger looking than twelve. Petite. Danny had had dark hair, a thick shock of it, a wide grin and what Ruby would bet were twinkling eyes. Cheeky, the pair of them. And just so full of life.

There weren't many photographs of them on the Net. There weren't many articles either, the inability to find their murderers – the shame – possibly responsible for that. It was as if everyone, the public and the police, had just wanted to sweep the whole sorry, unsolved incident aside and move on, focus on things that kept you sane rather than what didn't, that made you believe the world wasn't such a bad place after all. Could she blame them? She too found she could barely bring herself to look at the children, shot in black and white and always with that grainy quality to them, haunting images that spoke of way too much tragedy, Corinna and Ness also quickly averting their eyes.

As they refocused on words rather than pictures, Ness apologised again for Lee's refusal to get involved with help on finding family members of the children.

"His stance on this is clear," she said.

Although Ruby understood, she couldn't help but sigh. "Let's just see how we get on today, shall we, and take it from there. If we need his help, I don't know, maybe we can find a way to persuade him. After all, he cares about Theo too."

Theo, whom they'd last checked a couple of hours previously, when they were told there was 'no change' and that her family were with her, all keeping vigil by her bedside.

"No doubt holding her hand," Corinna murmured, clearly wishing she could too.

"At least it frees us up to do what we have to," Ness consoled. "Gotta look for those silver linings, Corinna. Theo'd be the first to say it. What we're doing is just as important as the medical treatment she's receiving. It could make the difference."

Eliza's parents, Johnny and Maria Brooks, were dead – Johnny aged only forty-nine when he'd passed, Maria sixty-two. One had had a heart attack, the other cancer.

"The result of stress, I imagine," Ness surmised. "Given what happened to their child."

"She had an older brother, though, also called Johnny," Ruby said. "This article here mentions him. He should only be in his sixties."

Corinna, meanwhile, was zoning in on Danny's family. "Seems like he was an only child," she said. "His dad's dead, but I can't find any mention of his mum, Angela Bailey, having died, so I'll see if I can get a lead on her."

A short while later and all Corinna had found out was that Angela had been born in East Grinstead and then moved to Eastbourne when she'd married Nicholas Bailey, Danny's dad. She'd been a teacher at a school there, a private one in the Meads area.

"I'll call the school," Ness decided, having Googled

which one it was.

"Johnny Brooks is proving elusive," Ruby said, again sighing. "I can't find anything more on him."

"Doesn't help that it's a common name." Corinna joined her in that sigh. "There are probably thousands of them in the world."

Ten minutes later, Ness came off the phone to the school in Meads.

"Well?" said Ruby, both she and Corinna looking hopeful.

"I spoke to a very nice lady, the principal there for some time. She was a bit off at first, wasn't going to say a thing, not until I told her I was investigating on behalf of the police."

"Ness! *Did you, really?*" Corinna said, clearly impressed.

Ness nodded. "At this stage, needs must. I avoided giving a name, but, anyway, it got me nowhere. Angela Bailey didn't teach after Danny was killed. She just…left her post, as you might expect. They never heard from her again."

"Poor woman," Corinna breathed.

"But she might be alive," Ruby pointed out, "and so might Johnny Brooks. Ness, I know what you said about Lee. His view on this, but—"

Ness's chair scraped against the lino as she stood up. "Maybe you're right. He might have to reconsider. We're wasting too much time otherwise, looking for needles in haystacks." Grabbing her mobile from the table, she held it up. "I'll call him again, outside." Smiling wryly, she added, "Use all those feminine charms I never knew I had. Beg him, if I have to. He needs to run a search on the names we've found. Wish me luck."

During the time she was gone, Ruby and Corinna continued digging, including referring to census lists taken as recently as 2021.

"Why are some people so hard to find?" complained Corinna. "They just…disappear."

"The world's big. There's a lot of places you can lose yourself."

"And if you don't want to be found…"

"You don't contribute to documents such as a census."

Corinna sat back in her chair. "Wonder if Lee'll come up trumps."

"Better hope so."

"Ness is taking a hell of a long time."

"Which…you know…could be a good sign."

"You think?"

"Uh-huh."

More minutes passed, Ruby checking her watch. Where was Ness? Was this a good sign or not?

"Johnny Brooks, Johnny Brooks, Johnny Brooks," Corinna was murmuring, her attention back on the computer. "Why the hell are there so many Johnny Brookses?"

Ruby was about to answer when the door opened and Ness reappeared. Both Corinna and Ruby instantly swung their chairs round to face her, Ruby practically bursting with anticipation. *Justified* anticipation, as Ness's whole energy was charged.

Ruby stood up as she neared. "Ness?"

"He did it!" she answered, smiling widely. "He ran a check. God, I owe him a decent bottle of red for this! As we know, only some details of the Brooks and Bailey case have been digitised, likely only those deemed essential, but…it was enough. Taking a deeper dive into it, he found—" she swallowed slightly, had to take a deep breath "—he found that when Eliza was murdered, the alarm was raised by another child, Christine Whitmore. Covered in blood, she ran screaming along the road, shouting for help, alerting nearby members of the public. Statements were taken from various children and their families, kids in Eliza's circle of friends, most likely, and then when Danny was found murdered, more statements were taken, Christine Whitmore's name appearing again. Obviously, as most of those questioned were minors, no names were ever made public."

"Christine Whitmore," repeated Ruby, testing it on her tongue. Did it fit? Did it…trigger something? Nothing, only a growing impatience to hear the rest of what Ness had to say.

"After Eliza, the kids generally were deeply shocked. None would be playing out late anymore, neither did they want to, nor would their mums let them. Some were reported as sobbing uncontrollably, of being fearful they might be the next victim. I'm not sure what support mechanisms were like in the seventies, but, anyway, the strange thing regarding Christine Whitmore is that she told police Eliza was her *special* friend. She was totally grief-stricken at finding Eliza. 'She was just lying there,' she said, 'like one of the dolls.'"

"One of the dolls?" repeated Ruby.

Corinna went one step further. "If she had dolls, did she smash their faces in too, then?"

Ness nodded. "My thoughts exactly. When *Danny* was found and the police interviewed Christine, once again she described *him* as her special friend."

"Another one?" murmured Ruby.

"And this time, just after 'special friend'," Ness continued, "the officer who'd taken the statement put a question mark."

Corinna had also stood up, the three of them forming something of a circle, all looking at each other quizzically.

"Can the officer who took the statement be traced?"

Ness shook her head. "There's no note of a specific officer. Regarding details, things weren't as tight in those days. Let's not forget this was Eastbourne in the seventies. I seriously doubt anyone investigating had any real experience of anything like this."

"But I wonder why the question mark," Ruby mused. "Why there was doubt. 'Special friend' isn't that sinister, is it? So this Christine—"

"No. There's no death certificate for Christine Whitmore, none registered, anyway," Ness said, anticipating Ruby's question. "So, despite how it looks, we could be barking up the wrong tree here. Lord knows that's happened before. I think what we do is dive deeper with this new information, check everything online for any mention of her. It's going to be another late day, I'm afraid. Is that okay, girls?"

"It's fine," Ruby assured her. "Theo comes first, and Cash couldn't agree more. His mum's helping with Hendrix. The pair of them are having a ball."

"Good, good," said Ness. "Corinna?"

"Oh God, don't worry about me! We've got to solve this and then let Theo know we've solved it, reach her somehow and bring her back to us, where she belongs. Come on, let's get started. If we find out that Christine Whitmore died around that time, then it sort of confirms everything, doesn't it? That she's the one that begged Theo to help her? So we have to find a way to connect with her too."

"Whoa, hang on!" Ness said, holding her hands up to slow them down. "I'm not done. There's something else of interest that may help us connect with Christine, as you say."

Like Corinna, Ruby had turned from Ness, ready to retake her seat and get going, but now she turned back. "What is it, Ness?"

"Christine's mother was also mentioned in statements, just briefly – *Shirley* Whitmore – and a note was put in pencil beside her name too. One word: 'unemotional'. Like I've said, things really were very different in those days, and I'm not sure Eastbourne was coping, because after what Christine had experienced – she'd found Eliza's body, for Christ's sake! – wouldn't you expect the mother to fuss over her, be hysterical too? What her daughter had witnessed could leave her permanently scarred. And then for her second 'special friend' to die the same way a few days later? But no, Shirley Whitmore was 'unemotional', and it rang alarm bells with someone. Unfortunately, they let those bells ring off."

"Why was she like that?" Corinna wondered. "Fear of her own child, perhaps? Because she knew what Christine was capable of?"

"Maybe," Ness replied. "As I say, it was questioned by someone but clearly never followed up, despite the fact that not long before all this happened, there'd been the high-profile case of another murderer who was a child, Mary Bell. The thing is, no one wants to think a child is capable of such an act. Think of murderers in that era and you'd get Myra Hindley and Ian Brady; they'd become the stereotype. But someone, somewhere, thought differently, at least initially, and then either dismissed those thoughts or someone higher up did, becoming wary of complicated tangents. If this is the child we're looking for, she's dead, but in finding out further about her, focusing on her, visiting some of the places unique to her, we might connect with her. Then again, we might not – this gift we have doesn't always work that way. Lee couldn't find any death certificate issued for Shirley Whitmore either, so she too might still be alive. Our primary aim should be to find out if that's so. And if she is, we visit her, connect with her." Determination flared in Ness's eyes. "Find out *exactly* what went on all those years ago."

Chapter Twenty-Three

As far as Ruby was concerned, Lee deserved much more than a decent bottle of red – a barrel of whiskey, more like, a night on the tiles, a weekend away. If she could grant all that and more, she would. He'd given them a lead – a strong lead, the only one they had.

They'd dug and dug and dug and, at last, found an address for someone who fit the description for Shirley Whitmore, a resident at a care home just outside of Eastbourne on the road to Herstmonceux. Lee had got them access to that care home too, Ruby marvelling at his skill and how people bent to his will, didn't ask too many questions. Lee had been careful to explain that, although he was a police officer, this wasn't a 'current' case and was therefore 'off the record', pending a cold case being reopened if new evidence came to light. It was simply that Shirley Whitmore might have been witness to an unsolved case in the seventies, and there was no more to it than that.

Not an abuse of power, Ruby told herself, not really, but a necessity. Although technically there was the potential for this to become a police matter, for the team right now, this was about Theo's spiritual and physical well-being, and Christine's too. There was no doubt, though, that Lee had sailed very close to the wind for them.

When they'd first found her likely address, the air at The Keep was filled with a jubilant cry. Success when previously there'd been only failure because, regarding Christine, nothing could be found out about her except the address she'd once lived at, a council estate near Hampden Park that had since been demolished to make way for blocks of flats. She was a child that had existed under the radar, something far more possible back then, the digital age still being a way off. Sometimes Ruby resented how much documentation current living required, saw it as an intrusion of privacy, but, by God, for every con, there was a pro. It was easier to track people, usually, to get at least some information on them. *What an enigma you are, Christine.* Or perhaps there were other words for her, considering what she'd done, *feral* being one of them. And if that were true, then what kind of woman did that make Shirley for not being able to control her? Not that they were blaming the mother entirely, of course; they'd searched for Christine's father too, wondering also what kind of man he might have been, Ruby suspecting she knew already, but every alley they'd ventured down regarding him had proven blind.

A bit more digging and they found Whitmore was Shirley's maiden name, that she was the child of Helen and George Whitmore, her birthplace Eastbourne. On Christine's birth certificate was just Shirley's name, her birthplace Eastbourne too, at the same hospital, St Mary's. But just as they could find no death certificate issued for Christine, her name wasn't on the missing persons register either. An enigma indeed.

Ridge View Nursing Home was where Shirley Whitmore lived, Ness initially giving them a ring to ask about her and promptly being told *Ms* Whitmore was not receiving visitors. After Lee's phone call, though, it was all systems go. He'd secured an appointment for his 'colleagues' – the very next day, after lunch at 2:00 p.m.

Having returned home to get a good night's sleep, the team reconvened the next morning. More enquiries were coming in to Psychic Surveys, but all had to be put on hold. One or two potential clients got irate, insisting their cases were urgent.

"It may well be," Ness had said, having spoken to and calmed one of those callers, "but right now there exists varying degrees of urgency, so, if you want our services, I'm afraid you'll have to get in line."

"This is why it'd be handy to have more freelancers," Ruby said to Ness after that phone call, simultaneously sighing and frowning, "so we can field these cases out, but…the gifted, the truly gifted, I mean, prefer to live quietly."

Corinna, sitting opposite Ruby in her attic office, gave a shrug. "Can you blame them?"

Ruby didn't, she never had. To turn the psychic tap on full blast, to face that drama, took some courage. And maybe, she admitted, more than an ounce or two of stupidity.

Although visitors to Theo were being restricted, before the team left for Herstmonceux, they'd been granted a short time with her – 'mere minutes', they'd been told by a nurse who didn't look old enough to be out of school, according to Ness, anyway.

Each took it in turn to hold her hand, trying to reach a still sleeping Theo on a psychic level, but there was nothing, Corinna getting upset about it again.

"It's like she's—"

"Don't," Ness warned. "Don't even think it."

Immediately, Corinna apologised. "Sorry, sorry, I… She will get better, though, won't she? What we're doing, it'll make a difference?"

"We're doing our utmost," Ruby said, trying again to console her. "And on some level, she'll know that and be rooting for us. We *will* connect again, somehow, someway."

Ushered out of Theo's room once those minutes had passed, Ruby wanted to try Michelle again, both phoning and texting, but she got no response to either.

"What are we going to do about Willow?" she asked her colleagues, completely dumbfounded by her former friend's actions.

"Look, if we don't leave now, we'll be late for our visit with Shirley Whitmore," Ness insisted. "When we return, we can figure out what to do about the Bayliss family. You know the school Willow goes to, when she goes, that is. Maybe you can wait for Michelle there. No way she can ignore you if you're standing right there in front of her. Willow needs help. You know it, I know it, and so does Michelle. But for today, we deal with what we can."

Ruby drove them to the nursing home, bringing the Ford to a stop in the car park there. The three of them emerged into a day that had turned cloudy, a slight breeze stirring too as Corinna looked around her.

"Can't see any Ridge," she said.

Ruby smiled. "Maybe if you squint, over there in the distance, just beyond the trees."

Corinna duly obliged. "Nope, still not seeing it." Turning to face the building itself, she added, "I think maybe Colditz might have been a more apt name."

An old building, Victorian, and ramshackle with paint peeling in places, it did indeed have an austere air about it, slim bars on the lower windows a slightly surprising feature.

"This is a nursing home, right, Ness?" Ruby checked.

"*Just* that."

"I didn't think to check. I just…assumed. Oh dear," she added, "there I was, berating those given to assumptions only yesterday, and yet here I am, guilty as charged."

Corinna checked her watch. "Come on, it's nearly two. We'd better get moving."

At the entrance, Ruby pressed the doorbell.

"Jed here?" Ness queried as they waited.

"Nope, not yet, at any rate. Which I'll take as a good sign."

"Must be hard, though, mustn't it?" Corinna interjected.

"What?" asked Ruby.

"Being the mother of a murderer."

"*If* she knew her daughter was a murderer," Ness interjected.

The door was opened at last by a woman in a nurse's white uniform.

"Hello," Ruby greeted, "we're here to see—"

"Shirley Whitmore, yes, of course. Come in. I'm Nurse Winters."

Nurse Winters offered no welcoming smile. Her manner was entirely perfunctory, as austere as the building in which she worked, the two a perfect match for each other.

Colditz was what Corinna had likened it to, a place of incarceration, a jail. And that's what it felt like as Nurse Winters about-turned and, after signing them in, led them through a glazed door that had to be opened with a bunch of keys jangling in almost wicked delight.

There was nothing delightful about this place, though. It was indeed a cold, cold place, as stark inside as it was out, the corridor ahead of them and various rooms leading off it. Other members of staff could be seen coming and going, but none had smiles on their faces. Allegedly, this was just a nursing home, a place to see out your days. Ruby knew many of them weren't as pleasant as they should be, as the people who inhabited them deserved after making it thus far in life, but of the few she'd encountered, mainly due to work, none were like this.

"Ms Whitmore's on the second floor," Nurse Winters informed them. "Would you like to take the lift, or can you manage the stairs?"

Ruby was quick to answer. "The stairs are fine, thanks."

They reached another corridor on another landing, one that ran on and on in what was clearly an institution, not so much a nursing home after all. It reminded her of Cromer, that other institution she'd had dealings with, which had been knocked down to make way for the Brookbridge Estate, all except the high-security wing, of course, where Hames had been a onetime resident. A place that tried to help, which *did* help but sometimes couldn't.

Nurse Winters stopped outside room number thirty-three, and, with the keys jangling yet again, she unlocked the door, a slight gasp from Ruby that this was the case, Ness's and Corinna's eyes also widening. Just what state was Shirley Whitmore in?

"Come in," Nurse Winters said, venturing inside. "Shirley, you've visitors."

Ruby had stepped aside to allow Ness in after Nurse Winters, then Corinna. Finally, she entered. The room was stuffy, in need of a good airing. Although a relatively mild spring day, all windows remained sealed. A slight partition divided the room, another door set within it, likely leading to an en suite. There were some luxuries, Ruby thought, half fancying there'd be none. *Homely* touches, though, remained entirely absent. It comprised a table and a chair, a very small, very cheap TV, a shabby armchair positioned in front of it, bereft of any cushions, and some low shelving with a few books – Ruby could see the dust on them from where she stood. The walls were grey, and there was a grey carpet beneath her feet, no rug to break the uniformity. Soulless was how she'd describe the room, and yet a soul existed within it. Ms Whitmore. There in the bed, for the moment out of sight beyond the partition, Ness the first one to set eyes on her, swallowing hard.

"Gosh," Corinna whispered, as she too encountered her.

Then it was Ruby's turn.

Shirley Whitmore was tiny, birdlike, propped up against pillows, straggly grey hair resting on bony shoulders, her skin pale and mottled, equally bony hands in her lap and fingers entwined as she stared back, not at them but something distant, barely blinking.

Ruby turned to Nurse Winters. "What's…wrong with her?" she whispered.

Nurse Winters had no such compunction about keeping her voice low. "What's wrong with her? You tell me. That's what you're here for, isn't it? That officer fellow said you wanted to investigate. So—" she shrugged "—investigate." About to turn, she seemed to think better of her attitude, adding, "Catatonic. That's the term for her condition. She was admitted here three years ago after a spell in hospital, a *long* spell. It isn't many nursing homes who take people like this on, only the more—" she paused again, breathed in before exhaling "—*specialised* ones." All brisk efficiency again, she hurried on. "We've done our best by her. Tried to get her to talk. Used various methods. Nothing. So…good luck to you. I mean it. With whatever methods you're about to use." She raised her keys, the jangling of them especially jarring this time. "I'll be outside if you need me."

On leaving the room, Ruby was stunned further when she heard the lock turn in the door, trapping them with yet another enigma.

Chapter Twenty-Four

"Methods." Ness was not happy with that description. "Just what kind of methods do they sanction in a place like this for a woman like her? We're in the twenty-first century, as a society, as an entire world. We know so much more than we used to, what works and what doesn't regarding mental illness. There's so much research to access, and yet some"—she inclined her head towards the door, outside which Nurse Winters was allegedly waiting—"insist on sticking to the old ways, the *bad* old ways. There'll be more investigations after we're done here, you can bet on it. About this place, rather than just one of its patients. My God, this *room*! We've got to get a window open."

Corinna marched over to the windows, likely glad of something to do.

"How long has she been like this, I wonder," said Ruby, inching closer to the bed. "She's been at Ridge View for three years, but before that, she was in a hospital and, from the sounds of it, in the same state. And then before that, even, when her daughter was alive, she was 'unemotional'. Because of what? Terror?"

Ness nodded, her eyes narrowing. "*Possibly* because of terror."

Able to release the window only an inch, Corinna

returned to Shirley's bedside to join the others. The ensuing silence was as stagnant as the air in the room.

"Do we just…talk to her?" Corinna said eventually.

"It's as good a start as any," replied Ness, signalling for them to move a little closer.

The bed was a regulation hospital bed, bars on either side of that too. As Ruby stood there, all she felt was compassion, wondering if anyone had actually felt that way towards this woman in recent years. Or was she just seen as a burden, taking up valuable time, space and resources? She was another hiding deep inside herself, any misgivings she might have had, any suspicions, any knowledge, too burdensome to face. *I understand*, Ruby tried to project.

Ness made the address, speaking clearly, calmly and respectfully. She introduced the three of them, then didn't beat about the bush, got straight down to business as to why they were there – because of their friend, also lying in a regulation hospital bed, and because of Shirley's daughter too, Christine.

"We suspect, and we think you suspect too, that your daughter was…ill, that she was behind the deaths of two other children, both around the same age as her, Eliza Brooks and Danny Bailey, both from the same area of Eastbourne that you lived in back in the early 1970s and both murdered within days of each other. In fact, Christine was reported as finding the body of Eliza Brooks, who she called her special friend, and raised the alarm. She called Danny her special friend too. You spoke to the police alongside Christine regarding the deaths. You were noted as being…unemotional. Shirley, we don't want to add to your distress. Please believe us when we say we're only here to help, but we also need to help our friend and Christine.

"We believe Christine's dead, Shirley, something you may or may not know. I've told you we're psychic, and it was Theo she made contact with, that she begged for help. She's a grounded spirit, you see, unable to pass, to return to Source, where we all come from. Theo couldn't help, not at the time, but she wants to now. We don't know how your daughter died. There's no death certificate. She's not even on a missing list. She just…disappeared. Which must have been tough on you too. Perhaps you even feel terrible guilt about this because…because you may have wished it to happen. Shirley, we're all human, but we're all spirit too. Despite the crimes Christine committed, she deserves peace. If Theo can't reconnect with her, we will try to. Once she's on the other side and in the light, she can learn and evolve. There's hope for her, and for you and for Theo, for all of us. The one thing I think you've given up on is hope, and it's the one thing you can't afford to let go. None of us can. Hope *and* love. If you can hear me, Shirley, let me know. Like your daughter, you've been in the darkness for too long."

It was so still in the room, Shirley still too, giving no sign she'd heard a word.

Ruby dragged her eyes from the woman and surveyed the room again. There was no history here, no photographs of her when she was younger, certainly no family photographs, no obvious personal mementos anywhere on display. The woman was stricken and in the worst way. Emotions having smashed her against the shores of life, to leave her stranded there. What had been wrong with her daughter? Ruby remembered something a past client had said, one who'd called them in about a disturbance in his home, which had indeed turned out to be the rattling of ancient pipes. Whilst investigating, he'd offered her and Corinna the obligatory cup of tea, which they'd accepted, then proceeded to tell them his life story. He had said he was a Borstal boy, referring to the youth detention centres that used to exist for young offenders – their aim was to reform wayward behaviour but, in reality, they were brutal places that only nurtured more of the same.

"ADHD was what I had," he'd told them, "dyslexia, dyspraxia, the whole shebang. Except no one knew it, of course. No one tested you for things like that in the old days, not people like me, anyway. They just took you at face value, branded you a troublemaker 'cause you couldn't sit still, said you were disruptive instead. You got a reputation, and in the end you lived up to it. What else were you supposed to do? People thought you were bad, so that's what you became. A self-fulfilling prophecy. I spent so much of my youth in borstals," he'd said, "then after that, when I got older, the prison system, but don't worry, don't look so shocked! My wife, God rest her soul, saved me. Clever woman, she was. She knew what I was straightway, got me tested finally, then got me all the help and meds I needed to balance myself out. I calmed right down, but more importantly, I finally understood myself. Forgave myself too. So many slipped through the net back then, so many…suffered. I don't blame anyone, though, not now. We were all affected by ignorance."

Alan was his name, his blue eyes with a kindness to rival Theo's. Not bad at all, not at heart – but his problems were relatively mild compared to some other conditions. What about schizophrenia? Psychosis? Bipolar and dissociation? Christine could have suffered from any of those, or indeed a combination, and her mother, a *single* mother – which must have been a struggle in itself, a stigma attached to it back then – might not, as had happened with Alan, have known how to deal with it. Denied it, even. Until it was too late.

Ruby reached out, felt compelled to. *I know what it's like to deal with madness in the family, to feel helpless in the face of it.* And yes, she had to admit, afraid too, no matter how hard you tried to deny it. To wonder also where that madness came from, if everyone would stare at her, blame her somehow. Shirley was the mother; *of course* they blamed her.

Poor, poor woman. A child was a gift, a blessing, except when they weren't, when they were a curse. And yet still a mother would love them, even if that love destroyed them.

Skin touched skin as Ruby lifted Shirley's hand and enclosed her own around it.

I'm sorry, so sorry.

No one *had* touched her in this way for so long, with any form of understanding.

Therefore, she was doing a good thing, the right thing.

Compassion was at the heart of everything Psychic Surveys did, an essential part of their approach, very often the reason behind their successes.

Love, empathy and understanding.

So why was Ness's face contorting in sudden horror? Corinna's, too. She was shouting something. "No!" Was that it? Ruby couldn't quite make it out, because the world around her, the room she was in, that awful room that was as much a shell as its occupant, was fading. Not fading into darkness, though. There were images; there was life. Another person's life: Shirley Whitmore's.

She'd connected with her, truly connected.

It's okay, she wanted to tell Ness and Corinna, *this is what we came here for, to see, so don't stop me now, don't stop…us. Shirley was listening after all, Ness; you broke through. This is what we wanted, remember? She's trying to help us, and, in turn, we can help Theo and Christine. No way you should stop me.*

It all happened so fast.

No chance of stopping any of it.

Chapter Twenty-Five

Ruby was standing in another room, looking around, disembodied somehow, or rather…buried in the body of another. That might be a more accurate way to describe it. Like being…imprisoned? Surely not. She could break free whenever she chose. Ness and Corinna would help her to do that, force Shirley's hand from hers, sever the link. She could try to do it herself right now, put it to the test, at least, but she was just too curious, and it seemed Ness and Corinna had hesitated too, complying with her wishes.

Ah, this gift. What she was dealing with was yet another aspect of the paranormal, but not one totally unfamiliar to her. She'd done this before, entered another person's psyche, not a living person, though, that of a spirit, Cynthia Hart of Highdown Hall. She'd seen and felt exactly as Cynthia had, the crushing blow that had been delivered. Had she thought the same thing could happen again here, deep down? Is that why she'd done it, taken Shirley's hand? Actively *willed* this to happen?

She might have ventured into Shirley Whitmore's mind, but she had to remember the reasons why, that this was ultimately about Theo. If she had indeed actively willed it to happen, crossed a line, a divide, then it was because Theo *wouldn't* connect, not with them, her closest friends, because she was on a crusade of her own to find

Christine. It was Ruby who'd done that, though, because look, there she was in front of her, *in front of her mother.* Christine was standing in this other room, in this other era, aged twelve or thereabouts and staring upwards, such…defiance in eyes that were as dark as coal.

Ruby had thought Christine was feral, *wild*. Certainly, that prior appraisal appeared correct because she *was* unkempt, smudges of dirt smeared across her cheeks, clothes with holes in them and hair that was greasy and lank, and, oh God…something was crawling out of it! Trudging along her forehead, something tiny but which made Ruby flinch – a louse? The girl was infested with them? *What the fuck?*

Able to drag her eyes from the child, Ruby studied her surrounds further, just as she'd done at the nursing home. A living room. The décor not light and airy but with a somewhat claustrophobic feel. And yet, although tiny in proportion, it was neat enough. The walls were covered in a floral pattern, something that should have lent some cheer, tiny flowers in an abundance of colours, but they failed entirely to do the job, the background upon which they resided stained brown with nicotine. As for furniture, there was a sofa, also brown, room for only two people to sit on it – mother and daughter? Shoulder to shoulder? There was a TV, but as it had been in that twenty-first-century room, its screen remained blank. As well as a sideboard, there was a low coffee table with an ashtray upon it, one overflowing with lipstick-stained cigarette stubs. The light that hung in the middle of the room gave off a stark rather than comforting glow, a sickly yellowish tone to it, but at least a lampshade covered it – although that too was nicotine stained. And it *stank*! Ruby wished she could dull that sense, at least.

There were no knickknacks or ornaments of any sort, no framed photographs. No pictures hung on the walls either, something to relieve that relentless floral landscape. Similar to the room Shirley Whitmore lived in now, it was entirely devoid of personality.

But of the personalities here, at least one was twisted and dangerous.

Words were being spoken, and someone was trembling in response to them.

Such a strange thing – she was observing this as Shirley, the one she'd connected with, and yet it all seemed so distant, the scene clear in front of her yet mysterious too.

The words being hurled were terrible to hear, awful, and yet her focus had shifted from the child to something far more benign, as if Shirley couldn't bear it and averted her eyes.

"Filthy whore, scum, bitch. *Poisonous. Rotten.* Look at you, trembling in fear. You're scared, aren't you? So scared. Weak! Pitiful! Can't look after me, can't look after yourself either. One day…know what I'm going to do? Hurt you too. Soon. Soon. You don't deserve to exist. Burden. An insult. Crying! You're crying! Weak, weak thing!"

Other than the absence of all things personal, this was a normal room, the kind that had existed all over the land in the seventies, and yet what was happening, on so many levels, was as far from normal as it was possible to get and so, so confusing.

For the umpteenth time, she questioned it: how could a child say these things? From what source had she learnt it? She was conducting a reign of terror inside her own home, away from the prying eyes of the world. A horror story unfurling.

The scene changed, just switched from one to the other with no warning, growing dark. Ruby wasn't standing anymore. She was…lying down – that was it. In the house still? In one of the bedrooms? She tried to turn her head, to confirm that was exactly where she was, but found she could only gaze upwards at the ceiling. There were shadows flitting across it, performing some kind of dance macabre. Those that had broken free from the darkness? Gorging themselves on the terror of the situation.

Whispers… Was that a voice? Travelling through the wall towards her, no respite from the attack the child was waging, a child that had to be possessed. To look like that…to talk like that…the lowest energy of all finding a haven inside her.

Whore…bitch…filthy, filthy, filthy. You don't deserve to exist. Burden.

They were similar words to before, when they were standing in the living room, an onslaught she'd correctly surmised was without end, delivered day and night.

Such violent trembling. A whimper too. Ruby was experiencing all of it, and yet still she remained so distant – both a blessing and a curse – unable to intervene, to call out, to offer any kind of solace. It was like she was the one catatonic, not Shirley. And yet Shirley wasn't truly either, not if she was reliving this in her mind, the torture of it embedded there.

Another swift change of scene. She was in the kitchen, another tiny room that contained only the basics. It was so different to the kitchen of Ruby's childhood home, which was a warm and cosy space, always so welcoming, her grandmother practically a permanent fixture there, baking an assortment of cakes and biscuits, the smell in the air mouthwatering. Here there was a stench, worse than in the living room. Even if your throat was desert-parched, no way you'd accept a drink of any kind, imbibe further what was putrid.

Something went flying past her head. Ruby ducked, or thought she had, although she half suspected Shirley had just sat there and endured it. *Unemotional.*

A plate was what it was, with some kind of mush on it that Ruby couldn't identify, smashing against the wall and breaking into several pieces, the mush drip, drip, dripping down it. There was other muck on the wall from previous plates hurled, which had become encrusted, the will to make this house anything other than a shell, a place to exist, long since diminished. More plates were smashed, about six or seven, all pitched in fury, a piercing scream erupting that reached a terrible crescendo, that Ruby wished she could shut out. Why wasn't Shirley lifting her hands, attempting to do just that? Too scared to move, perhaps? That's the impression Ruby got. Because any reaction would be met with further attack. The scream, though, was unbearable.

A bang at the door somehow overrode it, also furious. Neighbours? It had to be. This was a tiny house, no doubt in some kind of terrace. Screams like that would be heard the length and breadth of the street, surely!

There was a rush of something. Shirley moving? Down the hallway?

A door opening. Light! Only now did Ruby realise how much the light had forsaken this place, been deliberately shut out, curtains closed and blinds closed too. Light was the enemy. But there it was, trying to cut through the congealed atmosphere.

She heard more garbled words. An explanation.

"Sorry… Difficult, yes. Tantrum. No. No. Fine. Will be fine. Really sorry."

Ask for help! Ruby wanted to yell. *Don't suffer this alone!*

But people did. Even in today's world, they suffered without a word to one another. She was a woman who couldn't control her child. Was there any shame greater?

The thought, the realisation, made Ruby shudder. She flinched too when the door closed. The woman swung around, and Ruby could see – caught in the gloom at the far end of the hallway – the girl again, Christine, just staring at her, a demon in disguise.

There was a rushing sound, the sound of the child rushing at the mother? Armed with yet more threats. But then everything went black again, and Ruby heard not threats but sobbing. Quiet sobbing. Restrained. Something of a plea on Shirley's lips: *Help me, help me, help me.* If only she'd been brave before when the neighbour had come calling, if only she'd said that then. Yes, there existed evil, but there also existed such good! The neighbour had come calling, maybe not solely to complain about the screaming but also to see what was going on – to offer the help Shirley needed. Because this battle, no way could it be fought alone.

Such deep, deep grief. Such…bewilderment. Such questioning too. *What did I do to deserve this, deserve her? Am I what she says I am? Is that why? Filthy. Scum. Rotten inside. Is this my punishment? I must be that! Worthless. A burden.*

Ruby had connected with Shirley, but it was on too superficial a level, because she was replying to her, telling the woman that none of it was true, not to absorb it, believe it, or succumb but to get out of there, get help, yet still there was no hint Shirley could hear her, only the child, who was whispering, continually whispering, who was laughing – a maniacal sound. What Shirley had bred was mad. And it would end in yet more madness.

Another scene change, a bedroom, but different to the other Ruby had been in. Her head not caught in such a vicelike grip, she was able to look around, discovering it was packed with junk, the bed at its centre floating in a sea of debris. Such a huge jumble of stuff, it was hard to separate any of it, although she scrutinised further. An arm. Was that a baby's arm poking out of the debris? Ruby's heart thudded. Could it possibly be? Then she saw a hand – just that – reaching out and pulling the arm from the debris. It was the body of a baby indeed, a doll, though, its pink, mercifully plastic body naked and its head shoved in. More dolls appeared. They were everywhere. All perfectly intact except for their heads, which had been crushed or sometimes ripped from the body to lie there staring through beady black eyes at nothing.

Dolls…dolls… dolls… She'd heard mention of dolls recently. *Think, Ruby, think! What was it about the dolls?*

Eliza, that was it, and Danny…their heads shoved in too. *Like one of the dolls.* Yes! That's what Ness had said, or rather what had been reported when taking a statement from Christine after she'd found Eliza – *She was just lying there, like one of the dolls.*

This room she was in, it was her room, Christine's – the epicentre – the chaotic surrounds again a reflection of the occupant. That was what Shirley was trying to tell her.

Look! Look at this! What she's capable of! The dolls were mere practice, so many of them, so much fury, *delicious glee*, visited on them before she had moved on to bigger things, to real-life dolls, other children, her friends, those she deemed special.

Oh God, Shirley, why didn't you stop it? If you knew what she could do. Why?

A shrieking again, the howl of a banshee. Ruby closed her eyes, refused to see any more. This room, this house, this pair. She had to escape it all. She'd seen enough horror, could take no more, her heart at bursting point.

Don't show me the victims. Don't show me the victims. The words kept repeating in her mind. *I don't want to see…kids that way. Please. Don't.*

What was taking Corinna and Ness so long? Why hadn't they broken the connection, forced her from Shirley? A memory flickered, which she tried to catch hold of but failed – they'd tried to warn her, hadn't they? Against doing this, touching the woman?

It was no use. She couldn't recall the details, her mind too preoccupied with determination not to see the ruined faces of what had been flesh and blood. Eliza had been such a cherub, and Danny cheeky. Beautiful children. Destroyed. By her. Christine.

Ruby would *not* be witness to that. Her will was something valid too.

She was falling, and she knew what it meant: that once again she was retreating inside herself. This time to hide. And no matter that it was dark in there, that it was bleak, because anything was better than being in the Whitmore household.

Let it go, Shirley. You have to let it all go too. Don't keep reliving this horror.

Shirley? She didn't matter here. Nor Christine.

Deep inside herself, it was empty, lonely.

But some hells were better than others.

In the void she'd returned to, Ruby curled up tight, as small as a child herself, and wept.

Chapter Twenty-Six

Was it possible to dream in a place like this? Or was it dangerous to even attempt to do so, because such dreams would inevitably become nightmares? Ruby didn't have the answer to this or any other question. *There's so much we know about and so much we don't.* Knowledge was a vast ocean in which you could endlessly swim, going round and around and around as the shore drifted further away.

A gift. A blessing. An ability. What she channelled was something she sought only to use for the good of others, a power that exceeded the natural. Which she'd encouraged, had been taught to respect and nurture from a young age, and yet she knew, courtesy of her mother, how perilous it could also be. Jessica, though, had used it with bad intent, at least when she was younger – *abused* it. Ruby hadn't. And yet what did it matter that she'd denied the temptation? Where was the reward? Her mother was currently living life in the light with her partner, Saul, and Ruby was here in a place like this. Anchored.

Who's the fool now? Who's the idiot? Just as they'd discussed shutting it down in Willow, she should have shut it down in herself. The world was not hers to save! And now look, who would save her? Ness hadn't, or Corinna, and there was no Cash here, no Hendrix.

Children. Whether or not it was a dream, she could

suddenly see them. Not the sweet smiling face of her baby – which she longed for – but a group of friends playing, dressed in T-shirts and shorts or summer dresses, their laughter and shrieks high-pitched as they engaged in a game of tag… Ruby baulked to see them, because she knew in amongst them were *those* children, the killer and her victims. The sun was shining, the birds were singing; there was no hint of what was to come. It was an innocent game for now, but soon another would take its place. Two would peel off and then again, a couple of days later, another two, one of them the same person.

That was why she'd come here, because she'd felt certain she'd see their faces in the violent throes of death, Eliza's and Danny's, and she didn't want to.

So why was she dreaming of them? Was there simply no escape, not now she'd come this far? Was it inevitable she would see? All part of the package, the experience?

Not if she could help it. If she just screwed her eyes tighter, became smaller, hid deeper, ventured further into the void, would all this end? The promise of pain.

She'd do just that until all dreams of children playing innocent and not-so-innocent games faded.

Oh, Christine, how come you opened yourself up to such evil?

Slowly, slowly, their images faded, Ruby alone now in yet another vast ocean, suspended. A dark place but a shelter too. It didn't matter how long she stayed: seconds, minutes, hours, days, months or years. All that mattered was that she was alone.

No way of knowing how much time was passing. She simply…drifted. Slept again, but this time dreamlessly. She was tired. So tired. Had been for so long. In her late twenties, and yet she felt so much older, ancient even. Every bone, every joint ached.

But there was also comfort, also relief. She was happy to sleep forever if sleep was like this. Funny how people feared nothingness, the possibility that once life had ended, they'd be erased just like a flame, snuffed out.

Ghosts exist, don't they? She'd lost count how many times she'd been asked that. *I've seen one. I have!* That insistence coming from those who tried to convince themselves. But yes, spirits existed. There was indeed something else out there beyond the veil, the great divide, whatever anyone saw fit to call it. But not here where she was. There was nothing, and because of that, surely nothing to fear? This place was different from that other one she'd been in, the one she'd been taken to. It was a place she'd found on her own. Oh, she mustn't think any further, keep contemplating. It was entirely possible to still the body – Shirley had done that in the nursing home, in her hospital bed, staring into nothing – but the mind? That took some doing.

The mind was all part of the soul, that was why; they were hooked up together.

No! No! No! She was analysing still! Trying to work things out, the reasons for everything. There might be spirits, other realms, but sometimes, just sometimes, there was no reasoning. Best to accept that, be content with it. And close her eyes again.

Be still, Ruby. Be still.

Silence. Beautiful silence. Nothingness in all its unheralded glory.

A prison?

Maybe. But a comfortable one.

She even smiled at one point, forcing serenity further.

Who knew it could be this good? A place in which she wasn't special, not in possession of any heightened ability, where she was simply nothing too.

Bliss! It really was.

Perhaps she'd stay forever.

Drifting.

Ruby…Ruby…

Blot out everything.

Ruby…

The bad, the ugly, even the good, the magnificent.

Ruby!

If that was the price she had to pay, so be it.

Spooky Ruby!

Ruby's eyes snapped open. She was still in the darkness, which was a relief, but she wasn't alone.

Who'd just called her that? A male or a female? And who had called her that before, a long time ago? *Think, Ruby, think!* A girl, a friend, a *child*, Lisa. That's who. Not just a friend, a best friend, one whom she'd told her secret to, that she could connect with spirits, thinking Lisa would keep that secret, maybe even…admire her?

Oh, come on, who'd admire someone like you?

Ruby swallowed. Peace was far too fleeting, chased away as older memories returned.

Lisa hadn't admired her; she'd been horrified, had stopped being her best friend. Tried to get others to taunt her too. *Spooky Ruby! Spooky Ruby! Spooky Ruby!*

A terrible memory, but not the worst.

The worst was the person who'd just called her that.

Worse by the fact he knew what had happened and how much it had hurt.

Aaron Hames.

She wasn't alone. She'd *never* been alone. A fool indeed to think it.

He was here, both a conduit and her nemesis, in these dark depths, which wasn't a happy place at all. On the contrary, it was the *un*happiest.

She'd entered his prison, the one she kept him in. He was all around her.

Told you, didn't I, the last time we met, about that Lisa. If I was around then like I was fucking supposed to be – as your father, Ruby, your father! – I'd have sewn her fucking mouth shut for saying that. Or...I'd have taken her by the hand and congratulated her for outing you, for letting everyone know what walked amongst them. Not someone normal like all the other kids but someone mad...as mad as they say her old dad is. Oh, it's in there, Ruby. You know it and I know it, that same potential. That's almost more frightening, isn't it? The thought of going mad. Or...I don't know...maybe it's already happened. You've succumbed, finally, the seed of my loins. You must have done, because here you are, in the darkness alongside me. Able to hear me so well.

Ruby swung round, tried to see the man behind the voice, then questioned what she was doing. No way she wanted to see him! Gazing on his face would be even more terrifying than Eliza's or Danny's face after Christine was done with them. Could she go any deeper than she already was? There had to be a place Hames didn't exist! Where he couldn't follow her.

You just don't listen, do you? There's nowhere, Ruby, none at all. We're connected, you and I, mind, body and soul. Did you really, really think you could escape me? You came to visit me, then just turned your back and walked out, resolved never to contact me again. Oh, Ruby, Ruby, Ruby, how stupid can you be? We've been in contact ever since. Every time you look in the mirror, boom! There I am! Standing in front of you.

True, all true. Every word. She *did* connect with him every time she looked in the mirror and saw his likeness, every time she…

Ah, yes, yes, of course, every time you look at your baby! You see me in him too.

Deeper, deeper and deeper. There had to be a safe haven! Or was he telling the truth about that also, that actually he was at the core of her? Always.

All she could do was as she'd done, curl up small again and try to disappear, become the nothing she craved. Eyes screwed shut, body like a foetus, she was something pathetic, vulnerable, and still he showed her no mercy.

Mad. Deranged. Abnormal. Like me, you're all that and more. We walk in the shadow of each other. Through the years we've done that, ever since you were born. Ruby, lift your head and listen to me. Let the truth sink in: you cannot escape me. In life. In death. I'm coming for you. Recently, you checked up on me. I know you did. To see I was still in there, in that filthy, disgusting place full of people like you, those that think they can make a difference, save me. Fucking fools! The true imbeciles! Just like you, my own fucking daughter. I said lift your head and listen! You bitch! You fucking, fucking bitch! Nothing can keep me from you, not least a cell with bars on the windows. I'm free, Ruby! My mind is. And I'm coming for you. All of hell is! All those creatures your bitch of a gran sent after me when I first visited you, not the other way around, when you were a kid – they're with me still, and they're hungry still. They want to gorge on your blood, which is my blood. They will feast, Ruby! Feast! Soon! Very soon! LISTEN

TO ME! LISTEN! There's no escape.

Ruby...Ruby...don't listen to him. Listen to me. Ruby, please. You have to.

What fresh horror was this? Besides Hames's, another voice was commanding her. She mustn't listen, not to either of them, but focus on her heart, which was beating wildly in her chest, stop it from continually lurching. Stop everything, the whole damned ride. "Leave me alone, just leave me alone. Both of you."

Turned out, hell was hell after all. There were no soft versions of it.

Ruby...listen.

Ruby screamed as something touched her hand, tried to pull back.

It was something cold that wouldn't relinquish its grip, something...stronger than her.

That man, her father, was still screaming. She could hear him calling her such savage names, for that's exactly what he was – a savage. She knew she would hear his words forevermore ringing in her ears. No more silence. Ever.

Ruby!

Who was this other person calling out? Who had taken hold of her hand and wouldn't let go? Hames was at her core, but so too was someone else. Had followed her there.

Who'd be that stupid?

That brave?

Ruby, raise your head and look at me, only me.

Whore, bitch, scum, filthy, filthy whore... Miraculously, Hames's voice was at last growing fainter. But should she give in, be so easily fooled? This thing that had hold of her, what if it was him? Hames? Trying to mimic someone gentler, a friend, then cackling, roaring with laughter if she believed.

There was a hand on her chin too, just as cold, pushing upwards, forcing her to look.

A bark.

Jed?

That at last persuaded her to look – that wondrous possibility. He was the one that had followed her in, her dog, her protector?

But it wasn't Jed.

It wasn't Hames either but another monster. And yet…in her eyes there was only concern.

"Don't let him talk to you like that," Christine Whitmore said, "the way my mother used to talk to me."

Chapter Twenty-Seven

Ruby was rising, pushing upwards through layers and layers of darkness. This child, this supposed monster, the one she'd seen through Shirley Whitmore's eyes, a grubby, filthy, feral little thing upon which lice crawled, was dragging her…where? What realm would she next inhabit with this child beside her, what further horrors witnessed?

"No, no, no," she said, trying again to pull her hand from Christine's. "I don't want to see what you've got to show me, not that, not *them*. There are boundaries. Please."

Their progress didn't halt. "You have to see," was all Christine said, so calm in the face of Ruby's increasing panic. "It's the only way."

A feral child – or the product of neglect?

As the thought entered Ruby's mind, the child turned towards her as if, like Theo and Ness, she could catch thoughts. She *acknowledged* it.

"Where's Jed?" Ruby said, remembering what else she'd heard in that other place – a bark. When there was no reply, she called out instead, praying her voice would carry, that this was not a place that swallowed sound, deadened it. "Jed? Jed, are you here? Ness, Corinna? Where are you all? We're supposed to look out for each other, be there."

As despair threatened to surge once again, the scene

changed. There was no more darkness but the four walls of a living room instead, the one she'd stood in before with Shirley and Christine.

The girl, her hand still in Ruby's, gave a violent shake of the head. "Shirley…*Mum*…" She spat that last word as if it had got stuck somehow. "She manipulated everything."

Ruby stared at Christine, saw how anger had pushed her former concern aside, and knew she had to be careful. *Which one of you is telling the truth?*

Before, Christine had stood in front of Shirley, Ruby seeing this as well. She'd been staring defiantly upwards at her, and Shirley had been…trembling, that was it. Terrified by the strangeness of her daughter, this creature she'd produced. And yet when Ruby now peered closer at the child by her side, she saw it was Christine who was trembling, who was terrified, although still that spark of defiance shone in her eyes, something Ruby couldn't help but marvel at, for there was a bravery there too, a resistance. Again, like before, she heard words, the threat that accompanied them: 'You're so scared, aren't you? One day…know what I'm going to do…hurt you too.' She'd wondered how a child could say such things, the violence in them a match for Hames. Remembering him, she jolted, and Christine tightened her grip. Ruby got the message, and she was right: *One step at a time.* Right now, this wasn't about her own parent; this child had rescued her from him and his ongoing torment. Perhaps, then, what she was being shown, this new version of events, was the truth, and Christine needed rescuing too from a mother who kept her trapped in memories, reliving them over and over. *Twisting* them. The world might not know of

Christine, this child who had lived – and died – under the radar, who'd been neglected indeed, but that didn't mean she was free to just disappear.

As quickly as it had done previously, the scene changed. She was in a dark room, lying next to someone – Christine? – their hands still entwined. Despite this, she tried to turn her head, wanting to check, but she couldn't. Again, as before, her eyes were fixed solely on the ceiling, upon which those strange breakaway shadows played.

The incessant whisperings began. *There's something rotten in you, something poisonous. You're evil, evil, evil.*

No sanctity, not anywhere in the house, not when the walls were so thin and night's silence carried whispers loud and clear through bricks and mortar. This time, they were both trembling – she *and* Christine, listening to the mouth pressed against the opposite wall, drumming the message home, day and night, for years and years and years – *You're evil, evil, evil.* Trying to deflect, perhaps, what was in herself, like someone suffering from a type of Münchausen, pushing what was rotten inside her deep into her daughter instead, *enjoying* the process, the very act of torture and the power it gave her. From trembling, from being so frightened too, Ruby also felt a spark of defiance, the one that had eventually lit in the child. Anger too for what had played out here behind closed doors – and was *still* doing so in Shirley's mind. There was no greater power than a parent over a child, and in a free world, no restraint over who could wield it.

At last Ruby found she could turn her head. It *was* Christine beside her. Rather than catch Ruby's glance, though, she carried on looking upwards, caught in this web of horror, entrenched, but no longer alone, Ruby there for the ride. The pair of them in this together.

Just as the child had squeezed her hand, Ruby squeezed back. Was this the truth, all that she was thinking, the conclusions she was reaching? Shirley's catatonic state was one she'd willingly imposed on herself because she wanted to live in these types of memories, where she still had power? Christine was dead, and so a world without the object of her abuse in it was a world no good to Shirley.

It made a dreadful sense, more sense than that other scenario in which Christine was the perpetrator – a child dominating an adult, although that did happen, she had to remind herself; there'd been instances documented. Basically, as she already knew, *anything* was possible, and so she must be careful. Separate fact from fiction.

Another change of scene, a kitchen, a plate being hurled, screaming that made Ruby at least want to raise her hands and protect her ears – impossible when the child refused to let go of her hand. A door being banged on, someone hurrying down the hall in response to it. Voices. One heated, full of complaint. The other placating…explaining. *Blaming.*

Ruby was sitting in the kitchen, and the child was with her, an…unemotional child. Shirley had been described that way in police notes, and yet Christine was now the same. Had the note been in reference to them both?

Another squeeze of the hand.

One emotionless when dealing with police, trying to reign in the beast within, prevent it from showing itself, the other emotionless in private…because she had to be. A survival technique, that defiance again, a refusal to give the beast what it wanted: matching fury.

Another squeeze of the hand, just as all murmurings

ceased and the front door closed.

Silence followed, and Ruby's heart beat faster because of it. She and the child were no longer sitting but in the kitchen doorway. Ah, so much defiance in the child, so much fear! There was that rushing sound Ruby had experienced before, just before everything had gone black, before the sobbing had started. Pleas for help that were useless because kept private.

It didn't go black this time; the rushing was Shirley flying down the hallway right at them, the very stuff of nightmares, her features – so ordinary otherwise, unremarkable – distorted beyond recognition by the gloom and by rage, by what she harboured.

Ruby opened her mouth to scream, tried to backtrack, desperate to avoid her, but Christine squeezed her hand again, tighter still. *Do what I do* the message this time.

This scene would change again soon. Wouldn't it? Before she reached them and did whatever she was going to do to Christine, raise her hand, then bring it down upon her flesh. Ruby could just imagine it, the child suffering the beating, swallowing her screams. Burying them. There was no change of scene, though, and Shirley was almost upon them.

What a whirlwind she was! Bursting with all things bitter.

Don't react! Don't react! Don't react! That's what Ruby kept telling herself. *If you want to survive, do not react.*

Unable to help herself, to bear what was coming, she closed her eyes.

There was no impact of flesh against flesh but a hissing in her ear instead, the breath that wafted over her bitter too, a fetid stench, all things ugly spewing from one psyche into another, trying to claim yet more real estate, to infect and keep on infecting.

With her eyes still closed, Ruby clamped her mouth shut, hardly breathed. No neighbour would come running at this, because just as the child had been, it was below the radar, but the woman's fury would spill over again at some stage, again become louder. Any control she had slipping. And when it did, would they come running a second or third time? Armed with complaints? *Stop that noise! I can't bear it any longer, can't hear myself think!* Or would they think they'd done enough, had tried to intervene? Maybe they'd grown a little afraid too, sensing what was truly happening a few feet away, albeit on a subconscious level, drowning out that fear and the Whitmores by turning up the TV a little louder, or popping to the shop for more supplies of milk and bread, even though milk and bread were already in the fridge, just until the drama was over.

Ruby wished so hard this woman would stop the flow of vitriol, shut her mouth as tight as Ruby's, find it in herself to fight back against whatever it was that possessed her. *It doesn't have to be like this!* she wanted to scream. *Get help! Go to a church, speak to a priest.* Or was it just too late? The woman that had been Shirley gone.

Ruby felt someone snatch at her hand, her *free* hand, and her eyes flew open. Shirley had grabbed hold of her. Ruby was linked to them both now, mother and child, was being yanked forwards, back up a hallway even gloomier than before, shadows again breaking free and dancing along the walls, just as they'd danced on the bedroom ceiling, lively, gleeful things that were welcomed here, allowed to accumulate, rejoicing in that.

Where are we going?

Ruby fired the thought at the child, but Christine remained mute. Too emotionless, too frozen. Desperate to protect herself against this new onslaught, Ruby tried to visualise the light, the greatest protection of all, but the shadows and the darkness fought against her, made it difficult to even *remember* the light. The journey continuing, Ruby and Christine were forced up the stairs, Ruby's heart freezing right alongside Christine's. She knew what was coming next, the bedroom with the dolls in it.

Christine's bedroom?

The hissing voice of earlier returned. *That's it! That's right! Her bedroom. Whatever I've done, remember what she did. What she taught herself to do!*

No more dragging. They were in the bedroom. It took a moment for Ruby to realise, but both hands were free now, and she was on her own in a corner, huddled and gazing outwards. Immediately, she reached for Christine. *Where are you? Where'd you go? Come back! Don't leave me alone like this, with her, your mother.*

It was another room riddled with gloom, but not so dark she couldn't see. Oh no, she could witness perfectly well all that was happening in front of her. There were dolls. Hundreds of them, thousands. And the fist that she'd feared whilst standing in the kitchen doorway came down on them, with almost tribal repetition, to bludgeon every one, their faces caving easily under such pressure, sweet smile after sweet smile vanishing.

A fist...*just* a fist, clenched tight and the knuckles white. Who the fist belonged to, Ruby couldn't work out. Christine was tall for a twelve-year-old, Shirley petite for an adult. It could be either of them doing this, practising for the ultimate crime: murder.

It's her!
It's her!
It's her!

That phrase was repeated with the same rhythmic intensity by not one voice but two, which screamed in almost perfect unison, again blurring the possibility of identification as each one protested their innocence by blaming the other.

Ruby only added to the mix. "Christine? Christine! Why'd you let go of my hand?"

Christine was the victim here; Ruby was certain of it, that she wasn't being fooled. Shirley had abused her, possessed by something other than the spirit of maternal goodness. But…and Ruby had to think clearly, get it straight in her head when it all felt so skewed…she'd tried to *infect* her own child too. Spent years doing so. Chipping away at her innocence just as, at some point, her own innocence had been chipped away at.

The question was: Had she succeeded?

Were both guilty of terrible crimes?

Her!
Her!
Her!

Again, the voices matched, the tone, the intonation, the sheer fury behind each one. There'd been a spark of defiance in Christine's eye when she'd stood in the living room, something Ruby had marvelled at. But which route had that defiance taken her down?

Two twelve-year-old children's deaths were at the heart of this. Their murderer or murder*ers* never found. Only a link forged by Theo, who'd slotted the pieces of the jigsaw together. A psychic, not the police – the police had had the

Whitmores in their sight, then let them go. *Unfinished business.* But one of these two wanted it done with, the truth to be exposed.

But again, which one was guilty of something other than torment?

Eliza and Danny were children – the same age as Christine or thereabouts – and therefore easier targets than an adult. No way a child could overcome an adult, only someone of a similar or lesser build. Shirley had said to the child that there was something rotten in her, something poisonous, trying to make her a mirror of herself, to forge another conduit. And then later, after the murders, the dead Christine had appeared to Theo and had questioned whether she was indeed something rotten, something poisonous…maybe her way of admitting it? And there'd been blood all over her, on her hands. Another admittance?

Her!

Her!

Her!

With the two voices screaming, it was so hard to think, to believe in who'd done what. And those faces, the dolls, they taunted her. No use even closing her eyes. They'd still be there before her. *Calm down, breathe easier. They're just plastic faces, Ruby. And think!*

You have to see!

That's what Christine had said earlier, that she had to see, *wholly* see.

Are you guilty, Christine? Because one of you is. One of you killed Eliza and Danny.

A crime that was over fifty years old, being forced into the light.

One hand was grabbed again, a split second before the

other was too.

Both leading her to the real crime scenes at last, the real bludgeoned faces.

Chapter Twenty-Eight

Not this! Anything but this! A truth too terrible to witness, an abomination.

You have to see!

There was no escape, not now that both Christine and Shirley had hold of Ruby again, determined for her to do just that – see. But what would she see? The truth manipulated?

A child – a cherub of a child, small for her age, rose-cheeked and fair-haired. Eliza was now in front of her. A grainy photograph come to life. A sweet child. Simple? Ruby hated to think it, but she seemed almost ethereal, unattached to this world, too good for it.

There was a smile on her face as she played in a wooded park. A…grubby child, although not as bad as Christine. She definitely had an unkempt air about her, though. *Left to run free.* Something that didn't happen so much these days, but the seventies had been a different era entirely – children were definitely more free-range then, and conditions, perhaps *this* child's condition, just like Christine's, were more likely to be ignored, as Ruby's previous client Alan, the one who'd ended up in Borstals and prisons, had told her.

Sweet, sweet child! A child Ruby wouldn't have let out of her sight if she were her mum.

Just the shade of her, in amongst trees dappled with sunlight on what looked to be an idyllic summer day. A gorgeous scene, Ruby strangely relaxing into it until something else approached: Christine.

A squeeze of her hand, the left one – which one of them held that? Christine? Telling her to focus, to concentrate.

Eliza had been drawing pictures on the dusty ground with a twig, but now she lifted her head to smile at Christine. Christine crouched down by Eliza, selecting a twig and creating her own drawings.

They were talking, although Ruby couldn't hear what was said, Eliza emitting bright bursts of laughter that made the leaves ripple all around her. Then they abandoned their twigs to play another game, hide-and-seek – Christine's idea – taking turns, playing again and again…

Tears pricked at Ruby's eyes. They seemed happy enough, these friends.

Special friends.

But the sunlight was fading. The scene growing darker. Christine didn't want to go home, was putting it off as much as possible. Eliza hid again. She was found. Growing tired, she at last wanted to go home. But still Christine refused, insisted she take another turn, got a little spiteful about it: *Go on, hide. You have to!* Then her whole body had seized as her head whipped round. *Hide! Hide! Hide! Quickly. Now!*

The shades of the children blended with the darkness to become indistinguishable. Had someone else appeared on the scene? It was so frustrating! She needed to see but was also being blocked. The only thing she could make out was an arm lifting, something grasped within its hand, a rock or a stone of some sort? It had to be. She could hear a scream, *several* screams, then a shadow breaking free and running. Christine? She was the one screaming now. *Help me! Help me!* Not help *her*, Eliza, the child who'd been attacked. There were the shapes of others now, those alerted by her screams, who had answered the call, and the child pointing. *There! There! It's her! It's her!*

Ruby peered harder. Confusing. The entire scene was. What did Christine mean? Was the 'her' she referred to Eliza or someone else?

Had Shirley been there too? Spying on them, perhaps?

A squeeze of both hands.

Who was telling the truth here? And who was denying it?

Tread carefully, Ruby.

Another wooded scene, the same park or another? Surely, the area where Eliza had been killed would have been cordoned off? Despite Ness's disparaging view of the police back then, some red tape must've existed, some rules and regulations!

If it was the same park, what a bold move. The evil of it, the arrogance. Not to care.

There was another walking along and limping slightly. Danny? It was; she recognised that impish air he had about him. Why was he limping? Ruby wondered. Had he hurt himself, or was it more than that? An affliction of some sort?

Vulnerable, both Eliza and Danny. The kind that always got picked on. Lonely. And, therefore, also the kind that would welcome the hand of friendship. Even from someone like Christine. Another loner. A child on which lice crawled.

As with Eliza, the sweetness of the boy moved Ruby.

She wanted to scoop him up in her arms and run with him to safety, but evil had spied him and had him marked.

Christine, Shirley, which one of you did this? Between you, which one unravelled first? Succumbed wholly. An agent of the darkness, a disciple.

Another warm, sunny day, the boy dressed in shorts, a T-shirt, socks and sandals, trailing a stick beside him as he walked, idly batting at the foliage with it.

A whisper.

Someone from deep inside the foliage was calling out.

Danny? Danny, is that you? Oh, Danny!

Danny turned his head towards that whisper, frowning slightly, curious.

Don't do it, don't go in there, Ruby wanted to shout, but what good would it do? What she was seeing was merely a replay.

He disappeared into the foliage, Ruby following him, but she could go no further than the edge, could see again only an arm rising, same as it had before, another large rock in the hand, coming down with all the force of a thousand demons behind it. Barely even a scream this time, more a whimper.

Silence again.

Only that.

And Ruby standing there, staring into the woodland, both her hands still being held, another squeeze from one of them, an insistence.

It was her! Her! Please believe me. It was her!

Whose voice was she hearing? Why couldn't she distinguish them?

If fury was behind the actions of the perpetrator, it rose in her too.

Bastard! she breathed. *You bastard! Who committed these crimes?*

Fury overcoming everything, she whipped her head from side to side. She had to see, not the crime but the guilty party. *Which one of you was it?*

Another whimper – but whose? *Her! Her! Her!*

"Stop saying that!" she demanded. "I want a name. Christine, if it was Shirley, say so. Shirley, if it was Christine, just fucking tell me. Stop what you're doing – this sick game!

A scream in her ear, not a whimper but a response that was lightning quick: *It was her!*

More voices joined in, those that she could distinguish: Ness's and Corinna's.

"Ruby! Ruby! Don't do it, don't touch her!"

"Ruby, stop! Just wait a minute. Look!"

Ruby's head was spinning, her vision too. What was happening now?

She felt sick, dizzy, unable to reason.

"Ruby, listen to my voice, okay? Only mine. Let her hand go!"

Was that Ness commanding her?

You have to see!

She had seen, though. Some of it. But not enough. The process interrupted.

Another voice joined the melee, a cry in it so pitiful it could crack your heart. "It was her! Don't you see? A wrong 'un from the start. She infected *me*, not the other way around. She was so, so dangerous. So…clever! Able to twist things, turn it all around. The devil's liar! Oh, Ruby. That's your name, isn't it? Such a…nice name. Pretty. It was her. All her! Don't be fooled. That's what you're so afraid of, isn't it? That you'll side with the wrong party. She was at the rotten heart of it all. Still is. I've tried to hide from her, tried so hard, but she's found me. Finally, she's found me. It was her, Ruby. Please! Help me!"

That voice she knew too – although she'd only heard it in visions – could now see where it was coming from, the spinning in her head slowing. It was Shirley, no longer catatonic but fully aware and clinging on to Ruby with both hands, her eyes laser focused on Ruby's, a naked plea in them: *Don't be fooled, Ruby! Don't be fooled.*

What if…what if…

"Ruby, let her hands go!" Ness had come closer, as had Corinna, their hands also upon Ruby's and Shirley's, straining at them, trying to sever the connection.

But what if…

There wasn't the savagery she'd expected to see in Shirley's expression, just utter desperation. If she was guilty, would she be able to hide it so successfully?

Who killed Eliza and Danny? Who killed Christine?

"Did you do it?" Ruby whispered, her voice heard by Shirley, as she knew it would be despite the commotion going on around them, Nurse Winters having opened the door and entered the room too, demanding to know what was happening before stopping dead in her tracks and gasping loudly. Ruby's gaze, however, remained solely on Shirley. "Did you kill Christine? Were you forced to, to prevent the possibility of more victims?"

Such terror in Shirley's eyes, such…suffering. How could you feign something like that? And there was spite as well as defiance in Christine; she'd seen it during the game of hide-and-seek with Eliza when Christine had forced her to play on and on. Spite that had built and built?

"Oh, Shirley," she said. "You poor, poor—"

Jed materialised on the bed, right in front of Shirley, not only Ruby able to see him this time – Shirley could too. She howled, just as Jed howled, bared her teeth at him, just as he bared his teeth at her, *growled* even.

Thank God for Jed. For setting the record straight. Finally.

"Let go, Ruby," Ness continued to beg her. "Let her go."

"Unhand that woman! Unhand her right now!" Nurse Winters had finally found her voice.

"She's dangerous," Corinna insisted. "I saw it in her eyes just before you touched."

She'd seen it? And yet Ruby hadn't. Shirley was the devil's liar, and she'd believed her.

No time to wonder at it, to be *aggrieved* by it. That time would come soon enough. Another thing to plague her. Another…failure. Shirley was the murderer, the manipulator, the one who'd followed her child into the woods, the wickedness getting worse, wanting to show what it was capable of – show *her*, Christine.

Help me! Help me! Christine had said that first time, running from the trees, an appeal for Eliza but also for herself. *She was my special friend.* Because any child that didn't flinch at the sight of her as she drew near, but saw beyond the dishevelled exterior and welcomed her, was special. Danny, who knew the whispering voice in the woods because he and Christine had also played together several times right there, the only happiness Christine had ever had – with them, Eliza and Danny. And Shirley knew it. She'd followed her, and she'd seen the smiles on her child's face, in place despite everything, and had taken care of the situation, for there must be no happiness. Ever. Happiness was undeserved.

That second time, Christine had been hiding from Shirley, pining for Eliza, trying to feel close to her friend again by revisiting the place they'd last been together, a place she'd mistakenly thought of as safe, that her mother wouldn't go near again, not so soon. Even so, when she'd called him, she'd been trying to tell him to run, to go home, to stay indoors instead, somewhere she'd hoped was a haven for him. But Shirley had been close, very close. If only Christine had kept quiet, said nothing at all; Danny might have stood a chance then.

After Danny, when the police had come calling, when someone had written the word 'unemotional', it was perhaps describing them both. For Christine's part, another cry for help – *Look at me, look at me. He was my special friend. I've told you that. Would I react like this to his death?* She'd mystified the officer enough to make a note of it, but later, they'd dismiss it as shock, and therefore it wasn't mystifying at all.

And so, after that second murder, the door had closed on the officer. Ruby could see it now in Shirley's eyes, everything that had happened, the *truthful* version, and Shirley knew she could, her lip curling, her hand wriggling, trying to let go of Ruby's hand, to thrust it from her, but Ruby wouldn't allow it and clung on.

"You're next," Shirley had said, rushing down the hallway again at Christine. "I'm growing tired of you. So, so tired. And what I did to the others…I liked it."

More profanities, such dark, dark promises.

Defiance. That spark within the child burning brighter. Her mother had been growing tired of her because, despite her best efforts, she was *not* like her. And nor would she ever be.

As Shirley at last straightened and walked past Christine into the kitchen – *sauntered* past – the child seized her chance. She too hurled herself down the hallway with preternatural speed towards the door, opening it and rushing onto the street.

Surprise rooted Shirley to the spot, giving Christine yet more of an advantage.

She ran and ran, her mother finally in pursuit, calling out for her to stop, for anyone to stop her, but people went about their business, as people were wont to do, hanging their heads lower, thinking it best to ignore the drama, not get involved. Christine ran right down to the sea, and there she stopped, but only to stuff her pockets full of stones. Not a beautiful summer's day, not this time. The weather had broken, become quite stormy. The beach was no place to be on a day like that, with the waves growing higher, the roar of the sea deafening. If there were any passers-by, some who'd ventured along regardless of the pending storm, they didn't see her, the child that strode into the waves, so heavily weighed down, a child no one had ever really seen or heard except Eliza, except Danny. And the darkness.

"Christine! Christine!"

Shirley, panting and spluttering, couldn't stop her.

And the darkness, its fury increasing at being thwarted, turned on Shirley instead, the one who'd failed it, and brought her, by degrees, to a dark place, the only place she could keep her child alive – not through love but the continued desire to persecute. A desire that had sent her mad, as such desires always did. A place that truth had ejected her from.

"You killed them," Ruby declared, releasing the woman's hands at last, although her reptilian touch was a memory that joined so many others. "Eliza Brooks and Danny Bailey. Then you hid, deep inside yourself, and continued to blame Christine. That blame grounding her because it was so unjust. She wasn't poisonous or rotten. You were."

"Fucking kids!" Shirley spat back, her empty hands flailing. "Fucking Eliza! Fucking Danny! Fucking Christine! Yes, I killed those other two, but I would never have killed Christine, despite what I said. I'd have got her to submit eventually. And she knew it. That's why she did what she did! Because deep down she was like me. She was!"

As Ness stood there, bewildered, Corinna too, Ruby addressed Nurse Winters.

"Did you hear that? What she said? The confession."

"Oh, I heard it all right," Nurse Winters replied, her eyes darting between Ruby and Shirley. Quickly, she held up her phone. "What's more, I've recorded it. Every vile word." As she revealed this, three people burst through the door, others that worked there, just as Shirley thrashed and arched, spewing forth a torrent of filth again. As they restrained her, as Ness, Corinna, Ruby and Jed stepped back, allowing them to do their work, Nurse Winters joined them. An ally, not a foe.

"I'll be calling the police," she said. "Just as soon as she's sedated. You know something? I never bought that catatonic nonsense. Whenever I came in here, whenever I had my back to her, I could feel her eyes on me, like...like she was trying to *worm* her way inside me. It was like she was searching...you know?"

"She was," Ruby answered, "for vulnerability. That's what the darkness always searches for." As Nurse Winters contemplated this, nodding in agreement, Ruby smiled. "Thank God you're strong and good at heart. As with Christine, she never stood a chance."

Chapter Twenty-Nine

She was innocent. Christine Whitmore. Not rotten or poisonous but a veritable lionheart!

When Ruby and the team burst into Theo's room, Theo was sitting up in bed, not just feeling well, feeling *great*, a smile on her face, one she smugly suspected had a hint of serenity about it.

Theo spoke before Ruby had a chance to. "I know," she told her. "I know all about it."

Ruby, Corinna and Ness all stood there.

"You know?" Ruby managed at last. Not *Oh God, look at you! You're awake! You're so much better!* But she was better for a reason – because of Christine Whitmore.

Theo patted her bedside. "Oh, for goodness' sake, close your mouths, you three, will you? You're in danger of catching flies. Come on, come on over here and sit down. Yes, Ruby, I know everything that happened between Shirley and Christine Whitmore, because I found her, you see, inside me. I searched, and I searched, and finally I found her, the memory something fresh rather than stale – and, as I suspected, it was enough to enliven her again, for us to connect. And then she connected with you, didn't she? At that nursing home where that dreadful mother of hers hides herself, busy persecuting her child still, twisting and turning everything, insisting it was Christine who was to blame and that she was innocent of everything. Oh, I'm so glad the truth has broken through at last. What a glorious, glorious thing!" She sighed as Ness, Corinna and Ruby took their seats. "That's why she haunted me all these years, why I could never forget her, try as I might. Because I had a sneaking suspicion she was an innocent. Want to know how I knew that?"

"How?" asked Ruby, her eyes practically on stalks.

"When she asked if she was the devil, she shuddered at that possibility, was horrified by it. And well, as we've since learnt, nothing devilish would ever do that."

Corinna let out a burst of laughter. "Simple, really, isn't it?"

Theo chuckled too. "It is on occasion, and yet darned complex too."

"You're better." It was Ness who finally stated the obvious. "You're positively radiant."

Theo nodded. "I keep telling you, I plan to be a thorn in your side for a lot longer yet."

To Ruby's and Corinna's surprise, Theo's too and perhaps even Ness's, Ness got up and gently enfolded Theo in her arms. Her eyes as misty as her own, Theo would bet.

"Bloody make sure of it," she heard Ness whisper.

When Ness was back in her chair and noses had been blown and eyes wiped, Theo gazed again at Ruby. "Tell me, then, how it was that you reached the truth."

Ruby obliged, visibly trembling as she related certain parts of the story. Words either tumbling from her or hesitant. Afterwards, she leant back in the chair she was occupying, clearly exhausted. "The thing is, Theo, we've faced the darkness before, together as a team as well as individually, but…this time, it just…it got so personal."

Theo contemplated her words, knew what she was referring to, what had also reached out in the darkness for her, that fear of what she'd inherited.

"Ruby, Ruby, Ruby," she answered, "there's a balance of emotions within us, dark and light, you know that. We've talked about this before, many times, about choosing sides, feeding the good wolf and the bad wolf. And you *have* chosen your side; all of us in this room have. Nothing can change that. We don't just keep the light balanced, we use it to outweigh the darkness. But even so, darkness is still there in this wild terrain we call our heart and soul. It's all part of the human experience, so don't beat yourself up about it, about harbouring anger, about harbouring fears too, about harbouring anything you perceive to be a weakness. We're flawed beings, we have to accept that, but some of us are *magnificently* flawed, and that includes you, Ruby, and you, Corinna, Ness too, and me."

Ruby began nodding, but then she stopped, her head to one side. "The children, Eliza and Danny, there was nothing flawed about them, Eliza particularly. She was so…pure, Theo. She *shone* with purity. What happened to her…"

As Ruby's voice cracked, Theo reached out, took her hand and gave it a gentle squeeze. Ruby brought her other hand over to lay it on Theo's.

"Exceptions to the rule will always find themselves targets," she said, sad about that too. "You say they might be grounded after all, at St Martin's, she and Danny? Well, we'll just have to go and sit there on occasion, won't we, Ness? See if we can't rectify that."

Ness nodded, as did Ruby, but there were no more

words, not from any of them, just silence instead, a time to reflect, to understand that somehow, someway, justice had happened because Christine at least had soared – finally – and was now where she needed to be.

Oh, what a journey it had been to find her, though! Wading through such sludge, other memories taunting her, almost causing Theo to abandon the quest she'd been on and turn back or do as Ruby had and try to hide, erect four walls around herself – four *padded* walls. Sanity – all four of them clung to it by their fingertips, and little wonder given the things they'd experienced! Things that were sometimes too big for them, and yet Theo expected it was only really the tip of the iceberg. What more would they discover, in this life, in other lives, in different realms, even? Just what were they in training for here?

Memories of Reggie had hurt her the most when she'd been under Willow's influence, her beloved husband and how he'd suffered at the end, illness eating away at him. And Theo, for everything she could do, could do nothing to halt it in its tracks. He'd clung to her in those final days with such pleading in his eyes – *Help me, Theo! End this. Find a way.* And she'd stared back as helpless as a babe. If she could turn back time, she'd do it, crush some pills, dissolve them in water, hold that cup to his lip, and he would sip, and in his eyes there'd be only love still, the love they'd shared from the moment they'd met, in the doorway of Woolworths, sheltering from the rain. In that space deep inside her, that wild terrain, as she'd dubbed it, she'd fallen to her knees and cried out, hoping that wherever he was, he'd hear. *I'm so sorry!*

She'd then decided she couldn't go on after all. Had lingered for an age, it seemed, regretting that failure. As

Ruby had found, there was so much to fear when examining yourself. Inside existed a sorrow that was all-consuming, that could crack you so far apart you'd never be whole again. She'd got stuck in the hell of her own life, forgetting what she'd been searching for. Forgetting too that someone had followed her this far in – taken her there in the first place – skipping alongside her, dancing and clapping. Charming gestures. Normally. Whispering in her ear, *It's hell in there. Go on! Go!*

She'd forgotten the reason she'd gone there, but the reason hadn't forgotten her.

There'd been another child besides Willow. A hazy memory of her, her face, the blood – not hers but Eliza's, the child she'd cradled in her arms as Shirley stood over them, Christine begging for Eliza to come back, to hold on, just hold on, before finally releasing her and running, reaching a more crowded area of the park. *Help me! Help me!*

She'd said the same thing to Theo. *Help me! Open your eyes and look at me. Only me. Let me show you the truth. The time has come. Please.* And still Theo might have ignored her but for another voice that had overlaid the child's – and maybe it had been imagination, sheer hope, the stuff of fantasy – but it had sounded so like Reggie. A Reggie who wasn't in pain, begging for relief, but whose voice was like it used to be, full of humour: *Theo, come on! Chivvy yourself up. I don't want her weighing on your mind when we're finally reunited. Do what you were born to do and help her. Oh, and Theo, I want to say I'm sorry. I should never have asked of you what I did. Weighed you down with the burden of that responsibility.* Another throaty chuckle. *Ah, but what can I say in my defence? I was a desperate man. All's well now, though, sweetheart. Rather heavenly, in fact.*

She'd lifted her head. *He* was apologising to *her*?

"Reggie?"

It was the child's face she'd seen instead, a child with dark hair, not red.

"I'm Christine. Will you help me now?"

A mobile phone ringing cut through Theo's reverie.

"Sorry," Ruby said, reaching into her jacket pocket. "I forgot to put it on silent."

As she checked the caller ID, she gasped, her gaze then bouncing off each of them.

"It's Michelle," she said. "Willow's mum. Calling me back at last. What do I do?"

More silence as each contemplated an answer.

"Take the call," Theo said at last. "See what she has to say."

"Okay, all right," Ruby responded, hurrying from the room.

In her absence, Corinna began fussing over Theo, wondering if she had enough water, if she was comfortable enough, whether she'd like her to bring in some sandwiches from M&S. "You know, those fancy ones. They do some great salads too."

Theo endured it all, occasionally throwing Ness a look when Corinna's head was turned, and Ness smirking back at her. All good-natured, their love filling the room, bolstering her further, making her glad to be alive, grateful, the memory of being in that darkness, wanting to curl up and scream, to die alongside Reggie, just that…a memory. Not to be harboured.

Another memory, though, she couldn't vanquish. It wasn't yet time.

As Ruby reentered, all fussing stopped, Theo taking a deep breath, steeling herself.

It was as she'd thought.

"Michelle's in a dreadful state," Ruby told them, her complexion as white as the hospital walls. "Willow…she's…spiralled out of control. She's hitting out, screaming, and, God, she keeps hissing! They've been trying to deal with it, keep it contained, terrified in case…I don't know…the authorities get involved and try to take her away or something. Michelle was whispering all this down the phone because she didn't want Willow to hear. She was crying too. She's petrified, absolutely petrified! Of her own child! Her partner's left, taken Leo and gone to stay with his mother. He said it was just too dangerous for them to stay, as Willow attacked Leo. They found her practically throttling him."

"Jeez!" Corinna's face had drained of colour too. "They've got to call the police!"

Ruby turned to her. "It's her child, Crin! What if she's right, and they take her away? She's called us. So it's us who has to help. We've got to try, at least."

As Ness rose from her chair, Corinna too, Ruby focused on Theo.

"That's right, isn't it? This is down to us?"

Oh, how could she say this? Theo wondered. She feared for Ruby. No way could she go back to that place Willow had so effortlessly plunged them…with him there, her father. Because he'd know if she was there again. He'd sense it, her vulnerability. Attack.

And Willow, she'd sing and dance and clap to see it.

"Theo?" Ruby urged. All eyes on her now, not just Ruby's but Ness's and Corinna's too. "We can't just abandon her."

Theo cleared her throat.

"Of course you can't abandon her," she said eventually. "Of course you must try to help. But not in the way you think."

Ruby frowned. "What do you mean?"

"The child has a grandmother, doesn't she? Whom she inherited this – what did the woman call it? – 'fey' streak from."

"Well, yeah," Ruby said. "Anne Murphy. But she wants nothing to do with her. And nor did her son, Shaun. They felt Michelle had tried to trap Shaun by getting pregnant."

"A honey-trap," mused Theo. "Such a sweet term for something so unfair, isn't it?"

"Unfair?" This time, Ness was the one questioning what she was saying.

Theo nodded. "Tell me, Ruby, how did Michelle feel about Shaun? Has she said?"

"Um…yeah, kinda. She loved him. Hence, why she did it. She was young, you know. She just wanted to be with him, wanted to find a way. Any way."

"Exactly," concluded Theo. "She loved him. Go to Michelle's, by all means, but one of you must go to Anne's too and tell her that, make her understand that Michelle only did what she did because she loved Shaun. There was no malice in the act. Stupidity, agreed, but not malice. And then ask her to help too. Oh, there you go again, all of you! Standing with your mouths wide open. Think about it. The 'fey' are a breed apart, an *ancient* breed. As such, they've developed their own way of dealing with things. Ultimately, Willow is her family's responsibility, and Anne, whether or not she likes it, is very much family.

Bringing Willow back to the light may well be a long and perilous journey with no easy answers and no shortcuts, so any help that's out there, we make use of."

"The thing is," Ruby replied, "a lot of the men in her family, Shaun included, couldn't deal with the darkness. Like him, some took their own lives."

Theo tapped at her forehead. "Women are stronger. Up here. Where it counts. So thank your lucky stars it's Willow we're dealing with here and not a Shaun Junior."

"Anne won't help." Ruby was sure of it. "She'll turn me away again."

"And maybe she won't. She couldn't help her son, and I'll bet a pound to a penny that deep down she blames herself for that rather than the darkness. Guilt must be eating away at her. Maybe all she needs is an extra push, because she can ease that guilt by helping another instead, the one who has her son's blood running through her veins. It's all about how you put the challenge to her, Ruby, but you're clever. You'll find a way."

Acceptance transformed her colleagues' faces.

"Gotta be worth a try, huh?" Theo cajoled further.

Before they left, rushed off to the Baylisses', Theo had to press home one more point. "As I've said, though, don't expect instant results, and make sure Michelle knows that too. This *will* take time. And ramp your protection up to the max. I'll help from here, sending all the love and light in the universe, and the luck."

"The luck?" Ness questioned. "Theo, what is it you're not telling us?"

"Honestly, I've said most of what's needed except, perhaps, this." Before continuing, she took a deep breath. "As you know, Willow took me into the darkness. She danced and sang and clapped beside me whilst doing so. And then, just before I went further, she turned to me and spoke, the very same words Christine had said all those years ago: 'Is this hell? Am I the devil?' Unlike Christine, though, she didn't shudder, didn't look even remotely bothered by the likelihood. She just skipped off, still clapping, still singing. *Joyously.*"

Chapter Thirty

Theo was right, there were to be no instant results, not with a child like Willow.

When Ruby, Ness and Corinna arrived outside the Bayliss home, they could hear her shouting and screaming from within, curtains twitching at the neighbours' houses, but only that. No one was coming out to ask what the hell was going on.

Hell. That'd be it exactly. A version of it.

Michelle opened the door. She looked at least ten years older than when Ruby had last seen her. Had it really been only a few days ago? Wretched was how Ruby would describe her. Her pale complexion now almost completely grey.

"I don't know what to do anymore," she kept saying as the tears poured down her face. "I just don't know what to do. The neighbours will call the police eventually. They're bound to. They can't put up with this either. She screams for hours sometimes now, through the day and through the night too. And she says such…terrible things. Words she doesn't know. That she hasn't heard from me, certainly. They stream from her mouth."

Stepping forward, Michelle threw herself into Ruby's arms, clinging to her like the drowning person she was. "I'm sorry, Ruby," she whispered. "I'm so sorry."

As expected, the child was enraged further to see them, hissing and spitting, recoiling from the light they'd brought with them, Theo sending an abundance more. It *burnt* her; that's how it seemed. Whatever had hold of this child, whatever she'd opened herself up to, allowed right in through the door of her humanity, Ruby could not – would not – believe it was wittingly. The child was *not* evil. But evil was a lure sometimes. All the Psychic Surveys team knew it. It promised so much, and it preyed on the vulnerable. It *adored* them in its horribly warped way. No matter. It must not be allowed to consume her. Because if it did, if they couldn't get the child to fight back, she'd end up like Shirley. Lost.

Theo had advised them to get Willow's grandmother involved, the blood of her blood, the fey – Anne Murphy. 'They've developed their own ways of dealing with things,' she'd said. Not the men, perhaps, but the women, who could be stronger in mind and therefore more capable of managing the burden. When Ruby thought about it, she realised that was true of Anne, at least. She was still here, still coping, despite having suffered the worst thing possible, the unimaginable, the loss of her son, but still getting through every day.

She was a strong woman indeed if she could do that.

The team of three tried with Willow. In the living room whilst she sat on the sofa, staring wildly up at them, alternately swearing and hissing, thrashing out and screaming, they stood in front of her, sending wave after wave of love and light to the child who was buried beneath. Solid, assured waves that were breaking shore but prematurely.

Eventually, a Ness almost as grey as Michelle turned to

Ruby and told her to do it, to go to Anne and bring her into this.

To leave Ness and Corinna with Willow…she was resistant until Jed appeared, standing just in front of the two women, his brown eyes trained entirely on the child.

It was the reassurance she needed, no time to explain her change of heart, not even to Michelle, who was closer to Willow than them, on the sofa with her, trying to wrap the child in her arms – an impossible task as Willow proved as slippery as an eel.

Ruby left, but not before she'd caught a brief glimpse of something else in the room – something that shone as brightly as Jed. Theo. She was certain of it. In the hospital bed but also there. All of them pitting their wits, and yet they needed more. They needed blood.

Ruby drove as fast as she could from Lewes to Uckfield, cursing traffic lights and, indeed, the traffic whenever they hindered progress. Once parked, she flew out of her car and towards the flat where Anne Murphy lived, furiously jabbing at the doorbell.

Despite this, it took an age for Anne to respond, but when she did, her dark eyes wide with confusion, Ruby pushed her way into the flat.

"What in God's name—" Anne began, but Ruby grabbed her hands, spoke over her.

"You have to come with me to see your granddaughter, Willow. No, don't do that, don't shake your head. Hear me out, okay? Just hear me out. She was a honey-trap. I know that's what you felt, and Shaun too, but, Anne, I want you to know this: Michelle loved your son, and she loves her daughter too, so, so much. She was not conceived in malice. And yet…it's something malicious that's got hold of her. The same something that had hold of Shaun, perhaps, but she's a child, just a child, and…and…it's not fair. You know what this something is; you've a family history of it, as you said. You're cursed. It's destroyed members of your family, and she *is* your family. Willow's your blood."

Ruby faltered, found she had to blink back tears. "We're trying everything we can to help her, my colleagues and I. We're trying to make the darkness let go, but…" She swallowed, remembering Theo's words. "Willow seems to cling to it as much as it's clinging on to her. Please come back with me to Lewes and stand beside us, shoulder to shoulder. Blast this thing back to where it came from. Do it for Willow, but most of all, do it for Shaun." What she was going to say next pained her – the truth of it. "The fact he wanted nothing to do with her doesn't change the fact she's his daughter, that she's your granddaughter too. Oh, Anne, she's in so much trouble."

Still holding on to Anne's hands, Ruby stood there with her, Anne's eyes so guarded that Ruby couldn't tell what she was thinking. Then she realised: they were guarded for a reason, not just because of what was happening right now, but because she knew how to block this thing out, this curse, this attachment, whatever it was that had befallen her family, and, yes, she might well have tried to teach her son, but for whatever reason, it hadn't worked. With Willow, she had a second chance. And there were people who'd give anything for that. If Anne lowered that guard and looked deep inside herself, would she find herself one of them?

"Anne," Ruby pleaded, "help Willow. At least try."

More seconds ticked by, painfully slow. *Anne, please!*

Anne spoke at last, and when she did, Ruby's shoulders slumped with relief.

"Best get my coat, then, hadn't I? Best go and meet this Willow."

* * *

Theo had said it would take a long while to treat Willow, and she was right. It would take time, and it would take patience, alongside a whole heap of love, understanding and firmness. Plus the total absence of fear, for if what possessed her suspected you were afraid, it would go to work on that and exploit it, something Anne knew all too well, the lesson of generations, something, she told Ruby in the car journey over, that she had indeed tried to teach her son. Going so far as to take him away from his family in Ireland, his grandparents, aunts and uncles – what remained of them – and not even leaving a forwarding address.

"I still don't speak to them," she said, "because…I can't. And maybe there's shame in the mix about that, but I wanted a clean slate for me and my son. As you know, though, I failed. I taught 'im everything that had worked for me, my sister, my ma, and he was good. He protected himself. Then he reached his teenage years and started taking drugs."

"Drugs?" Ruby said, briefly dragging her eyes from the road. "Shit."

"Drugs," Anne repeated, "and drink. Just like other teenagers the world over take drugs and drink. But for some—" her chest heaved "—it's not an option."

"Opens too many doors," whispered Ruby.

"That's right, then just you try closing them again. I'll do what I can for 'er, for Willow. I'll try again, but even with some women in our family, once they're older, start dabbling…"

"The only thing we can do is try. That's all I'm really asking here," Ruby told her. "I'm extremely grateful you're willing to do that."

When Anne arrived at the Baylisses', not only Michelle gasped in surprise as Ruby introduced her, but so did Willow, or rather the something that was in Willow.

Something that recognised Anne.

Anne, however, walked right up to where Willow was and stood before her, dark and diminutive and so resplendent.

"Enough," she said, "d'ya hear me? You took my son from me, and so many others, but this is where it ends. It ends because I say it does. Because I'm so, so *bored* of you."

She raised her arms then, held them high, for all the world like an exorcist of old, standing there in a long black coat that she hadn't yet discarded. Michelle, who was beside Ruby, gasped to see it, made to rush forward to intervene, but Ruby stayed her.

"Just wait," she said. "Give her a chance."

Corinna was also looking perplexed at the spectacle before her, Ness more intrigued. Jed was barking and wagging his tail, clearly excited.

"Let her do what needs to be done," Ruby whispered again to Michelle.

"Quake!" Anne yelled, her voice making even Ruby tremble. "Shudder with fear at the very sight of me, demon! That's it, that's right, squirm, like the coward you truly are. Oh, you love the innocent, the vulnerable, those that can't fight back, who try and hide. I've been hiding too, I know it now, but I won't anymore. Never again will my heart quicken at even the mere thought of ya. Over the years you've come for us, picked us off, those that you can. Well, now my wrath is coming for you. I know what you'll do, that you'll also try and hide, deep inside the child, waiting to strike, always waiting, but I'll be waiting too, just as vigilant, as persistent. And the minute you rear your ugly head I will pounce! Now be gone, you vile and lowly thing, and know this: I'm not like these others behind me. I won't use the light to break you down. I'll do it with yet more darkness, with an energy worse than you, which also lies in wait, and doesn't care who calls it. All it wants is to feed. So it'll listen, it'll answer. It may destroy me to summon it, but it'll destroy you too. And I will laugh, all the way to hell."

How the child on the sofa stared at Anne, such defiance in her eyes, her body jolting, more hissing on her lips, the kind that scratched at every nerve ending. But then…against a background of Michelle's sobbing, Willow's defiance faded, her body and mouth quieting.

She slumped, and again Michelle made to dash forwards, but it was Anne who reached her first, who the child held her arms out to, seeking her embrace.

Anne willingly complied, sitting beside Willow, the pair of them entwined, Michelle at last taking a step back, just standing there, staring.

"Well, well, well," Ruby heard Ness mutter. "Someone who goes even further than Theo on occasion."

At last, Willow pulled away from Anne.

"Who are you?' she asked.

"Who am I?" Anne replied, her voice something soft

and melodious now, the Irish lilt in it coming to the fore. "Why, I'm your granny, darlin', that's who. Granny Murphy."

And the child laughed, an innocence in it, delight, but also, Ruby noticed – and so did Anne, as told by the way she narrowed her eyes – a slight rasp.

A long journey, an ongoing project, but if they fought it together, it was one they could win. The light was always stronger than the dark; that was the age-old lesson, the age-old truth, although to be threatened with a darkness greater than you, to be made to realise such a thing existed, and that you'd use it, despite the danger to yourself – that could work too. Spectacularly.

As Michelle also drew near to Willow and Anne, wonder had replaced horror in her eyes. There was wonder in her own eyes too, Ruby imagined, and perhaps even a touch of anxiety, to realise that curses, even those that stretched back generations, didn't have to endure. That *everything* could be broken. Eventually.

Chapter Thirty-One

"Happy birthday, Hendrix Christopher Wilkins! One today! One! Can you believe it?"

Cash was holding Hendrix in his arms as Ruby proffered the cake she'd made for him – or rather a semblance of a cake. It had sunk in the middle and was therefore more icing than cake, a single candle stuck determinedly in it, with an increasing lean. Nonetheless, her baby's face broke into a delighted smile as immediately he reached for the candle and tried to grasp it in his fist. Ruby, however, took a quick step back.

"As glad as I am to see you reaching for the light, son," she continued, her smile as wide as his, as Cash's too, "fire is something you're going to have to learn about."

Ruby blew the candle out on his behalf, a huge cheer going up in the kitchen of the house on Sun Street, stuffed with a few friends she'd made from a recent mother-baby group she'd been attending with Hendrix at a nearby church hall. There was also Ness, Corinna, Theo, Jed, of course, Cash's mum, Cassy, Ruby's mum, Jessica, and her partner, Saul, as well as Michelle, Leo, Anne – and, yes, Willow was also there.

A *very good* Willow, who sat beside her gran and eyed the cake greedily. *Now, there's a kid that loves icing*, thought Ruby, extending her smile to include her.

The child had indeed been smiling and clapping her hands along with everyone else, but when their eyes met, Ruby's and Willow's, that smile immediately vanished, something cold and glittering appearing in those green eyes instead, saved just for her. Something that tried to hold Ruby's gaze and connect again.

Ruby broke the stare, and as she did she thanked God for Anne – that she was there to take the burden off Psychic Surveys' shoulders, allowing Ruby in particular to put some distance between herself and the child. But not Michelle – their friendship had endured, genuine at last, as genuine as the friendships she had with these other mothers, none of whom knew the extent of what she did for a living. When they'd asked, she'd simply replied, "I'm a mum, foremost, but with an interest in the spiritual." If they found out more through other channels, so be it. She'd deal with it, accept too that she'd lose some friends along the way, those that found the spiritual just too strange a concept to deal with, but that was life. *Her* life. An unusual one that right now was as normal as could be.

She set about cutting the cake, everyone declaring it a success despite her protestations.

"Too hard on yourself," one woman said, Laura, clutching her baby girl, Aria.

Ruby kept her smile as she handed over the cake. *If only you knew!*

People continued to chatter and eat, heading from the kitchen into the living room, where Ruby had laid out various toys so the babies could play, Cash and Hendrix joining them, such laughter coming from there as Ruby cleared the dishes. Theo came over to help, Ness and Corinna too, whilst Anne and Willow continued to sit there at the kitchen table, Anne's arm a permanent fixture around the child's shoulder, the child's gaze still burning.

"Just ignore it," Theo told her in a whispery voice, all too aware of what was going on.

"I am, don't worry," Ruby said. "She won't get to me again."

"Anne's doing a great job."

"She is. And you know what? I think the child loves her. I know Michelle does. Anne's stood by her, normalised everything, talked to her partner, Tim, too, told him in no uncertain terms to man up or ship out. He chose the former, and he's moved back in with Leo, which is a step in the right direction. Anne's there most of the time too. She's practically moved in."

Theo nodded. "That'd be good. Very good. As you say, all going in the right direction."

Stacking the dishwasher, Ruby could only agree. "She might be one of the lucky ones."

"Indeed," Theo said. "Now, shall I set the kettle to boil? Get some teas on?"

"I'll do it," Ness said, overhearing.

Meanwhile, Corinna had stopped helping and was gazing wistfully into the distance instead. "I'd love a baby," she said. "I feel quite left out here!"

"It's not all fun and games," Ruby assured her. "It's mostly bloody hard work."

A bang resounded as Willow kicked the table from underneath, Anne whispering words into her ear, a sharp reprimand that saw her sitting still again.

Corinna eyed her before turning to Ruby. "Maybe you're right. Maybe I'll embrace *not* having kids, actually. You know, just to be on the safe side…"

Ruby laughed, Theo did too, and Ness – who'd also remained childless. Navigating life alone was certainly challenging enough without adding to it. Although, as Ruby looked at Theo grabbing a selection of clean mugs, Ness now busy searching for a teapot, and Corinna leaving all wistfulness behind to hand Ruby more items for the dishwasher, as she heard cries of laughter from Cash, Cassy and Jessica in the front room, the squeal of babies and a bark from Jed, who'd joined the merry throng, she had to revise that statement. No one *ever* lived life alone. Even those who, like her – as she caught Willow's eyes again, quickly, surreptitiously, trying not to curse her further for doing this, for picking on her, *only* her – felt lonely…so very, very lonely…in a crowded room.

* * *

As she lay in bed that night, staring up at the ceiling, Cash sleeping beside her, Hendrix spark out too in his cot with Jed at the foot of it, Ruby felt blessed. A bit like a yo-yo too, if she was honest, because there were times when she also felt cursed, veering between the two options like a driver that had slid off the road and was trying to regain control.

What a great day it had been, though! A huge success. The house filled to the rafters with people and laughter, babies cooing and gurgling, presents being unwrapped, cake eaten, no matter how sickly, and cup after cup of tea or lemonade drunk. The perfect children's birthday party, and she'd hosted it, the first of many.

Families. A double-edged sword. *Can't live with 'em. Can't live without.*

She couldn't live without her family – Cash, Hendrix and Jed, and, despite everything, her mother too, Jessica. As for Sarah, her grandmother, she kept her deep inside, in her heart, at least the memory of her because if she knew Sarah, she'd be having a whale of a time on the other side, so much to discover, so many mysteries to unravel!

Some families, though, Christine's… Ruby was so glad the child was untethered. As for Eliza and Danny, that'd be an ongoing case too, not just Theo and Ness visiting St Martin's; they all would, just to make sure the children had flown and, if not, continue to persuade them.

As for Shirley…she'd been moved from Ridge View Nursing Home to a facility not unlike the one Hames was in, although she remained in the south rather than being sent north. Catatonic again. Hiding again. Mired in the darkness, but what was that darkness like now with no Christine? She'd tried so hard to be a friend to the darkness, but it didn't want friends, just people it could use. Despite everything, Ruby still felt compassion for her, sent her healing and light. The team did as a whole, hoping, praying that she too would break free one day, not get trapped in the afterlife as well as this life.

Nurse Winters had provided the police with the voice file she'd made, but there would be no prosecution, no trial. Shirley was in no fit state. Plus, Ruby surmised, she was imprisoned anyway. Maybe the room she was in now was more comfortable than at Ridge View, some members of staff as good at heart as Nurse Winters despite their gruff exteriors, maybe even on a crusade to help, just like Ruby felt she was. There was, perhaps, an ornament on a shelf there, bright cushions scattered around, the TV turned on. And yet, a prison was still a prison, whether or not there were bars at the windows. Shirley Whitmore was a monster but also a human, flawed, but in her case not quite so magnificently. Sending love and light to her was the only way the team knew of trying to 'cure' her, Anne's way deemed effective for sure, and something to learn from, but not employed. Not yet.

Still lying there, still staring up at the ceiling, Ruby continued to think and muse, her mind taking her down paths that were, by now, well-trodden. She remembered too the words she'd said to Anne regarding Willow and Shaun: *The fact he wanted nothing to do with her doesn't change the fact she's his daughter, that she's your granddaughter too.* Words that – with only a slight change – applied to herself. *The fact you want nothing to do with your father doesn't change the fact he's your father, that you're his daughter.*

He wasn't free, and nor was he ever likely to be. But in stark contrast to Shirley, could you ever imprison a man like him? Not when he could reach out with his mind the way he did, dark tentacles with suckers on the end that probed and probed and probed, and all in Ruby's direction. Something Willow knew – the same energy in possession of them both.

There were shadows on the ceiling, just like there'd been in the Whitmore house, in Christine's room, and Ruby would swear they were getting darker, some breaking away from the mass to form shadows and shapes of their own. Faces that leered down at her, *his* face.

She screwed her eyes shut. *Stop it!* When she opened them, they were nothing more than shadows again. *Rein in your imagination. Don't let it be used against you.*

Two foes, not just one, Willow *and* Aaron Hames. Cut

from the same cloth. Innocent once, maybe, but also just so damned willing, so damned curious. Naïve. That was what they were. For you had to be naïve to believe what the darkness promised.

The two of them, with Ruby in their sights. *Just two*, Ruby reiterated. *Just.*

Hardly a legion. But a legion of them were out there. Blakemort had taught her that. But there was a legion of her kind too. So many that would help in the fight against them, so many different ways to do it – fey ways, even.

Did she feel alone right now? Like she had earlier in the kitchen, in a house crowded with people? Like she had countless other times too. Was she afraid?

No!

She was on a high still from the party. And Jed, her protector, was taking care of Hendrix, which was her preference, which didn't leave her feeling more vulnerable but the very opposite. A child was every parent's weakness, but not every parent had a Jed as another pair of eyes, or rather realised they did, and, along with Cash, protectors didn't come much better. *Guardians.*

So, no, she wasn't afraid right now. She wasn't beating herself up about the fact she'd sympathised with Shirley there at her bedside, hadn't seen immediately what Corinna and Ness had, that she'd been taken in, or very nearly, which was why she allowed her mind to do this, continue to wander, to countenance Willow and Hames. Because right now she was driving along a straight track, her route a solid one. But if another roadblock should present itself, a diversion? As she'd already said, others would be there for her, all those that loved her. She could draw on their strength and knowledge as well as her own.

Not be fooled again.

Ah, just so easy to talk the talk…

She yawned, tiredness finally swamping her.

So bloody easy.

Even so, as she drifted into further darkness – a softness to it, though, the welcoming arms of sweet respite – there was a smile on her face, a frown too.

So cursed. So blessed. You're a conundrum, Ruby, an anomaly. But so what? Perhaps you're meant to be. Whatever. You know what to do. Break it down, bit by bit.

Deal with it all like any other person would: one step at a time.

Epilogue

Ruby was asleep when Cash woke that night, which he was pleased about; she spent far too much time ruminating instead of getting some rest. Now, though, it seemed to be his turn.

As he shifted from side to side to eventually lie on his back, he smiled. It had been such a great day, and Ruby so nervous about it beforehand, worrying endlessly about every little detail. Okay, admitted, you had to have a sweet tooth to enjoy the cake she'd made, but people had gamely tucked in, nonetheless. So many had come to celebrate their son's first birthday. There'd been so much laughter, but no grin wider than his own, surely?

Family. What a glorious thing it was. Funny, though, because he could never imagine himself married with a kid when he'd been younger. He'd tried to. Most likely everyone did at some point. But, nope, just couldn't picture it. And now look at him!

No ordinary girl. Oh no, he'd married a stunner! One with a gift, an…*incredible* gift.

As he thought this, Ruby stirred slightly, a low but brief moan escaping her. He reached across and patted her, whispered that everything was okay. Straightaway she settled again.

A sigh replaced his smile. God, he wished he could help

her more! Chase away all the fears she concealed. Always trying to wear a brave face, that was Ruby, and he both admired her for it and felt frustrated. More the latter, actually, especially recently, but he too tried not to show it, to keep floating along in their happy bubble.

But what if that bubble should burst? And why was he frowning now, suddenly so worried that it would? He was…*gripped* with worry. The memory of the happy day they'd spent fading far too quickly in the face of it.

Someone was coming for them; that's the feeling he got.

Someone with a big sharp pin in their hand. Not a spirit or an entity, a living person.

Why did he think that?

And who could it possibly be?

Again, he turned to Ruby, but this time he didn't touch her. Strangely, he didn't want to. Instead, anger flared. *What's going to happen…it's your fault. All of it. It's because of you – your weaknesses – that hell will rain down on us.*

What the…?

Cash released a deep breath, sat up, felt hot and then cold…so cold.

Where'd that thought come from? He didn't blame Ruby! He loved her. Plus…he still had no clue who he thought was coming after them.

Think, Cash, who could it be?

No one he knew. So, therefore…it had to be someone to do with Ruby. He gulped as realisation dawned. Her father?

She hadn't mentioned him, not in a long while. And why should she? Like that dreadful Whitmore woman Ruby had dealt with earlier in the year, he was incarcerated, with no prospect of release on the horizon. A man she barely knew.

No way it could be him.

The devil himself. The very worst.

Again, such a weird thought – and not one of his, he was certain of it. It was just there, as though another had scrawled it across his mind.

Coldness continued to seize him.

Isn't that what Ruby had said happened to her in that place that kid Willow had taken her? She'd invaded her personal space like some virus, got in there and tarnished it. Christ, the paranormal! It did his head in sometimes.

Fuck this! He couldn't deal with it, not right now at this hour.

He turned to the clock. It was 3:00 a.m. Listened out for Hendrix too. Was he okay?

There was nothing but silence.

A silence he was both grateful for and which made his skin crawl.

Too much silence, too much darkness, too much of *anything* was never a good thing. The day would dawn soon, though, and slice right through the night. The birds would start up with their chorus, normality resumed. As normal as it got around here, at any rate.

He should just lie back, close his eyes, try to get some more sleep. He had a busy day ahead, another project he was in the middle of that needed completion.

So much needs completion…

Stupid thoughts. Stupid feelings.

If only Ruby were awake, he'd pull her into his arms and hold her. He would! No doubt about it. She'd chase his fears away, not the other way around.

Enough already. He had to sleep.

That kid, though, Willow. Ruby had insisted on inviting her to the party – a channel, she'd said she was, a conduit. She'd kept on catching his eye, kept…staring at him.

He wished now Ruby *hadn't* invited her.

Because he could still feel her eyes on him.

Scratching claw-like below the surface.

Seriously?

He shook his head.

No. No. No. Of course not seriously!

She was just a kid, under the wing of her grandmother now, who was also psychic, or 'fey', as Ruby had described her.

He listened to Ruby snuffle again before falling quiet. Where was Jed? His pal. And no matter he couldn't see him, their invisible dog; they were the best of friends. Was he in Hendrix's bedroom? Ruby had said he was, that just as Jed guarded her, he also guarded him.

Something which got Cash smiling again, which at last helped him to relax.

Funny old life. Like he'd said, one he couldn't have possibly imagined.

It had been a good day that had just passed. And sure, in Ruby's line of work, there'd be more dark days ahead, and sometimes he'd stand on the sidelines, sometimes he'd get roped in, the latter inevitable. But he was prepared. She was too. And no way, whatever happened, would he blame her. Ever. All these creepy thoughts that had entered his head, he'd just…tuck them away. No way he'd share them, no need to freak anyone out.

Yep, whatever happened, they were in this together.

They stood side by side.
Vows had been exchanged.
He shivered again as he closed his eyes. *Till death do us part.*

A note from the author

As much as I love writing, building a relationship with readers is even more exciting! I occasionally send newsletters with details on new releases, special offers and other bits of news relating to the Psychic Surveys series as well as all my other books. If you'd like to subscribe, sign up here!

www.shanistruthers.com